CRIMES OF PASSION

CRIMES OF PASSION

Samantha Lee Howe

First published by Telos Publishing
139 Whitstable Road, Canterbury, Kent CT2 8EQ, UK.

www.telos.co.uk

ISBN: 978-1-84583-225-4

Telos Publishing Ltd values feedback. Please e-mail any comments
you might have about this book to: feedback@telos.co.uk

Crimes of Passion © Samantha Lee Howe, 2023
Cover Art © Iain Robertson
Cover Design © David J Howe

Previously published stories:

'The Curse of The Blue Diamond' (as Sam Stone) first published in
Further Associates of Sherlock Holmes. Ed George Mann (Titan Books,
2017)
'Trophy Wife' first published in *Black Is The Night* Ed Maxim
Jakubowski (Titan Books, 2022)
'Slash' first published in *Criminal Pursuits: Crimes Through Time* Ed
Samantha Lee Howe (Telos Publishing, 2022)
'The Curse of Guangxu' (As Sam Stone) first published in *The
Mammoth Book of Sherlock Holmes Abroad* Ed Simon Clark (Robinson,
2015)

The moral right of the author has been asserted.

British Library Cataloguing in Publication Data.
A catalogue record for this book is available from the British
Library.

This book is sold subject to the condition that it shall not by way of
trade or otherwise, be lent, resold, hired out or otherwise circulated
without the publisher's prior written consent in any form of binding
or cover other than that in which it is published and without a similar
condition including this condition being imposed on the subsequent
purchaser.

CONTENTS

DEDICATION

With thanks to:

Stephen James Walker, David J Howe, Camilla Shestopal, Maxim Jakubowski, Karen Krushinsky Deal, Cathy Gilberto, Tracey Garside, Kelly Beckett, Katherine Easton Campbell, Heatherlynn Nickles Gonzalez, Chrissie Wood, Karen Woodham (Blazing Minds), Mark Fearn (BookMark) and Susan Hunter (Crime Fiction Addict), Caroline Marston (UKCrimeBookClub), Samantha Brownley (UKCrimeBookClub), Steve Matthewman, Susan Springer Coleman.

Mine

You were in the coffee shop when I first saw you. A battered paperback, an old historical romance, in hand while you sipped at a tall latte. The choice of drink, the literature, all told me the first things I needed to know about your story. You were a romantic, as was I, and it was only right that we should meet and talk and become friends.

That day didn't come for some time though, and all the days in between have changed us so much. This was the lull before the full force of my storm.

Can you see that now?

I followed you home, discovering so much more. You were a loner, I realised, no parents to fall back on, no family at all, living in a small rented flat. Friends, too, were few and far between.

You were *perfect* for me.

There was no vanity, or ego. No need for designer labels – even if you could afford them. You were an understated beauty, simple in dress with shoes old and worn down, only replaced when you were forced to buy new ones. And that coat that you wore all year round, bolstered by sweaters in the coldest days. It was too deliciously ugly. I loved it.

I knew right away that my father would like you, as he never went for the posh girls, always the down to earth sorts.

'They make the best wives and mothers,' he'd say. 'Just look at the lovely life you can give a simple girl. They'll appreciate you for ever.'

It always made me chuckle: he was old fashioned but not wrong.

Throughout the changing seasons, I got to know how the sunlight fell on your dark brown hair and how it curled when you were caught in the rain. It wasn't until you looked my way, that I saw your sea green eyes. Later, I learnt how they changed colour to hazel depending on your mood. And you have moods, don't you? *I've been on the receiving end of some of those!*

There were other traits I found both endearing, and sometimes irritating. How you ran in order to avoid missing the bus, when really you should have just left earlier. How you were late most of the time, no matter where you went. How you ignored the homeless begging on the street, behaving as though you didn't see them at all, displaying a complete lack of empathy to the world around you.

But even so, I grew to love you at a distance, knowing all along, one day you'd be mine.

I even saw your blindness to me as a challenge. Sometimes, I was near you, a person at the bus stop; queuing in the coffee shop behind you; walking towards you in the park. I was the man who held a door open for you that you never acknowledged or thanked. You were always miles away: lost as you were inside your own internal world. Maybe your mind was on the hero in your latest book. Were you wishing you would be ravished, just as the heroine within those pages was?

All along I knew one day you would know me, see me, love me. I'd be your hero, sweeping you off your feet in such a way that you couldn't resist. In the way you deserved, taking all control and decision out of it. Just as, I knew, you really wanted!

I daydreamed about the day when you'd look into my eyes and smile. A million kisses would be on your lips. You'd praise me for my devotion and patience. Stoic in my resolution, while I wooed you the old-fashioned way. You wouldn't make it easy: love, after all, has to be earned, but I would do my part to fulfil your fantasy; dreams do come true for those who wish hard enough.

There was a time when your head was turned even further away from me. Another you met in your favourite haunt, more forward than me, asked you out. A few dates later and things were getting serious. Though not ready to pursue you in earnest, this person had to go because the way had to be clear.

I suppose you wondered where they were that night they never showed. Why they stopped calling, or didn't pick up when you tried to get in touch? I guess you thought they were a player after sleeping with them the night before – they got what they 'wanted', didn't they? It was a lesson learnt on who not to trust. A lesson you needed before you could be mine. A moral lesson on keeping yourself for me, and only me.

Don't look so surprised ... I reacted as any man might if he were scorned. It had to be dealt with swiftly and with no remorse.

As for my rival, the roses benefited from what remained. My love for you by then, you see, was so deep, and all is fair in love, as well as in war. And sometimes the strategy to win is one and the same anyway.

After a year, I made a note in the new diary of when we would start to date. You'd be readier after the holiday isolation. The Christmas holidays would not be kind to one so alone. I'd swoop in on Boxing Day, a mix up on the delivery of some flowers that would come to your door, instead – I would tell you – to my girlfriend. You'd see me then as datable, romantic: a caring potential lover. All the things I am.

I had it all arranged. All mapped out

My plans were ruined when you stayed away from home for those three holiday days. It took some investigation to learn where you were. I'd been a little too sure of your movements, had predicted you'd be where I thought you to be. But then there was a new curve ball ...

I hadn't counted on you starting the new job, and making new friends in the shape of colleagues. It was shocking seeing you working in a bar, where you met people all the time. A girl like you, collecting and washing glasses, waiting on tables – serving drinks. I'd have never thought it your thing!

I had to take a step back. Rethink things.

You changed a lot after that and I watched your confidence soar, sat in the corner of the bar, nursing a pint of lager. Your smile was out in the open, free to anyone but me.

There were no more days spent in the coffee shop reading romantic fiction.

My vision of 'us' crumbled.

You bought new clothes, which weren't as reserved as your previous style: competing as you were with the other women who worked there. Most nights then, you were never alone. I had to do something before it got worse. They, your new friends, would start to care about your whereabouts.

And so, it wasn't how I wanted the beginning as you know. But the idea of traditional courtship had to be shelved. You were never going to see me … not until I *forced* you to.

I missed those days before the new friends led you astray, but still I wanted you – you were always loved. Always going to be idolised, put on a pedestal, treated like the princess you deserved to be.

Do you remember when I brought you home for the first time? This house, so much better than that awful flat you lived in, with its chintzy wallpaper and tiny one bedroom, little more than a studio really and now you have this place to ramble.

My father used to call it an 'old pile', even while my mother nagged him to decorate, and he would to please her, every few years.

You weren't happy then though, were you? Even though I gave you all this. Even though I promised you could have free reign over your new domain, you had to learn to appreciate your new circumstances. I was a bit surprised at how ungrateful you were. But hard lessons are soon learned …

Don't look so worried, you fret too much. The *box* was necessary at first, but we understand each other now, don't we?

That's it my dear, smile through the tears. It is all for the best, and one day you'll understand that you won't miss the old life. It wasn't good for you, going out clubbing with *them*, they just wanted to use you. That's what young men are like these days. Father explained it and he brought me up to respect women as you can see. I will give you everything and you'll never have to worry again.

Now stand still and let me look at you. Mother's clothes

suit you, don't they? Go and show her, you know where, this place isn't so big that you can't find their room again now that I'm giving you some freedom.

Once I can trust you, you can help me more with them. The drip is always in, just change the bag when it is empty and of course we must drain the catheter bag regularly.

I'll tell you what happened to her, *since you asked*. She tried to leave once father became incapacitated. He'd grown old and frail, lost his grip … well … *control* over her, you see. She never understood that this was all for the best. She didn't have the same versatility as you, and after years of being with him, she decided she wasn't going to stay anymore. And me, as my father's son, couldn't possibly listen to all that crazy talk of hers. She wanted *freedom* … had to *escape* … that kind of thing. The stuff women say when they get all worried about their situation, and if things aren't going all their way.

I realised, as she ranted, that what father had always said about her was true. She was stupid. She was selfish. She didn't appreciate everything he'd done for her all these years, protecting her from the outside world. I didn't see it earlier; I'd just sometimes thought he'd been a bit hard on her. I'd often felt sorry for her. But this attitude – abandoning him after all he'd given her – well it was so wrong! She couldn't see that he'd done everything for her own good.

When she talked of 'going to the police' I knew I had to deal with her. I pointed out how he'd let her have her own way too much … how ridiculous to say he'd tortured, abused her … I couldn't let that kind of slander besmirch his memory could I, as his only son? I mean! Such lies!!

Others? Oh yes … He let her have other children, but I'm the only one left. Too many girls. Father was set in his ways like that. He wanted sons and mother only managed that once – with me. A failing that, sometimes, I do think he punished her for … in ways I didn't agree with if I'm honest because I don't think she understood what she was doing to him then, and she probably didn't mean it. You see, I'm not so bad after all, am I?

I guess you are wondering where the girls went?

Some are in the roses, keeping your old friend company, whereas the others … well, I don't know what he did with them … I was always his favourite and from the beginning I saw things his way. Mostly. And he made sure my education was good, so that I'd know what to do when the time came. Like when he got sick and he taught me how to find someone who could be mine.

Yes, he showed me everything. *The box too.* Although I do hope you won't have to go in there again because you've promised to be good, haven't you?

And now you're having a baby all your own, aren't you? I'm so proud of you!

But don't worry. I won't mind what sex it is: I could never get rid of something that's going to come from both of us. Father was so old fashioned, but you see, a daughter can be taught proper values too, maybe we can find someone worthy for her in time? Someone we approve of, who has the right attitude and worships her of course.

But back to mother. Father wouldn't have been happy if I'd let her go, after he faded away, despite how much she begged me to at first. He'd said they *had* to be together for all time and I couldn't deny him his dying wish, could I?

I drugged her the first night, just to get her in position, but when she came round, and found she was tethered to him: she wouldn't stop screaming. No one wants to see their mother losing it like that, do they? I mean it is not dignified.

So, the drip keeps her calm, feeds her too. She's half alert but feeling no pain. I had to do it, and you can see she's happier now. And father's wish is achieved. So, it's a win win all round!!

Look at them lying side by side. She like Sleeping Beauty, he the prince after her icy lips took him down with her kiss.

Women can destroy you once they have your love. You know that! You almost finished me off with that barmaid escapade! But now, you're being a good girl again, otherwise … well you know where the box is … and it's not good for you in that condition.

Look what you've done! Now mother's carpet is ruined!

Is it the baby making you sick like that? Only I know it isn't my parents, lying as they are, him dead and taxidermized and her, well she's not offending anyone.

Come on now. Let's clean you up. We can't have you like that, not now you're mine. Not now our baby's inside you. You're going to make a great mother. I can see you'll be just as good as mine was ... well, until she lost it ...

But you can see you have inherited her legacy, can't you? Look at you now, mistress of all you survey!

And, every night, when you finish looking after the house and me, and our child, I'll stand you back on the pedestal and you can pretend you can't see me again. Beautiful in your tattered shoes, and old dreary coat ... Won't that be wonderful for you?

Just like the old days.

The *Fukushū* Club

Clara Charmers was parked outside an exclusive hotel in the centre of London. She'd never been inside this one, but she'd collected clients from here many times. Clara knew that a room for one night cost more than most people's monthly mortgage. Now she opened the back door of her limo as the actor, James Bryant, and his latest girlfriend, climbed into the back before passing fans could notice who he was.

Clara closed the limo door, got back in the driver's seat, and switched the engine on. There was no reason to ask where they were going, the journey was already detailed and, she wasn't supposed to talk to the people she chauffeured – not unless they asked her a direct question which wasn't usual: to them she was invisible. But before she pulled away, James surprised her by knocking on the glass partition that divided the passengers from the driver.

James made a winding motion with his hand and she lowered the privacy glass.

'You're not the usual driver,' James said.

'No sir, Beverley is ill,' Clara explained.

'The limo service should have warned me,' he said. 'Can we count on your discretion?'

'Of course, Sir,' Clara said. And indeed, she saw herself as the symbol of the three wise monkeys: 'see no evil', 'hear no evil' and 'speak no evil'; a motto her father, the owner of the limo company, had drilled into all his employees.

Clara considered telling James she was Andrew Charmer's daughter, but thought better of it. Too much chat never went down well with celebrities: they didn't want to know anything about you: everything had to be about them.

'What's your name?' James asked surprising her again.

'Oh James! Leave the girl alone and let her drive. We'll

never get to the party at this rate!'

'Shut it, Faye,' James said. Clara tried not to react to his rude put down of the woman. Their relationship was none of her business but it jarred anyway.

'Well? What's your name?'

'Clara, Sir. And please don't worry, we'll make it to your party on schedule. One hour fashionably late, as you requested.'

Clara closed the glass without another word, cutting him off, and turned her attention back to the journey. She released the handbrake and pulled the limo out into the traffic. She heard the pop of a champagne cork, glanced quickly at her passengers, and saw James filling Faye's glass. Good, they would be distracted now, and would leave her to do her job without further interaction. Just the way she liked it.

The party location wasn't that far from their current position but she'd drive around the longest way to give her passengers time to drink the chilled champagne.

Clara turned the speaker off, cutting out her passengers' conversation in order to give them complete privacy. They had an intercom if they needed to speak to her. She wasn't interested in Faye's inane prattle, though she would never let her opinion of the passengers show. But within seconds of her silencing them, the intercom pinged, and Clara, glanced again at James and Faye. Faye was sitting back in the seat smiling at her as though she found her amusing, and James was once again by the partition.

Clara quelled a surge of irritation. Bev had never mentioned how needy James was, and he was starting to get on her nerves.

'Yes, Sir?' she said through the intercom. 'Do you need anything?'

'Faye has forgotten something. Can you turn back please?'

Clara nodded and took the next available turning.

A short time later, she pulled the limo back in front of their hotel. Clara got out and opened the door of the limo. Faye climbed out and rushed inside without giving her another glance.

'She could have at least thanked you,' James said as

though reading Clara's thoughts. 'For that she deserves to be left behind, don't you think?'

Clara looked at James not understanding what he wanted.

'Now close the door, get in the driver's seat and take me to that party.'

'Without your ...?'

'I'm the paying client. I said let's go. And she's a bitch so I'd prefer to go alone.'

As requested, Clara closed the door. She looked back at the hotel reception. There was no sign of Faye and so she climbed back into the driver's seat and set off again.

'Go straight there this time,' James said. 'And open the partition. It's weird talking to you through this thing!'

The glass rolled down between them again. Clara kept her eyes on the road, but she was aware that James moved once more to the seat by the opening and just behind her. For some reason his proximity made her feel uncomfortable, stifled.

'Tell me about yourself, Clara,' James said now.

'Sir?'

'How long have you been driving limos?'

'Ever since I could drive, pretty much,' Clara said.

'Do you like it?'

'I get to meet interesting people,' Clara said.

'Hmm. Or spoilt little rich and famous people,' James laughed.

'I would never say such a thing,' Clara said.

'Of course, you wouldn't.'

Clara turned the limo right at the next set of lights. They were approaching the address she'd been given, and she would be glad to drop James off. There was something about his over-friendly behaviour that set her teeth on edge. It was weird, and the guy, despite being attractive, was somehow creepy. She began to wonder if Beverley had thrown a sicky just to get out of driving him. Though, Bev had never complained about James that she knew of and gossip about the clients did get back to her as a rule.

Clara let a small smile flick across her lips. At least her shift ended with the drop off, and someone else would collect James later. She didn't fancy hanging around all evening until he decided to go back. And what about the girlfriend? How pissed off was she going to be when she realised James had left without her? Clara had a vision of the girl turning up in a taxi, furious. Perhaps there would be a scene? She was tempted to at least wait around to see him get a dressing down.

'This is the address,' Clara said as they approached a venue in Soho.

She noticed a group of photographers hanging about outside the building. People thought that celebs were caught out and about by accident, but Clara knew that was not the case and that their PR companies leaked their client's locations for free publicity.

'Do you want me to go around the corner to avoid the paps?' Clara asked, expecting James to say no.

'Keep driving. The party isn't there, it's somewhere else,' James said.

'But … this is what was booked.'

'My dear Clara, didn't I tell you earlier, I'm the client? There's a party at this address, yes, but the one I'm going to now is somewhere else. Pull over further down.'

When she stopped the car, James gave her a new address in Wimbledon. Clara programmed it into the sat nav.

'That's an hour away,' she pointed out. 'I'll have to call it in as my shift is due to end shortly.'

'Beverley usually stays with me all evening,' James said.

'I know. But as I'm covering for her, this was a split shift …'

'I don't need to hear it. Just take me to the party.'

Clara closed the partition, cutting off the sound between the front and the back of the limo and she dialled the office number.

'Charmers Limos?' a male voice said.

'Hi, Bill. Mr Bryant has changed his destination. You'll need your next driver to take over and collect from the new location,' Clara said. 'I'll text the address when I get there.'

'Oh, that's not possible, Clara. The replacement driver has

gone down sick too. I was just about to ring you to ask you to stay with Mr Bryant.'

'What?' Clara said. 'Another one sick? What's going on?'

'Sorry. You'll need to stay on this, Clara. We've no one else.'

Clara glanced at James through the rear-view mirror again. He was drinking from his glass of champagne and watching her, smiling as though he knew exactly what she and Bill were discussing. The crazy thought that he'd planned it all came into her mind, but it was impossible as they'd never met before.

'Okay,' she said. 'But you owe me Bill.'

Clara hung up and keeping her eyes firmly on the road, she followed the sat nav to the new location.

James didn't speak to her again. It was almost as though he'd forgotten she was there and Clara was grateful for it. She just didn't like him and couldn't even pinpoint why.

An hour later, they pulled up into the grounds of a huge house just on the outskirts of Wimbledon common. There were a few cars near the entrance, but not as many as he might have expected for a party.

'This is an intimate do,' James said as she opened the door for him. 'Come inside and wait for me.'

'That's okay, I'll wait in the car,' Clara said.

'It wasn't a request,' James said.

Then he marched off to the open door and went inside.

Clara got back in the limo and rang the office again.

'Bill, he's driving me crazy. He's *ordered* me to go inside the house he's at.'

'What's wrong with going inside?' Bill asked. 'It'll be warmer and you can have a hot drink and toilet breaks ...'

'I just don't like it. It's making me feel very uneasy.'

'Jeez, Clara! Why you overreacting? You know what these celebs are like. He probably thinks he's being generous by inviting you in.'

'Can you come and take over and I'll man the phone?' Clara said.

'You know I can't do that! I'm not a licensed driver anymore. Look, Bev always says Mr Bryant is considerate. She's never once complained about him. That's got to mean he's okay. Go in and take advantage of the offer.'

Clara glanced at the still open door.

'I'm just not comfortable with any of this,' she said.

'Then stay in the car, but honestly you have to wait this out, either way. I've no one else to cover it.'

Clara hung up. Despite the open door of the manor house, the place was dark and quiet. There was no sign of life and certainly no sounds of a celebrity party. *Weird.*

Clara closed her eyes. She was tired and it was part of the reason she'd only wanted to cover the first half of this shift.

A few days earlier, she'd taken an old friend in and she hadn't been getting much sleep because of it; a situation Clara hadn't shared with her father, let alone her work colleagues.

Alison had breast cancer and the news had been a shock to them both. Now Clara wanted to get back and see if she was okay after her first chemo session that day. She had no idea how bad it was going to be for Alison, and she'd wanted to be there for her.

Clara opened her eyes, wondering if she'd dozed off, but it was only moments since she'd looked at the clock on the dashboard. Alison had messaged her earlier to say she was back at the flat. She was tired and had gone to bed. Now Clara looked for further messages from her friend but there weren't any. She didn't want to call her as she might wake her. Rest was something Alison would need lots of now, but even so, she couldn't help worrying about her, alone, sick, scared.

Even though she knew what she was getting into when she invited Alison to come and stay, Clara was dreading the hair loss, the sickness, and the frailty that she imagined would come. But all of it she would endure with Alison for her sake, because what else could she do? She owed her this and she knew it.

They'd been friends since their teens, and Alison had been through a lot since then. Clara thought that no one deserved this less than her. From Children's home to foster parents, Alison had been banded from pillar to post and now Clara wanted her to feel safe and not alone. It was important for both their sakes. Especially because ... Clara turned her mind away from any bad thoughts. The past was gone and she was a changed person. She was helping Alison. That was all that mattered.

Clara glanced at the manor door again. Nothing moved inside and she was starting to wish she'd taken James up on the offer to come inside. Just as she thought this, another chauffeur appeared and walked up to the limo.

Clara rolled down the driver's side window and waited for the uniformed man to reach her.

'I've been asked to come and get you. Don't be shy, we're all in the kitchen. There's hot and cold drinks and even plates of buffet food. You should take advantage, as this sort of offer doesn't come often,' he said. 'I'm Barry by the way. Alfred Limos.'

Clara glanced at the door once more, 'I can't hear any music,' she said.

'The basement is sound-proofed,' Barry said.

'Basement?'

'Yes they have a bar down there, a pool and a gym. Perfect party area.'

'Sounds like you've been here before,' Clara said.

'Third Saturday of every month,' Barry said.

Clara studied Barry for a second and then she closed the window while simultaneously opening the door. 'Okay, you've convinced me.'

Locking up the car she followed Barry inside.

The food in the kitchen was piled high on platters that the catering staff were running out to wherever the steps to the basement were. Clara sat down near Barry, there were three other drivers – all male – and they sat around a small breakfast table where a few plates were placed down for them to pick at. Clara wasn't hungry but she took the offer of coffee from one of the waitresses and sat with her hands warming on the mug.

The kitchen was vast, hotel or restaurant standard with highly polished stainless steel work surfaces, huge fridges, two gas cookers. There was a head chef who occasionally barked orders at the sous and pastry chefs that were plating up the food; usually he complained about garnish and there being too much or, too little, of it being used. Clara tried not to stare at the man for fear of drawing his attention.

Whoever owned this house, certainly never cooked for themselves, Clara observed.

'So how long is this thing likely to go on for?' she asked.

'Just after midnight usually,' Barry said. He exchanged a glance with the other drivers, none of whom bothered to introduce themselves.

'Same group every time?' Clara asked.

'Usually, but your client is new. Just been brought into the fold,' Barry explained. The chauffeurs exchanged a glance that Clara didn't understand, but which made her feel excluded. There was something they knew that she didn't, but she didn't ask any questions regardless.

'Gossip is a bad thing,' one of the other drivers said.

'The fact he brought her means she'll be here every month anyway,' another said. 'One of us now.'

'I'm covering for someone else tonight,' Clara said. 'I doubt I'll be back.'

Barry's lips curved up in an attempt at a smile that didn't quite meet his eyes.

'Well, you best make the most of it this trip then,' Barry said.

Shortly after midnight a butler came into the kitchen and nodded to the drivers. Barry was the first to stand.

'We're up then,' he said to Clara. 'They've finished.'

Clara pulled her uniform jacket back on and followed the other drivers out to their cars. No sooner had she unlocked the limo than James came out followed by four other men: all of whom were wearing hoodie tops, which were drawn around their faces. Clara turned her attention to James as she opened the door for him. She noticed how his face was blanched white and gone was the cocksure attitude he arrived with. Subdued, James got into the back of the limo. His eyes stared ahead and he no longer tried to speak to her. She wondered if he'd eaten, drank or taken something that didn't agree with him and hoped, for her own sake, that he didn't throw up in the back of the limo.

Clara saw the other executive cars and limos leave the grounds and turn away in various directions and then she started the engine, backed the limo up and drove the car from the grounds, heading back to the hotel in the centre of London.

To her relief, James didn't speak all the way back.

A few weeks later, Clara had forgotten about the job. She hadn't been working any of the late shifts because Alison needed her. She was sick every time she had chemo and as a result, Clara was feeling the pinch financially. Then, another evening shift fell her way and she saw it was James again.

'I thought Bev was his regular driver,' Clara queried with Bill again.

'He asked for you and he's paying triple if you'll do it,' Bill explained. 'You must've done something right last month.'

It was then that Clara realised it was the third Saturday again, and she recalled the other driver, Barry, explaining this 'party' happened regularly.

With the money James was offering, Clara could work one night every month and subsidise the rest of her income enough that she could just take day shifts the rest of the time, leaving her freer most evenings to be with Alison. It was a win win, even if James was a bit of an arsehole. She checked in with Alison, to see if she thought she'd be okay alone that night.

'Of course, I'll just have a bath and watch a chick flick. Don't worry if you have to work,' Alison reassured her. It helped that she wasn't on Chemo that day, and so Clara was less concerned.

Clara took the job and it became a regular event once a month. If she was honest, it wasn't an unpleasant gig. And James, deep in his own thoughts, was silent now in the back of the vehicle. A situation that Clara was glad of as she could live inside her own thoughts, while taking them safely to the party.

Meanwhile, Alison began to lose her hair. They made a video of Alison shaving it off: she cried while the remaining clumps fell onto her lap. Clara found it heart wrenching, and also couldn't help thinking how grateful she was that it wasn't her. The cancer and especially the chemo treatment, disgusted Clara but she always tried to show a sympathetic face to Alison, being as kind and thoughtful as she could be.

'Keep filming, Clara,' Alison told her as though she saw through the façade anyway. 'When this is all behind me I'll have a record of the lowest point.'

'It's all up from here,' Clara said trying to reassure her. But it was traumatic watching her friend go through so much and she repressed the shudders, only letting them out when Alison's attention was elsewhere.

The months went by. Alison finished the chemo. Her eyebrows, lashes and hair began to grow back. Clara noticed it was finer, curlier, than it had been, but the Macmillan nurses had warned that her hair might be different and so every change was accepted as the norm, and they didn't dwell on it, even when they noticed a difference.

Every month she picked up James and took him to the Wimbledon manor, noting how quiet he was whenever he came out after the so-called party. He'd stopped trying to talk to her at all by then, not even greeting her when she arrived at the hotel, but she was always grateful for his silence as it was so much better than his faux friendship and curious questions. In the end, it was a well-paid job and it required little effort. She'd even started to eat some of the delicious food on offer, treating it, like the other chauffeurs did, as perk of the job.

The months passed and Alison was in remission. Clara was able to take on more work again. The whole thing now had a positive impact on her finances. She'd been worried, at one point, that she'd have to ask her father for help. But he'd never liked Alison, not since the fall out over the wedding that didn't happen and Alison had been left at the altar. Somehow, her father had blamed her jilted friend for being the victim. These days Alison never mentioned her ex, Steven, and it was just as well, because he was the last person Clara wanted to talk about.

As Alison got better, with the worst days of her recovery behind her, Clara thought her friend would want to move out and take on her old life again. Surely she could now return to the job that had been kept open for her? But Alison showed no signs of doing so, nor of moving back to her solitary flat in Putney. Why bother when she could share in the beautiful dock location that Clara had, a gift from her father on her 21st birthday? An 'investment' he'd said in her future and it had been the only 'gift' he'd given her in her entire life, making her work as hard as he'd had to when he was building his business empire way back when.

As the months rolled on and half a year had passed, Clara began to wonder how to broach the subject of her friend moving out. She was living off her completely, ordering groceries on Clara's account, not paying anything towards the bills. In fact, Clara didn't know if Alison had any income at all, as it didn't seem as though she did nor did it bother her. Clara on the other hand was working harder than ever.

She was about six months in on the Wimbledon job when she noticed a change in the chauffeurs. Barry disappeared first and the other two drivers changed soon after. There was never a familiar face again and she was the only returning regular driver. Clara never saw any of the other guests either because James always left before everyone else, immediately after midnight, and she'd feel a sense of urgency when he didn't allow her to linger, but insisted, in the only dialogue they exchanged all evening, that it was 'important' to leave 'right away'.

Clara noticed a change in him as the actor lost weight, became gaunt, as though he were slowly starving to death and had forgotten how to eat. Yet food went down into the basement on those Wednesdays and empty plates returned.

Clara found herself wondering what was happening that was distressing James so much and why he returned, month on month, regardless? But, as she drove him back to central London, Clara had no right to ask such questions. It wasn't her place, and went against the code that her father's mantra insisted on.

That night she arrived home, tired, stressed, and she found the flat in darkness. Alison usually left the lamp on for her return, and so she went to check on her, but found that her friend wasn't home.

Clara looked at her phone for the first time that evening hoping for a message of explanation but there was nothing. She sent Alison a text, asking if she was okay, but no reply came. As she had been responsible for her for months now, Clara began to worry that something had happened. She went into her friend's room, glanced around as if looking for a clue of where Alison had gone.

This is ridiculous, she thought. Alison was a grown woman. Maybe she'd finally gone out with other friends for the evening and lost track of the time? Or maybe she'd gone back to her own place at last, and was starting to get her life back on track? But the spare room was still full of Alison's things, and so Clara didn't think this was the case. Even so, she forced herself to go to bed. She had to work tomorrow and needed the rest. Alison would have to take care of herself from now on anyway and Clara had done all she could so far for her anyway.

A few days went by before Clara really began to worry. Alison didn't return, nor did she reply to any of her texts and Clara's calls went through to voice messenger which she never answered.

After ringing a few friends, Clara decided that she ought to go to the Putney flat because no one had heard from Alison. She had to be there, where else would she go? There was the worry, of course, that Alison had relapsed and as Clara travelled up in the lift to Alison's flat, she feared that she'd find her ill or dead inside.

When Alison's treatment had begun, Clara frequently went back and forth to the flat to collect things for her and the key was still on her keyring. She tried it now in the door and the lock didn't budge. Had Alison changed the lock? Was she avoiding Clara, and if so, why?

She rang the doorbell now and she heard movement inside, which gave her a few seconds' relief as someone fumbled with the chain and lock on the other side, but when the door opened, Clara found herself face to face with a stranger.

'I'm looking for Alison,' she said.

'Who?' the woman said.

'She lives here?'

'Oh. Must have been the previous tenant,' the woman said. 'I've been here a few months now.'

'That's not possible. I've been here in that ...' Clara stopped. She hadn't been back since the first month that Alison moved in with her. And never again since, because Alison hadn't asked her to.

'Do you have a forwarding address?' Clara asked.

'Sorry. No.'

The woman closed the door, ending the conversation, and Clara found herself confused and afraid for the first time in months. Where was Alison? Why had she given up her flat without telling her?

Clara returned to her place and for the first time opened all the wardrobes in the spare room. She hadn't wanted to pry before and therefore hadn't searched the room beyond a cursory glance over the surfaces. Now she discovered the chest of drawers and wardrobes empty and she knew without doubt that Alison had left of her own volition and, for some reason, hadn't told her. Clara felt hurt by this behaviour after what she'd done for her over the last few months, letting her friend's illness all but take over her life until recently. And now Alison was gone without even a thank you. It was at the very least rude, but otherwise incredibly cruel to do that to a friend who cared, and then to not answer her calls on top of that!

Clara dialled Di: a mutual friend of them both who she hadn't spoken to in a while.

'Hey Clar ...' Di said answering the phone.

'Have you heard from Alison?' Clara asked.

'No. Why?'

'Well, she's been living with me for months. She probably told you … about the breast cancer …'

'Breast cancer?' Di said shocked. 'No. I didn't know about it. Is she okay?'

Clara explained. 'She told me you all knew, that she'd asked you to respect her privacy,' Clara explained. 'I just thought the silence was out of respect for her recovery.'

'Look …' said Di. 'Are you sure she was sick?'

'What do you mean?'

'Did you go to any appointments with her?'

'Well, no, but I looked after her in the evenings. Mostly she just slept … then we had to shave her hair …'

'Why?' said Di.

'Because she said the nurse told her it was falling out … I videoed it.'

'Send it me,' said Di.

Clara pinged the video through to her WhatsApp and after watching it Di called her back.

'Clara … there's no bald patches.'

'What?'

'Alison's head. Her hairline and scalp. It just looks like she's had a number one cut … I think she lied to you about her illness. She looks as healthy as anything. No weight loss. And the tears, she almost looks like she's laughing not crying … I hate to be mean. But she always had a weird sense of humour.'

'But … why would she do this to me?' Clara said.

Di went quiet on the other end of the phone.

'Di? Do you know something?'

'About nine months ago, Alison told me something. She said that you and Steven … well that you were behind him leaving her at the altar.'

'No!' Clara denied. 'Why would she think that?'

'I don't know,' said Di. 'I asked, but she refused to tell me. I thought she was just looking for someone to blame. But now, after what you've told me, I think she really believed you were involved. That you and Steven had a fling …'

Clara hung up the phone without saying another word. She couldn't admit to Di that in a way she was involved. Steven was a bastard. He was never good enough for Alison and Clara had known that all along. When she found out about the affair he'd been having, just weeks before the wedding, she'd warned him to tell Alison the truth. But he'd ignored her and Clara had had to resort to blackmail. She hadn't expected him to be a no-show at the wedding, letting Alison down like that. She'd hoped he'd come clean and Alison would have had her dignity, but the rat just hadn't had the balls to be honest. At the time she'd comforted Alison, told her it was for the best, but she'd felt awful too, and had wished she hadn't said anything at all. Maybe she should have let the marriage go ahead, but then, if Alison found out afterwards, wouldn't that have been worse for everyone?

'It's all for the best,' she'd told her at the time while she Alison sobbed her heart out.

But how could she know that Clara was the reason Steven didn't show? That coward would surely never own up to it, would he?

As a last-ditch attempt to reach out to her friend, Clara sent another text to Alison.

I'm really worried about you. Hope you're okay. Please just let me know!

But Alison never replied, and soon, Clara discovered why.

The letters started to arrive thick and fast. Clara's cards were maxed out. Her bank account cleared out. She'd been so engrossed in all she was doing; she hadn't even noticed the money dribbling out over the last few months. Now she wondered how Alison could have had access to it all, but she'd let her into her shopping account for ease while she'd been working, her computer was always logged into her many online shopping accounts and her handbag was always lying around with her purse and cards inside it. Plus, Clara had a terrible time remembering passwords and she kept a small notebook in a drawer in her bedroom with them all in.

Now she went in search of the notebook and found the page for her bank account ripped out. It was obvious she'd been scammed. And worst of all, her utilities bills hadn't been paid because of it.

She rang the bank and put a stop on all her cards and requested new passwords. After spending a long time on the phone with their fraud team, Clara was told that the police would have to be involved if she wanted to claim her money back.

She had to agree, but she agonised about it. It was, after all, her fault. But what a cruel person Alison was, to have gone to such lengths to betray her, and in such a detailed way. Clara couldn't get her head around it.

She found herself sitting in her lounge, wondering what to do for the next few days until her accounts and credit cards worked again. She had no money, no way of getting through this without the degrading phone call to her father. It was the last thing she wanted to do.

Just then, she received a call from Bill, giving her a booking from James.

'That's fine,' she said. 'But I need an advance Bill. In cash, or I can't fill the limo.'

She explained what had happened.

'That's shit!' Bill said. 'I'll let your dad know.'

'No. Please. Don't tell my dad,' Clara said. 'He never liked Alison.'

'Sounds like he had good instincts,' Bill said and the comment stung more than it should have. 'Look, pop round and I'll give you some petty cash. I'll take it out of your wages from the gig tonight.'

'Thanks Bill,' Clara said. 'I'll be there shortly. Can you spot me a grand so that I can go and pay some urgent bills, or I may have no electricity for the next few days until this gets sorted?'

Bill agreed and Clara took the limo around to the offices, collected her money and then spent the day paying everything that was urgent, as well as filling the car ready for the evening booking.

It was a relief to finally go to pick up James for his monthly event and to know that for the moment her finances were once again stable.

James looked different when she collected him that evening. He was back to himself and looked as though the thing that had bothered him for the past few months had passed, but Clara couldn't ask questions about his life or his health and so she behaved as usual with the professional dignity that was expected.

'Nice to see you Clara,' James said as he climbed into the back of the car. 'It's going to be fun this evening. There's an annual meeting and so there will be many more guests tonight.'

Clara picked up on the word 'meeting' but didn't ask for clarification. She'd always taken this trip as a party and suspected it involved some specific illegal substances that she was best not knowing about based on the condition that James often came out in.

'Things have changed,' James told her now. 'I haven't been in a good place, but with the help of the group I've now turned a corner.'

Clara didn't answer.

'Don't you want to know? Aren't you curious?' James said.

'I'm paid for discretion, Sir,' Clara said. 'Curiosity is not in the remit.'

James laughed. It was hearty and relaxed. 'You're a funny woman … Am I allowed to call you that? I'm never sure these days and the last thing any actor needs is to get "cancelled" because of a throw away remark.'

'You can call me a woman. Or a person. I don't mind,' said Clara. 'You're paying.'

James laughed again.

'I like you Clara. That's why you're still with me. You've always been better than Beverley or any other driver I've had. So, I'm going to be decidedly indiscreet with you. Do you know what we do once a month?'

Clara didn't answer, but deep down she hoped he'd tell her.

'Not even a clue?'

'It's none of my business, Sir,' Clara said because she thought she should.

After the day she'd had, she'd hoped for silence tonight but now James was starting to irritate her again with whatever game he was playing. If he was like this with her, someone he barely knew, what must he be like with his girlfriends or family? Clara realised then that she hadn't seen the girlfriend – Faye, wasn't is? – since that very first night. She also hadn't heard of any serious fall out either in the press. Not that she spent much time looking at celebrity gossip when she'd been so busy with Alison.

Thinking of Alison brought about a fresh round of anxiety that Clara hadn't been prepared for. If she hadn't needed the money, she might have cancelled out on this job tonight. The shock and hurt she felt went so deep. She couldn't understand why Alison would, or could, do what she had to her. All that trust she put in her friend, never knowing that she was being scammed. What would her father say if she did tell him? Clara shuddered at the thought. Charles, after all, never trusted anyone did he?

'You look sad,' James said.

Clara glanced at him in the rear-view mirror.

'Why not tell me about it? After all, I'm not about to judge.'

Clara took a breath determined to refuse the offer, but before she knew what she was doing she poured the whole story out, with one exception, she didn't mention her part in Steven jilting Alison on their wedding day.

'Shit. That is fucked up,' James said when she stopped talking.

'I'm sorry. I shouldn't have told you. It's unprofessional.'

'Bollocks to that love. That friend of yours is an evil bitch and she clearly planned to scam you. Did you talk to the police about it?'

Clara nodded. 'Well. On the phone as I had to report it or the credit card company and banks wouldn't insure the money. Which eventually I will get back ... but I have to make a formal statement yet. They all told me it's my own fault though. That I shouldn't have allowed her access.'

'Yeah. That sucks. But, you've known this girl how long?'

'We went to school together. Almost twenty years now ...'

'The thing is love; you can't trust anyone. They are all out to get you. It's one thing I learnt early on. Everyone has a motive. And if you're somebody, then they want a piece of that. She was obviously jealous of you,' James concluded.

'But why?' Clara said.

'Damn! You don't even know? You're a hot chick who drives a limo and probably mixes with some big wigs. Why wouldn't she be envious of that?'

Clara found herself laughing for the first time in weeks.

'I probably should say thanks for the compliment, but seriously, we shouldn't be having conversations like this.'

'I won't tell if you won't,' James said and he laughed.

'And, you probably shouldn't call anyone else a "chick". It's inappropriate and someone might get offended. I don't care though, to be fair ...'

'You're all right, Clara. You know that?' James said.

'Thanks. I'll deffo take that as a compliment.'

They reached the house in Wembley and James hesitated before getting out of the car.

'This thing I go to. It's kind of a meet up. A group. A sect. Some *might* call it a cult.'

Clara met his eyes through the rear-view mirror.

'But they help you. They help *fix* things for you. You know what I'm getting at?'

Clara shook her head.

'When you become a member, your problems are theirs. This girl that betrayed you. They'd find her. Make her face the consequences for her actions.'

'What are you saying?' Clara asked, even though she was afraid to hear the answer.'

'I can recommend you to the club … A few months in, the world's your oyster,' James said.

'I suppose it's expensive? I can't really afford to join an exclusive club …' Clara pointed out.

'It's based on percentage of the help you get. *Quid pro quo* sometimes. Not on actual money.'

'So, I'd have to do something for the club?' Clara asked.

'Something like that. Think about it, and maybe, next month, you'll be coming to the meeting instead of driving me to it,' James said.

Clara got out of the car and opened the door for James.

'When would I have to let you know?' Clara said.

'As soon as possible,' James said.

There was something bad and thrilling and dangerous about the offer and Clara didn't know if this was just another one of James' little games again. How could she possibly agree to something she didn't understand? It was insane.

'Okay. I'm in,' she said.

One month later Clara arrived at the Wimbledon house with James but this time she was in the back of the limo. To avoid gossip, James had ordered a different chauffeur service and Clara, on his advice, was dressed up and wearing sunglasses. She'd met up with him, prior to the car arriving, at the bar in the hotel, and one expensive cocktail later, the two of them were slipping into the back seat.

'Champagne?' James asked as he popped the cork.

This is a weird reversal of fortune, she thought as she took the offered glass.

She was relaxed, having restored her bank access and after hearing from the credit card companies and her bank just that morning that the money theft was going to be covered, and she was expecting it all back in her bank very shortly. She'd been working hard all month, feeling very insecure about money after all that had happened, and she'd taken every job that Bill had offered. She had earned a break. As she sat in the back of the limo, she checked her bank account and she was surprised to see a large transaction had gone in from a company called *FUKUSHŪ*.

'Everything okay?' James asked.

'That's weird!' Clara said. She showed James the amount and the name.

'No. Not at all. It means you passed the vetting stage. Tonight is the start.'

'What do you mean?'

'*Fukushū* is owned by the founder of our group, Kenzō Tanaka. You've probably heard of him because he's a film producer these days too. Tonight, you become one of us, and all your money worries are gone in one swoop.'

'But how? Why?'

'I told you. I recommended you,' James said topping up her champagne glass. 'This will take the edge off …'

Clara sipped before his words sank in. 'Edge off what?'

'Ah. We're here!'

The limo pulled into the very familiar grounds of the manor house in Wimbledon and James knocked back his glass of champagne as the driver pulled the limo up in front of the house.

The back door opened and the driver who, Clara realised, James hadn't bothered to ask his name, nor had he talked to him like he had always talked to her.

Clara was nervous as she climbed out of the back seat and then followed James into the house. Was this going to be all weird handshakes, rolled up trousers and some bizarre initiation ceremony? Clara just couldn't imagine what would happen next and James had been vague on the details. Even so, the nerves were tinged with excitement. Tonight, she was becoming part of something different. Something exclusive. Something that no average person was invited to, which made her feel unique and special. Every bit the 'hot chick' that James had said she was.

Once through the door, they passed the familiar route to the kitchen and walked on further down the corridor of what

Clara realised must have been servants' quarters of the big house back in the day. She saw the old bell pull system, still on the wall, probably still connected to all the rooms. There were around 30 bells which now gave her the real size of this place.

A door lay open at the end of the corridor and Clara followed James through and down some worn stone steps to the cellar.

They reached the bottom and Clara noted they were now in an incredible underground space that must run the entire length and width of the house. There were sofas, a self-serve bar, a water feature, subdued lighting that made her feel like was in a private nightclub. Over on one side of the space was a row of doors, two of which were bathrooms. On the other side of the room was a large glass bifold door that was pulled open to show a huge swimming pool beyond.

Beautiful people inhabited the space lying on sunless loungers. There was not one unattractive man or woman who lolled by the pool, or sat on stools at the bar, or reclined on the sofas.

James went to the bar and ordered drinks for them both; by then, Clara's head was beginning to spin because she was unused to drinking.

'Just a juice for me,' she told him but he returned with a potent cocktail instead.

Clara sipped it and grimaced. 'Seriously ... I can't drink this.'

'I strongly advise you ...' James began and then there was the sound of a gong being hit.

James stopped talking and knocked back his drink. The other people converged and curved around them in a circle. A tall Asian man walked into the centre. He looked like an older Gok Wan. James pulled Clara back to join him and the circle parted to accommodate them both. The group put their hands together in a prayer position and bowed from the waist to the man. Clara realised that this was Kenzō Tanaka, and he now returned the bow, showing equal respect to his guests. As though on autopilot, Clara returned Tanaka's bow.

And then the evening became very weird indeed.

The circle widened and all the beautiful people gathered around Tanaka, waiting for some speech or other.

'We have a new member to present this month, courtesy of James,' Tanaka began. 'Come forward Clara into the circle and let us salute you.'

Clara glanced at James and he nodded at her to step forward.

'Welcome to the *Fukushū* Club,' Tanaka said.

Tanaka offered her an empty champagne glass. Clara glanced at James, then took the glass.

Two women came forward and spread a sheet of plastic down on the floor between Clara and Tanaka.

'Bring the *Uragirimono* ...' Tanaka said.

James and one other man, a celebrity that Clara recognised but whose name she couldn't remember, went to the row of doors on the side of the cellar. They opened the end door and then they pulled a woman out of the room. Her hands were tied and she was wearing what looked like a pillowcase over her head. The woman was brought into the circle and stood on top of the plastic sheeting. James and the other man held her by the arm. She didn't struggle or attempt to get away as though she understood the part she was supposed to play in this ritual.

Tanaka walked around the woman and then glanced at Clara.

It's an initiation game, Clara thought. This was why James had warned her to hold her ground, no matter what happened, and now Tanaka pulled the makeshift hood off the woman's head and ripped away the silver tape that was covering her mouth.

Clara stared at the battered and subdued face of her former friend and scammer, Alison, and felt an immediate surge of concern.

'What hap ...?' she said.

James gave her a warning look, his face was blank, mask-like, serious, and Clara fell silent. It was all faked anyway: but they'd found Alison, brought her here for Clara to confront, and she'd be handed over to the police for her crime afterwards no doubt.

'Clara – face the person who wronged you,' Tanaka said. 'Tell her how you feel and free yourself of anger and hatred.'

Clara nodded to show she understood.

'Alison, you lied to me and stole from me. You put me in serious financial jeopardy. We were supposed to be friends and I thought I was helping you when you most needed it, but it was all a scam!' Clara said sure that this was the confrontation that Tanaka expected. 'Why did you do this to me?'

'You stole my fiancé,' Alison said. Her voice was weak and tired, she was playing the part of a tortured woman well. Clara wondered if they'd primed her to do it, or if she was genuinely afraid.

'Of course, I didn't!' Clara said. 'Why would you think that?'

'You were sleeping with him!' Alison said. 'He told me!'

Clara was shocked and visibly shaken by the accusation. It had never occurred to her that Steven would lie to Alison about the reason he'd been a no-show at the wedding.

'No. That's not true. *He lied to you.* I caught him cheating on you and I told him to 'fess up or I'd tell you. Instead, he jilted you. I wouldn't have been any kind of friend if I'd not confronted him! How could you believe that lying toe-rag?'

Alison lifted sad eyes to Clara.

'Why should I believe you? Your friends kidnapped me, beat me ...'

'Don't be rid—' Clara looked at Tanaka and she realised then that her first instinct to be concerned was right. Alison's injuries were real. She'd known it all along but had refused to recognise it. Clara felt a surge of panic and the blood rushed into her cheeks as the reality of what was really happening dawned on her with full clarity.

'And now for the ultimate *Fukushū* ...' Tanaka said.

Tanaka was holding a long sharp blade and the people in the circle began to chant. 'Kill her'. Tanaka held the knife out to Clara.

Understanding that the end had come, Alison began to struggle and pull away in a final panicked attempt to escape her obvious fate, but James and the other man held her firmly, then forced her down to her knees in front of Clara.

'This is your *Fukushū*,' James said. 'Which means *Revenge* in Japanese in case you haven't realised.'

Tanaka pressed the handle of the blade into Clara's hand even as it dawned on her that she would have to commit this crime, not just witness it.

Clara gripped the knife. This was insane and she knew it. She didn't want to kill anyone. She wasn't angry at Alison anymore but the look in James' eyes told her she had no choice. Alison was dead no matter what happened.

'Any advice on how to do this?' Clara said, keeping her voice steady.

'Up and under the ribs,' Tanaka whispered into her ear. 'Or slit her throat.'

Clara looked down at Alison. She'd stopped struggling as though she'd lost her remaining strength.

'Throat,' she said, feeling this might take less effort.

'Swift and firm,' James said and his eyes impressed on her that this would be for her own sake and not Alison's.

James tangled his fingers in Alison's hair and yanked her head back, exposing her throat.

Alison was foaming at the mouth in fear and shock. Clara avoided meeting her crazed eyes as she knew this would tip her own sanity over the edge.

How hard was it to kill someone? Especially when the crime didn't fit the punishment? For surely this was excessive? Shouldn't Steven be there, and not Alison?

Clara met James's eyes again. The colour was gone from his perpetually tanned face, and Clara considered that his fate, too, might hang in the balance because she was his recommendation. Now she wondered how and why he'd chosen her? Did he see her as someone capable of killing?

She pondered the question for a short second: this was a murder club, a cult of psychopaths, and Clara wouldn't get out alive if she didn't do this. Was there really any choice? It crossed her mind that she could go to the police afterwards and say she was under duress … Surely she would get away with it?

Without further hesitation, Clara pressed the sharp edge against Alison's throat, she closed her eyes and then swept the blade firmly along Alison's skin. The blade cut deep and blood immediately emerged from the wound. Clara tried not to think about how the knife slipped through Alison's throat like butter, snagging briefly on the taut sinew of her neck.

Tanaka took the knife from her immediately when the deed was done and she was left staring, numb with shock, at the gaping wound as James and the man held Alison upright even as the blood gushed and her lips flapped in silent panic.

Clara saw the significance of the empty glass held in her less dominant hand. She lifted her arm and held the glass near the wound, filling it now from the fountain of Alison's blood.

Clara stepped back.

James and the other actor lowered Alison's body down onto the plastic sheeting with a degree of reverence that they hadn't shown her when she lived. Then the two of them proceeded to wrap the body. A trolley was brought forward by the two women who'd laid the sheeting down and Alison was lifted onto it. They wheeled her away, stowing her back into the room they'd taken her from.

'Drink, then pass it on,' Tanaka said.

Clara sipped and swallowed Alison's blood. Then passed the glass to Tanaka. He took it to each of the attendees, all of them sipped the cooling fluid in a perverse replica of holy communion. Tanaka was the last to partake and he finished the glass with a flourish, then walked away taking it with him.

Clara was in shock when James pushed another glass into her hand. This one contained brandy.

'It's ok to throw up,' he said. 'I did. Multiple times. So did a lot of those here.'

She looked at him now, a feeling of unreality followed the moment. She didn't feel sick. Instead, she looked around at the other club members. They all dispersed to various parts of the room and resumed the party as if nothing had happened.

After the blood was drunk and the body stowed, the waiters appeared and platters of food were being taken around the room. None of the waiters had seen anything and now a bartender was pouring drinks behind the bar too, equally oblivious of the murder that had just taken place a few feet away.

Men and women alike, all witnesses to the crime she'd committed, tucked into the canapés, and ordered drinks as though nothing had happened. She wanted to imagine it hadn't, divorce herself from it, just as they seemed able to.

'You're very calm,' James said. 'I can't say I was – but I'm glad, because it's pleasing Tanaka.'

'What did you get for your revenge killing?'

'Get?' James said.

'Your reward? Mine was more money than I'd see in a lifetime of chauffeuring.'

'The Oscar,' James said. 'Best Actor.'

'Did you know what you'd have to do for it?'

'No. I was recruited. Like you were. Recruiters aren't allowed to tell you anything much … Would you have come if I had told you what would happen?'

Clara shook her head, 'I'd have thought you insane.'

'Exactly. There's no going back now. You're one of us. There's no escaping *Fukushū.*'

'You can never leave?' Clara said.

'Tanaka told me to warn you: you can't tell anyone Clara. This room is the only place you can ever discuss what you did because none of us will judge.'

James took her arm and led her towards the swimming pool.

She let him steer her to one of the loungers. They both sat.

'So, here's a scenario,' James said. 'One that crossed my mind. You leave here tonight; you go to the police. You tell them everything. And while they are processing you for murder, you commit suicide in the cell. Only it isn't suicide.

Someone got to you and silenced you,' James looked back at the main bar area. 'In that room are politicians, police officials, the deputy Prime Minister. All untouchable.'

Clara looked back at the partying celebrities. She knew he was right.

'Will I be expected to do this again?'

James glanced at the crowd. 'Maybe. If you recruit and they fail. Then you'd have to silence them.'

'You'd have killed me tonight?' Clara said. She recoiled. Strange how she'd gone from disliking him to a wary friendship over the past months and then back now to revulsion.

'I never doubted you and knew I wouldn't have to,' James said.

Clara looked down at her clenched hands. She saw a splash of red on the back of her hand.

'You should wash that off,' James said. 'The waiters, as you might have guessed, are all innocent. If any of them became suspicious, we'd have to kill them.'

Clara stood and made her way back through the party room. Crossing the main floor, she glanced down at the spot where Alison had died and saw no sign of the murder. They had all known what they were doing.

She reached the ladies toilet and opened the door, then went inside.

As she washed her hands, she studied her face in the mirror. Her face hadn't changed. There was no sign that showed she was a murderer. Clara marvelled at this. Surely, she had transformed and it must be visible?

As she dried her fingers, she noticed her hands were trembling, but she didn't think this was with fear, more the residual adrenaline rush the experience had given her.

Another woman came into the bathroom behind her. Clara glanced at her in the mirror.

'Well done,' she said. 'You've rid yourself of anger.'

'What do you mean?' Clara said.

'Tanaka's philosophy in life. Anger is poison that eats the soul. You'll live longer, healthier. We are all grateful for the change in our lives.'

Clara nodded. She didn't feel anything now. Not anger, not shame, not regret.

'I feel free ... if that's the right word,' Clara said.

The woman smiled at her. 'Yes. I think it is. You're truly one of us.'

Clara left the bathroom and as she wandered around the room, she was stopped frequently. Praised. Patted. Her hand was shaken. Some hugged her.

'Brave soul,' they said.

'You're one of us ...' was a frequent comment.

And Clara began to feel, as the evening went on, that she was part of something bigger than herself, bigger than all of them and Tanaka was at the heart of it.

It's a cult, she reminded herself and perhaps she was being radicalised by their mutual experiences but she somehow didn't mind.

Clara had lost sight of James but knew he was still present: no one left until after the witching hour. And now she would be here, the third Wednesday in every month. Supporting the members in their quest for revenge, their purging of anger as they cleansed their souls with blood.

Tanaka hadn't spoken to her since she arrived and since Alison's death and she saw him now across the room speaking to the Mayor of London. She experienced an odd sensation, as though she were waking from an awful nightmare. She fought the urge to scream and tear at her hair as though the reality of what had happened was clear to her at last.

'Hold it together,' said James appearing beside her. 'It's almost midnight.'

The group gathered once more as Tanaka came forth to give a final speech but this is where the formality ended.

'We welcome, Clara to the *Fukushū* family, and wish her pleasure and success for the next month when we reconvene. You have behaved with the dignity befitting a member of our exclusive club. We thank James for finding you. Forever ours, go and live your life. All your dreams will come true. Your life is forever blessed.'

James took Clara's hand. He raised her fingers to his lips and pressed a small kiss on them.

They left first. James leading her by the hand as though they had been transformed into a couple. At the doorway, Clara saw Faye, the woman James had been with on their very first trip and whom he'd left behind at the hotel.

'She was your recruiter,' Clara said.

James smiled and nodded as they passed Faye.

It was all for show, Clara thought. Faye had probably been here, at the *Fukushū* club, waiting for James to arrive and be initiated.

As they got into the back of the limo Clara looked at James.

'It was all planned, wasn't it? From the beginning you marked me for the club.'

'I knew all about you before then, yes. But not what your revenge would be. Your friend Alison did us a favour.'

'And now what happens?' Clara wanted to know.

'Tanaka wants us to be together. A power couple. Of course, I won't rush you.'

Clara looked at the limo driver as he climbed into the driver's seat and said nothing more for fear of what the man would hear. The car pulled away and she was left with so many questions that she needed answers for. What if she refused James? What would Tanaka do? Was he so powerful that none of them could resist? Were they all pawns in a game that only Tanaka understood?

She glanced at James through the corner of her eye. He looked happy, elated. The evening had gone better than planned. He was one of Tanaka's foot soldiers, moving up in the ranks. Clara could see that now.

A powerful ally or a fearsome foe ... She forced herself to see him through a lover's eyes. There were worse men to be associated with than a successful Hollywood actor and Clara knew they looked good together.

She glanced down at her hands as they rested, still, in her

lap. The hands of a killer … or perhaps of someone who had freed themselves from anger? It all depended on your viewpoint.

It was strange how Tanaka's philosophy made sense to her emotions. What was he after all? A businessman, a producer, or a spiritual leader?

Clara took James's hand in hers. He turned and smiled at her. Calm. Loving. Self-assured. She could see the logic of Tanaka's wishes. They could be an influential couple. There was no doubt in her mind that it was already preordained. For who else could she share the deepest darkest side of herself with other than the man who had watched her coldly kill her former best friend?

Clara took James's hand. Once more he raised her fingers to his lips.

It was the end of an era, but the start of something so much better.

The Curse of the Blue Diamond

It was a dark winter morning when a hand-delivered letter arrived at 221B Baker Street.

My friend and colleague, Sherlock Holmes, was away on some family business that he, in his usual style, refused to divulge to me. I was left holding the fort, so to speak, and so Mrs Hudson brought in the letter on a tray that also held a fresh pot of tea and one teacup, markedly reminding me that I was quite alone.

'Arrived a few moments ago,' said Mrs Hudson. 'It smells like expensive perfume too ...'

I took the envelope from her and, on instinct, raised it to my nose. Of course, Holmes would most likely have known which perfume it was, but 'expensive' covered it for me at that point. I met Mrs Hudson's curious eyes and felt a moment of anxiety that Holmes wasn't there to comment upon the mysterious note himself.

'Aren't you going to open it?' Mrs Hudson asked.

'Not at all. Bad form to open another chap's letter,' I said.

'My dear doctor ... it is addressed to *you*.'

'Oh!'

I read the writing on the front and discovered that my name was indeed on it.

'But who ...?'

Mrs Hudson smiled and waited. I realised then that she was as curious as I, a trait I had noticed she was developing of late, and I wasn't about to encourage that curious nature of hers any more than was unavoidable.

'Thank you, Mrs Hudson. I'll enjoy my tea and get to this sometime this afternoon,' I said.

I placed the letter down once more upon the tray.

Mrs Hudson frowned, then turned and left the room. I poured myself some tea, but my eyes strayed constantly to the envelope until finally I gave in to my own excessive interest and I lifted it up, smelling the paper once more, before turning it over and breaking the red wax seal on the back.

As if the perfume were not enough evidence as to the gender of the writer, the letter inside had been written in an unmistakably female hand. The writing was elegant and curved, with no sign of the aggression often found in male penmanship. However, I felt the hand rushed, and a smudge of ink on the corner of the page confirmed my suspicions.

Dear Dr Watson,

I am writing to you to ask for help. I believe you are the trusted friend of the detective Mr Holmes, and a respected physician.

The letter went on with praise for me and Holmes, and referenced how the writer had heard of us through a mutual friend, though the name of the friend was not given. Then it reached the reason for the missive:

A mysterious sickness took my father some months ago. Since then, we had barely begun to grieve when my mother's health began to fail, until she too was no more. I'm sure that you are, by now, wondering how you may be of assistance. This, as you may be able to tell, is very difficult for me. You see, my fiancé has recently fallen to the same affliction. However, our doctor can find no cause. What appeared to be an age-related illness in my parents cannot be the same in Jeremy's case, as a man of barely thirty years of age. Until now he has been fit and well; he remembers suffering few of even the most common childhood ailments.

It is peculiar that this all happened around the

same time: when we received, or rather my father did, a parcel containing a blue diamond. A rare and expensive jewel that was left to him by his brother, my uncle ...

I was startled that the lady had sent the letter to me instead of to Holmes. Maybe she was aware that he was unavailable, even though his private life was always kept undisclosed. I, as his closest friend, did not even know precisely where he was or how long he would be gone. So how would a total stranger know more? Then, when I reached the end of the letter, I discovered that the lady in question was none other than Hope Ballentine, a socialite of some repute – A lady I had met briefly some twelve months earlier. I was both surprised and flattered that she remembered me. I decided that I would help Miss Ballentine, even though I wasn't sure what I could do without my partner.

After dictating a quick reply by telegram, I was soon on my way to Brighton, on the south coast of England, as the letter instructed.

A few hours later my train pulled into Brighton station. I looked out of the window of my first-class carriage for Miss Ballentine's driver, but no one waited on the steam-filled platform.

Taking my travel bag and my medicine case down from the rack above my seat, I made my way onto the platform.

'Are you Dr Watson, sir?' said a small voice.

I looked down to find a boy of around ten. Intelligent eyes stared at me from a somewhat grubby face.

'Yes I am,' I answered.

'I'm to take you outside to your carriage, sir. The driver said you'd tip me for me trouble ...'

I doubted that the driver had told the boy this, knowing full well that any driver of Hope Ballentine's would most likely have paid the urchin already for his trouble. But I knew that such young ears and eyes were always valuable in an unknown town. And so, I gave the boy a penny, which he tested with his teeth, before placing in surreptitiously in the pocket of his short trousers. Then he led me outside to the front of the station, and I saw the carriage and driver waiting.

'Dr Watson?' said the driver as he climbed down from the front of the carriage. 'Please forgive my having to send a stranger to find you inside. My horses were skittish and I couldn't risk leaving them alone.'

He took my bags and heaved them up onto the back of the carriage, where he secured them with a piece of thick rope.

'I'm Samuel,' he told me. Then he proceeded to open the carriage door so that I could climb inside.

The carriage pulled away, rattling over the cobbles. I glanced out of the window, noting that we were not headed, as I had been told, to the townhouse owned by the Ballentines on the sea front. We were heading, instead, away from the promenade and back inland.

An hour or more later, tired and sore from the jostling carriage, I was relieved when the driver turned off the main road and began to follow a long dirt track that soon developed into an established driveway. I leaned out of the window as I caught a glimpse of an imposing house through the trees. The carriage turned and weaved towards it, and we pulled up at an impressive frontage with white marble steps leading up to a huge oak double front door.

As soon as the carriage had stopped, I climbed out before the driver had time to dismount.

The front door opened, and I saw impressive, white marbled archways, and a notable staircase that dominated the centre of the hallway of the house. The driver removed my bags from the back of the carriage and then led me up the stairs towards a waiting butler and, I presumed by her attire, the housekeeper.

Introductions were made. The butler was Anders, and the lady beside him, Mrs Anders.

'Miss Ballentine is waiting for you in the drawing room, but first you are to go and see Mr Richmond,' Anders said.

'Who is Mr Richmond?' I asked.

'Miss Ballentine's fiancé,' Mrs Anders explained. 'The patient.'

'Ah. Then I will need my—' I turned and saw Samuel holding my medical bag out to me. I found his anticipation of my request quite disconcerting but took hold of the case nonetheless and turned to follow Mrs Anders up the stairs.

But for a sliver of light filtering through the drawn curtains, the room I was led to was in complete darkness.

'I will have to light the lamp,' Mrs Anders said.

'Of course ... or I shall not be able to see the patient ...' I mumbled.

'Is that all right Mr Richmond? Will you cover your face?' Mrs Anders continued.

There was a groan from the bed in the centre of the room. A rustle of sheets, and Mrs Anders struck a match and lit an oil lamp that stood on a dresser by the door.

'He cannot bear any light,' Mrs Anders explained. 'This is the nearest that we can bring the lamp.'

'But I must be able to see in order to examine him properly ...' I said.

'I can creep closer once he becomes a little more accustomed to it,' Mrs Anders said. 'But you'll see ...'

I approached the bed, stumbling against a chair that I couldn't see in the gloom, and then Mrs Anders turned the lamplight upwards.

The patient groaned in the bed, pulling the covers up and over his face even as I drew near.

'Mr Richmond?' I said. 'I'm Dr Watson. I'm here to help you.'

Richmond groaned again. It was the sound of an aged and dying man who could barely articulate his pain and suffering.

I reached for the covers and pulled it back. Richmond was too weak to fight me; although he tried to hold onto the material, it slipped easily from his frail fingers and I came face to face with the reality of his affliction for the first time.

'Good Lord,' I gasped, as I couldn't hold in my shock at the sight of the man.

His skin was deathly white, and as the light from the lamp hit him, his flesh seemed to react to it. It blackened and began to char with a sizzling sound.

'Pull the light back for the love of God!' cried Richmond.

Mrs Anders responded and turned the flame down once more. My eyes had adjusted enough for me to still be able to just make out the other peculiarities in Richmond's state, and as the light dimmed further it became even more apparent that Richmond's eyes were flawed. Whatever colour the irises had once been was now bleached out. The man's eyes were as white as his flesh and they glowed somewhat in the gloom, oddly luminous.

I didn't dare bring the light closer now for fear of injuring him further but I leaned in and touched his skin. It was rough, scarred: it was the flesh of a victim severely burnt.

'What happened to you?' I asked.

Richmond shook his head as though his previous outburst was all that he had left in him, and now he could no longer speak.

'Can you see at all?' I asked.

Richmond nodded. 'A little. If it's dark …' he gasped. 'The light … it … it …'

'Turn the lamp off, Mrs Anders,' I said.

Mrs Anders complied, and I took the seat beside the bed of my patient and waited for my own vision to adjust. I could make out Richmond's shape in the bed, could hear his laboured breathing. I fumbled in my medical bag and extracted my stethoscope. I explained myself to Richmond, so as not to frighten him, and he allowed me to press the instrument against his chest.

I listened to the man's heartbeat for a moment and then looked into those peculiar eyes. I tilted his head so that I could observe the way the lenses captured light and reflected it, in much the same way that a cat's eyes did. But these were no cat's eyes. This was the symptom of some rare and frightening disorder.

'Are you in much pain?' I asked, but I knew the answer could only be yes and so I prescribed a dose of laudanum to help Richmond sleep.

'I must speak to Miss Ballentine,' I said to Mrs Anders as we left the now resting patient.

'She's expecting you,' the housekeeper replied, and I followed her back down the stairs and into the drawing room.

Hope Ballentine sat upright and stiff on a Chinese-style sofa. I was struck by her incredible handsomeness and paused in the doorway. When she looked at me it was as though I was released from some form of hypnosis. Miss Ballentine was ethereal. Like a muse, or a nymph, caught in a moment of complete reflection, as if by a pond and not in a place as ordinary as a drawing room.

'Dr Watson. It is good to see you,' she said, and then she indicated a chair near hers and I sat down beside her. 'You must be thirsty. The maid has just brought in this fresh pot of tea.'

'Thank you,' I said, though I felt in need of something far stronger after my initial examination of Richmond. I had seen many things during my investigations with Holmes, but this one had rattled me. Maybe because Holmes and his ever-present confidence were absent.

I took the proffered teacup and tried to hide the trembling of my hands.

'So, tell me what is going on here,' I said, placing the cup back down on the tray after a few slow sips.

'Well, that is why I've called you in,' said a familiar voice behind me. 'I wanted to know what you would make of this from a medical viewpoint.'

I turned to find none other than Holmes standing in the doorway.

'Good heavens, man!' I said. 'You gave me a turn!'

I stood and shook his hand then. I was glad to see him despite my surprise.

Holmes took a seat on a sofa some distance from me and Miss Ballentine, and I waited patiently as the lady composed herself enough to explain what symptoms had first manifested themselves in the patient.

However, I found it difficult to concentrate on Miss Ballentine, as beautiful as she was, because, despite my pleasure at seeing him, I was somewhat irritated by Holmes's appearance. And his declaration that *he* had sent for me, and not *she*, brought about a feeling of some disappointment: I had not been sent for merely for my own abilities.

'Come now, Watson,' Holmes said and I turned to him, noting how comfortably he sat in the drawing room, as if the house were his home from home. This clearly indicated to me, knowing Holmes as I did, that he had in fact been in the Ballentine residence for some time, perhaps for all the absence that he had conveyed to me was due to a family crisis.

Now he placed his long, musical fingers like a church steeple under his chin, and he watched me closely.

I felt a pang of guilt and wondered if he did indeed see the slight resentment I was harbouring. Holmes wasn't always the most tactful of people, nor did he care much for the emotions of others if they impaired his ability to work effectively on a case, and so I knew my antipathy would have to remain unacknowledged for the time being.

'Come now, Watson,' he said again. I blinked. Then I turned my attention back to the beautiful Miss Ballentine and began to question her at length.

'My parents went the same way. The colourless eyes, the skin so sensitive to light that it burned and scarred,' she said. 'But it was diagnosed as some sickness of age ...'

'Which quack diagnosed that?' I asked, and then remembered myself. 'Forgive me. But there is no illness of age that I have ever witnessed to cause such ... deterioration as this. Age often equals frailty, but not some sudden aversion or inability to tolerate light.'

I looked to Holmes for some endorsement of my words, but he appeared to be in his own thoughts. I noted how he tapped his fingers on the edge of the seat as though he were listening to his favourite opera. Was he perhaps composing something inside that magnificent mind of his, even as I struggled to make sense of a medical matter?

'I thought this myself,' said Miss Ballentine. 'That's why I invited Mr Holmes here in the first instances. But the day after he arrived, Jeremy fell with the same affliction.'

'What do you think this is, Holmes?' I asked, growing impatient with his silence, even while I knew that deep down his genius was cooking something up.

'My dear Watson, I'm more intrigued to know what you think,' he said. 'I'm not a medical man. This is a medical matter.'

I frowned. So that was how it was. Holmes was holding all the cards close to his chest for some reason. Or perhaps, and I preferred to believe this, he really did need my input after all.

'All right,' I said. 'Your note told me that your father received a diamond? A blue diamond?'

'That's correct,' said Miss Ballentine. 'Some months ago from my uncle who had recently passed on. My father's brother. It was peculiar because Father hadn't heard from him for years and had already thought him long gone. Then an Indian servant arrived one day, carrying the package, and we learnt that Uncle John had been living in India all the time. The servant told us that he had left him strict instructions to bring the jewel to my father. I remember they spent a long time in Father's office, and then the servant just left.'

'What happened then?' I asked.

Holmes was examining his nails as though he had heard this story so many times that it bored him.

'Father called Mother in, he showed her what was in the box and then he stowed it in the safe. A short time later he was just as Jeremy ... Mr Richmond ... is now. It wasn't long before he ...'

Miss Ballentine halted, tears in her eyes, and I pulled out my handkerchief and held it out to the lady. She took it gratefully and dabbed at her eyes until she was composed again.

'Then you say your mother took ill ...' I coaxed.

Miss Ballentine nodded. 'After the reading of the will she

took me into Father's study and opened the safe. Then she pulled a box from there. When she opened it I saw the diamond for the first time. It was like … an eye. If that doesn't sound too strange. A blue iris. Only large. As large as my palm.

'Mother took the diamond out of the box and held it, but I was too in awe to touch it. 'It's not in the will,' she told me. 'Your father had no time to change it before his sickness, and so I'm going to keep it to pass down to you. You are, after all, the only remaining heir of this family.'

'I forgot about the diamond as we continued to grieve, and then when Mother became sick it was the last thing on my mind.'

'That was some time ago?' I asked.

'Two months. And Mr Holmes came here a few weeks ago.'

Ah! Just as I had suspected: Holmes had been there all the time.

'Yes,' she paused. 'Mrs Anders reminded me that the servants were due payment and so I went into the safe to fetch out the yearly salary book and the money to give her to pay everyone. That's when I saw the box and recalled what Mother had said about the diamond. It all seemed so peculiar that I had completely forgotten about it. I didn't know what to think. So I sat at the desk merely looking at it.

'A while later, Jeremy arrived. We had planned to go for a drive to the seaside and I had forgotten that also. But he was quite used to me being like that since my parents died and so he came to find me in the study. I had the diamond box on the table, and Jeremy saw it. I saw no reason to keep the secret from my fiancé and so I let him look at it. That was the second time I saw the diamond,' Miss Ballentine halted as though this realisation was somehow important.

'And Mr Richmond took the diamond out of the box?' I asked.

'No. Not then. But later when we returned to the house after our day out he asked if he could see it again. This time he examined it closely.'

'So why did seeing the diamond again make you suspicious? Why did you send for Holmes?'

Holmes shifted in his seat and reached over to pour himself a cup of tea.

'Oh dear,' said Miss Ballentine. 'I really ought to get the pot refreshed.'

'No need,' said Holmes. Then he stood and rang the servants' bell himself, confirming his comfort in the house once more.

'You see, when Jeremy opened the case and removed the diamond a piece of paper fell out. It was written in a foreign language. Jeremy, fortunately, found someone to translate it and we discovered that it was Hindi,' Miss Ballentine continued.

'Of course, it was!' said Holmes. 'And here is the tea! Come in Mrs Anders.'

Mrs Anders was indeed on the other side of the door holding a fresh tray. Holmes held the door open and the housekeeper came inside and placed the new tray down on the table, and then collected the old one.

'So, what do you know, Holmes?' I asked, impatient to hear his prognosis.

Holmes remained quiet. He waited for Mrs Anders to leave, before closing the door and taking his seat again. Now with a fresh cup of tea and a plate of sandwiches, Holmes behaved as though he was alone in the room as he worked his way through two cucumber sandwiches.

I noted Miss Ballentine's distress and returned my attention to her after frowning once more at Holmes. His behaviour was more confusing than usual.

'So ... erm ... what did the paper say?'

'It was a warning,' Miss Ballentine said, 'of a curse.'

'It seems,' Holmes interjected, 'that Miss Ballentine's uncle was a thief. Or knew one.'

'Whatever do you mean?' I asked.

'The diamond was stolen. From a religious artefact. It was once known as the Eye of Shiva,' Holmes said. 'This very artefact is currently in the British Museum – *sans* its eye.' He indicated a place on his forehead. 'The third eye.'

'Mr Holmes is right. My mother told me that my uncle's servant, Rani, was incredibly circumspect when he was questioned about the origins of the diamond. He told them that my uncle won it in a poker game. However, he warned against 'holding' it for too long. I thought that meant *owning* it. But maybe it meant ...' Miss Ballentine said. 'I can only assume, as Jeremy and my mother held the diamond, that he meant not to touch it.'

'So, the common factor is the diamond,' I said, trying to keep my mind focused on the problem at hand.

'Yes,' said Miss Ballentine.

'Mmmm. What do you think Watson?' asked Holmes.

'Well. I suppose I should take a look at it. Wearing my gloves of course,' I said.

Miss Ballentine led us to the study. Wearing outdoor gloves, she took the suspect box from the safe and placed it on the desk. Then she stepped back, as though she were afraid of the contents.

I pulled on my own leather gloves and lifted the box, turning it over in my hands. I noted a smear of white and smelt a distinct scent on the contents.

I placed the case back down on the desk and opened the top, being careful not to lean over it. A burst of white powder emitted into the air.

'Step back,' Holmes warned. Then he threw his jacket over the case.

'What on Earth was that?' asked Miss Ballentine.

'A lucky escape for Watson!' Holmes said. 'And how curious that this did not happen when you showed the diamond to me. Watson, did you recognise that odour?'

'Yes, Holmes. It was lime sulphur, and that would explain the damage to your fiancé's eyes and skin. It is highly corrosive. But how was this possible?'

I held Holmes's jacket above the case, as he attempted to open it again. This time, no sulphur was released from the box, and I was able to remove the diamond from the case. I noted that it was now smeared with the white powder. Crystallised lime was covering the stone, and this could have certainly found its poisonous way onto the skin of anyone handling it with unprotected hands.

'How intriguing,' said Holmes, examining the box. 'It's an occasional emission. Guaranteed to catch the owner unawares at some time or other. See here Watson, there is a small clockwork mechanism that winds itself back up as the case is opened and closed. At full wind this coil releases. Then the powder bursts out through these small holes.'

'The lime would act as an irritant in this form,' I said, indicating the debris on the diamond, 'though wouldn't necessarily blind you without direct exposure – that would have to happen with the initial burst. Even so, it certainly wouldn't kill you.'

'Then what did kill my parents? And why is Jeremy so sick? I didn't see him sprayed with that concoction,' Miss Balentine said. 'So how ...?'

'We must ask him,' said Holmes. 'For certainly he entered your study, went into your safe and examined the diamond when you weren't present.'

Miss Ballentine was clearly overcome by Holmes's words. The implications that her fiancé may have been planning to rob her of the diamond hung in the air along with the smell of lime sulphur.

'One thing is for certain,' I said. 'The diamond must be washed and this container destroyed. Or a maiming may occur again.'

I went to check on my patient and found Richmond sitting up in bed in the dark.

'How are you?' I asked.

'Sleep helped.' He was groggy but better on the laudanum than without it and so I gave him another dose.

As he began to drift off to sleep I asked him a few questions about the diamond, knowing that it would be difficult for him to lie to me in his drugged state.

'I just wanted to see it again ...' he murmured.

Back downstairs I reassured Miss Ballentine that her fiancé was not a thief but had been merely fascinated by the diamond.

'Thank you Dr Watson,' she said. 'What an awful punishment to receive for mere curiosity.'

I met Holmes again in the study. He was sitting opposite the desk, looking at the closed safe.

'The Hindus have very strong beliefs on crime and punishment, which has much to do with penance. Although I have no evidence to support this, this case reminds me of the Sanskrit *Dharmaśāstra*s. In this document, Hindu law says that thieves should be maimed for their crimes, and sometimes even killed. Maiming is supposed to be self-inflicted too. But if the criminal refuses then the king must choose the punishment, and it often isn't pretty.'

'But these people aren't thieves, Holmes. They inherited the jewel. How can they be held accountable for its original theft?' I said.

'The Hindus believe you can also be punished for crimes you committed in a previous life,' Holmes continued. 'We need to discover what killed Miss Ballentine's parents. That way we may avoid the murder of Mr Richmond.'

'An autopsy might help,' I said. 'If we could gain permission from Miss Ballentine, of course.'

'Since she brought us in to help, it would be odd if she refused,' Holmes observed.

'Absolutely not!' said Miss Ballentine. 'I couldn't possibly let you defile my parents' graves!'

'Even to save the life of your fiancé?' I asked.

Hope Ballentine's hands wrung in her lap. She was torn between her respect for her parents and love for Richmond.

'But how can you help him?' she asked. 'Surely in his condition he is better off ...'

'Dead?' Holmes finished.

'No. Of course I don't mean that. Oh no. This is just too awful!'

Miss Ballentine's tears fell and, once again, I found myself handing over my handkerchief.

'You must do as you feel appropriate, naturally,' she said. 'It's just that it is so ...'

'My dear girl,' I said, 'don't take on so. Your parents won't know. This is not a desecration, but a search for the culprit. A way for the guilty to be punished for their crimes.'

'Yes. Yes ... certainly.'

With the aid of her driver and a footman, Holmes and I were soon at the Ballentine family graveyard towards the back of the extensive estate.

The body was decomposing but I immediately saw signs of emaciation: Mrs Ballentine's sickness has given her a poor appetite towards the end. There was some pigmentation visible on her skin. Localised oedemas prominent on both calves. We took the body out of the casket, and lay it on a white cloth on the ground so that I could have better access. Then I examined her thoroughly.

'I hoped this would confirm my suspicion,' Holmes said as I opened Mrs Ballentine's chest. We both looked inside and I saw the degeneration of her heart.

The obvious state of the body confirmed my fears without the need to do further testing. It was surprising that these symptoms had gone unnoticed by the coroner assigned to Mrs Ballentine's case. However, I was used to investigating the unusual and the symptoms I saw gave me good reason to believe that Mrs Ballentine had been the victim of arsenic poisoning.

'A victim of arsenic poisoning rapidly loses their appetite, hence the overly slender frame. Oedemas and the brown pigmenting are other symptoms, but the condition of the heart was the final confirmation to me. If Mr Ballentine is in a similar state then I would be definite in my assessment that they were indeed both murdered,' I said.

I closed Mrs Ballentine's chest and, with the help of the driver and footman, placed her body carefully back into her coffin.

Sometime later Holmes and I left the driver and footman to re-bury the bodies of Mr and Mrs Ballentine and set off on foot back towards the house. It was then that Holmes saw a man lurking in the woodlands surrounding the house. He was wearing a thick overcoat, and a hat was pulled down over his eyes as though he did not wish to be recognised.

'There's our culprit!' I said, drawing my gun from the pocket of my overcoat.

'Maybe he is, maybe he isn't,' said Holmes mysteriously. 'Put that thing away for the time being. He doesn't know he's being observed, and so we will wait and see what happens.'

Crouching down out of sight, we watched as the man approached the house at the rear. Then the back door opened to him as though he was expected, and the man entered the property.

'The picture becomes clearer,' Holmes said.

'Well, I do wish you would enlighten me, old boy,' I said. 'Only, the way I see it, there are several people who could have opened that door.'

'Precisely,' said Holmes.

It was Mrs Anders who opened the door to us when we arrived at the front door after first heading back to the graveyard. From there, Holmes had taken the driver aside and directed him on an important errand. While he did so I helped the footman to lay the last of the earth back over the coffins of Mr and Mrs Ballentine.

'Mrs Anders, can you please tell Miss Ballentine that we need to see her?' Holmes said.

'Certainly, Mr Holmes,' she replied and turned to leave.

'Oh, and Mrs Anders … I would also like you and your husband to join us.'

'Us, sir? But why, sir?'

'It will all become clear. We will be upstairs checking on Mr Richmond,' I said.

'Very good, Dr Watson,' said Mrs Anders, and then she hurried off in the direction of the kitchens.

'Interesting,' said Holmes. 'Miss Ballentine is usually in the drawing room, is she not?'

We entered Richmond's room to find him still sleeping off the laudanum that I had administered. Holmes went to the curtain and peeked out through the crack but did not make any attempt to bring light into the room. I lit the lamp, but kept the light down low as we waited for Miss Ballentine and the Anders and his wife to appear. It was quite some time before they presented themselves, but when they finally arrived, I made them all sit around the bed of Mr Richmond.

'Did you learn something that can help Jeremy?' asked Miss Ballentine.

'Certainly,' I said. 'It seems that your parents did not die due to the lime sulphur exposure. They were helped along.'

'Helped along?' said Mrs Anders.

'Poisoned,' said Holmes. 'A rather common poison at that too. Disappointing that it wasn't more inventive. However, most poisoners are opportunists and these things are rarely thought through.'

'Oh my God. My parents *were* murdered!' Miss Ballentine said. 'But how? By whom?'

'That is what we need to learn. And Jeremy, here, is the means by which we will have that truth …'

Holmes whipped back the heavy curtain and the remaining light of the afternoon burst in and fell across the bed. Jeremy, however, was not in it. What lay in the bed was something that resembled a scarecrow, wearing a fine white mask that gave the aspect, in the gloom, of the wounded man.

'This whole thing has been a charade!' Holmes said.

'Where is Jeremy?' asked Miss Ballentine. 'What have

you done with him?'

'My dear girl, he was never injured. It was all faked for your benefit. A simple chemistry trick that even a newly indoctrinated apothecary might know. You mix certain chemicals together to create a particular effect. That, coupled with a modicum of acting ability, is enough to fool anyone in dull enough light. Even my dear friend Watson.'

'But *where* is he?' asked Miss Ballentine.

'I don't know. But I suspect he is hidden in the kitchen. Or cellar. Wherever his parents want him to be.'

Holmes looked directly at Mr and Mrs Anders now and the two fidgeted in their seats.

'Now, Mr Holmes. What are you implying?' asked Anders. 'I'll have you know ...'

'Please make it easy on yourself Mr Anders. Richmond is your son ... by adoption. But he is the proper son of Mrs Anders, isn't he?'

'Look here. I won't stand around to be insulted...'

'It's no use,' Mrs Anders said. 'I told you he'd know.'

'His hands gave it away, Mrs Anders. Just as yours do. Sometimes the arsenic bleaching doesn't always work in all the grooves. You see, Miss Ballentine, you have been the victim of a hoax. I dare say that the Anders family hadn't planned to take things so far. The plan was probably to get you to fall in love with their son, and when your parents died, he, as your new husband, would have access to the family fortune,' I explained. 'I suspect when you invited Holmes here to investigate, they rather lost their nerve.'

'Watson is quite right,' Holmes continued. 'You see, Anders worked in India before he came here. I took the trouble to research you soon after I arrived. And after searching your room, I discovered a photograph of Mrs Anders in a sari, looking faintly darker in skin than she does now. Never truly Indian, but enough to have raised eyebrows had she not discovered how to lighten her skin with a common arsenic compound easily available from any local apothecary.'

Holmes pulled a piece of paper from the pocket of his

jacket and held it out to Miss Ballentine.

'Here is a receipt for the compound. Found in Mrs Anders' possessions this morning,' he continued.

'We've done nothing wrong!' said Mrs Anders. 'We're hard working. I wouldn't have been employed if Mr Ballentine had realised I had Indian blood in me ... More so that Joe had married me, even though he knew that.'

'Good Lord!' said Miss Ballentine. 'You've lied to us. But, Mr Holmes, the other things you've said. About Jeremy. Surely that is a mistake.'

Holmes had the evidence to hand and he held out a photograph for Miss Ballentine to see. I glanced at it also, but I already knew that it was a picture of Mrs Anders with her son, a young boy at the time, wearing the garb of an Indian. He was smiling in the photograph and the face, even though I had only ever seen it supposedly damaged, was without doubt, Jeremy Richmond.

'This isn't possible,' Miss Ballentine denied.

'I'm afraid he's telling the truth,' Richmond said. 'And in a way, Mr Holmes, you have done my family a favour. I was wondering how I could easily disentangle myself from this situation.'

Richmond was standing behind a Chinese screen at the other side of the room, and, I now noticed, it covered a door, probably leading to a dressing room, which in turn would lead onto the landing. He was wearing the overcoat and hat that we had observed him in as we had followed him through the woodland to the rear of the house, where, we now knew, Anders or Mrs Anders had let him back inside.

'Jeremy!' Miss Ballentine gasped as he raised his arm to show that he was holding a pistol.

'Mother, Father ... Get behind me. Don't try to stop us leaving, Holmes. I have no inhibition towards shooting you or anyone else.'

'I have no intention of stopping you,' Holmes said even while I slipped my hand into my overcoat pocket and found the butt of my own pistol. 'But first, clear something up for us.

You planned to marry Miss Ballentine and then your plan changed. Why? You could have easily disposed of her parents in a less brutal fashion once you were married. Or merely lived happily under their roof until they died of natural causes.'

'No one wanted to kill anyone,' Anders said. 'Then Rani turned up. He had worked for Mr Ballentine's brother. And so had Mrs Anders once. She thought Rani recognised her.'

'So, you killed him as he left?' I asked.

'No,' said Mrs Anders. 'Jeremy followed him. Found out where he was staying ... We wanted to know what he'd told the master.'

'There was no plan to kill him,' Anders said. 'It were an accident. And Jeremy weren't to blame.'

'Then Mr Ballentine got sick. He opened the casket and blinded himself,' said Mrs Anders.

'You saw it happen?' Holmes said.

'I was passing the study door. He always left it open. That stuff shot up into his eyes and I went in an' tried to help him ... I would never have hurt him. He were a kind man.'

'That's when you saw the diamond, though,' I said.

'I didn't steal it. I put it back. Closed the safe – just as Mr Ballentine told me too. He didn't want anyone to see it, or that letter that Rani had given him ... But I could read it and I knew what the diamond was.'

'So, you played on the curse?' Holmes said. 'And the plan to kill Ballentine and his wife was formed.'

'That's enough talk,' Richmond said. 'We're getting out of here.'

'You still haven't explained why you didn't carry on with the marriage, Richmond. Surely that would have given you access to everything. Including the diamond.' I said.

'Watson was right on that score. Your presence changed everything Mr Holmes. I had to take any suspicion away from myself. I had lost interest in the charade anyway. Why bother going through all that when I can just take everything that's hers anyway?'

At that moment I raised the gun in my pocket and aimed it at Jeremy. Without hesitation I fired, intending to injure him and make him drop the gun. The pistol in his hand went off, and Mrs Anders fell as her son's bullet pierced her in the back.

'Mother!' Richmond yelled.

Anders caught his wife as she fell, then Richmond's handsome face turned to rage as he pointed the gun at me and prepared to fire again.

'Don't do it!' Miss Ballentine cried. 'Jeremy, if you ever had any feelings for me at all ...'

Richmond's face turned and glared hatred at Miss Ballentine, and she crumpled in tears when she finally realised that everything she had believed in was a lie. Jeremy Richmond was the brains behind this crime. I didn't believe that Rani's death was an accident. I was certain now, that Richmond's cold bloodied scheme had drawn in his parents as much as it had taken in Hope Ballentine.

At that moment we heard the approach of pounding feet. Samuel, the coach driver, entered with a posse of policemen. They overwhelmed Richmond and surrounded Anders as he sat holding his wife. I bent to examine the woman as she breathed her last. Anders collapsed. He was a man ruined in every way.

'I cannot believe I fell for it all,' Miss Ballentine said.

'Richmond was certainly plausible, and, who knows, perhaps you would have been happy if the diamond had not appeared and the family's greed had not been so encouraged,' said Holmes.

'What will you do with the diamond now, Miss Ballentine?' I asked. 'It isn't cursed and, now that it's cleaned, no longer dangerous to hold.'

'Even so,' Miss Ballentine said, 'I feel like it brought us bad luck, and so I will pass it on.'

'Where to?' I asked.

'The museum. To be reunited with the original artefact,' Miss Ballentine said.

'A good idea,' said Holmes.

On the dresser, the blue diamond glittered in the sunlight. So beautiful, and yet so deadly.

Anger Management

'It's all about being in control,' Anthony said. 'Being aware of how close to the edge you are. And mindfulness is the key.'

Chloe, the quiet girl in the corner, was giving him her full attention.

'Be aware of your surroundings. Remember that anger and violence will only get you in trouble,' he continued.

The hardest part of his job was getting a new group to open up and admit that they were angry and then get to the bottom of why.

His meetings were modelled on AA meetings: anger was an addiction like any other. Anthony was the leading expert in this new way of thinking because he'd had so much success in the area. He led his addicts away from the darkness of that 'red veil' that they often described came over them in their most out of control moments. Some of them had restraining orders and ASBOs. But Anthony knew his methods worked. Anger was a poison. A cancer. It burned brightest in the most damaged minds and souls. It had to be cut out and tossed into a burning pit, expunged from the soul as soon as possible.

'The first step is to accept that you have a problem,' Anthony said. 'Who feels brave enough to tell us their story?'

His eyes went to Chloe, but it wasn't her that spoke up first. It was the little old lady, Mrs Badger, that came through. And her story was a good one.

'I hit my son over the head with a frying pan,' she said now.

'Why did you do that?' asked Anthony.

'He was always round. Wanting money. He's rubbish with money. Can never pay his bills, and there's me, saved up all me life so that I don't have to worry and I spend half of my pension on him. It started to fester,' she said.

'So, what 'appened?' Chloe asked and Anthony didn't discourage her asking questions.

'He sent social services round. Was trying to get me put in a home, went after power of attorney over me. He couldn't wait to get his hands on my savings. Of course, the social worker realised I had all me lemon drops. So, she went away and that's when he came round, all heavy. Insisting I gave him the money to help pay his mortgage. By then he was three months behind, because he hadn't used the last lot I gave him to catch up, as he should've done. Gawd knows what he spent it on. His wife was about to leave him, he said. But I'd had enough. I said, "no more". So, he hit me.'

'That's awful!' said one of the others.

'That's not right for sure,' Anthony said. 'Terrible behaviour.'

'I dealt with it, just like me Ma taught me. She used to say, there's only one way to deal with yer 'auld man if he got handy with his fists ... I waited until he weren't looking, then I whacked him one. Knocked 'im out cold.'

The group gave a collective cheer.

Anthony frowned, 'We don't condone any violence. No matter the provocation.'

'Oh, but you 'ave to see he asked for it,' Chloe said. Her eyes were gleaming now. She looked the most animated that Anthony had ever seen her.

'One bad deed doesn't deserve another,' said Reverend Frobisher, a vicar who had deliberately tripped up a parishioner after he'd seen them repeatedly ignore the collection tray.

'Yes, and the reverend has made very good progress in understanding that, haven't you?' Anthony said.

'Indeed,' said the reverend.

'The bible does say an eye for an eye ...' Mrs Badger pointed out.

'It does, but we aren't meant to take justice into our own hands,' Anthony explained. 'And we all need to understand that. It's for the law to deal out punishment. Not the individual.'

'Still, I'm struggling to see why this lady is here,' Devon

chirped up. He was a middle-aged, nervous looking man who was overly thin. 'It seems to me her son should have been punished for abusing his mother. I mean. It's just not okay.'

'He went to the police and told 'em I 'it 'im,' Mrs Badger explained. 'I told my side when they came to see me. They all agreed I needed some 'elp though, cos I boxed the young officer's ears when he wasn't listening to me properly. They just don't bring 'em up right these days!'

Chloe laughed. 'Sorry ... But *that's* funny.'

'Let's stay on track,' Anthony said and for the first time he looked flustered. 'It's all about thinking, before we act. We need to consider the consequences of our actions. And for some of you, that will mean imprisonment if you don't manage to control your addiction.'

'Addiction?' asked Harriet, a timid thirty-something who hadn't spoken once during the last three sessions.

'Anger is an addiction,' Anthony explained again. Even though he said this frequently during the sessions, some of them still refused to hear it.

'You know this, Harriet,' said the reverend.

Harriet shrugged, 'I just like to be sure. Only, I think addiction is something you can't stop doing. Crave it sort of. I don't think I crave anger.'

'Let's explore that,' Anthony said. 'What happens when you get angry?'

'Well. It kind of builds up. Inside me. Like a volcano waiting to explode.'

'And when you do explode. By that I mean lose your temper, give in to the anger?' asked the Reverend.

'Erm ... It's kind of a release,' Harriet said. 'Like I've let go of everything I bottled up.'

'Hence the addiction,' Anthony explained. 'If you were an alcoholic you'd feel a similar pressure, and drinking temporarily releases the compression. Resisting, going cold-turkey, can help you break the addiction, but it's a little different with anger because it's something we can't always escape from. It comes from us, and therefore harder to avoid. Giving into it though, is still feeding an addiction. Part of what we are doing here, is to learn our triggers and find better ways to ease the pressure of anger, dispel it before it becomes dangerous for example.'

'Oh,' said Harriet. 'I see it now.'

'Tell us what you did,' Devon suggested. 'It might help you.'

'Me? Well ... it was my boss really. He kept saying things. He was so rude. Suggestive rude. Hinting that him and I should go for a drink sometime. But he was a bully too. He was always picking at my work. Saying it wasn't good enough.'

Harriet fell quiet and everyone waited as they always did when a newbie came out with their worst day. Sometimes the stories made them all realise that their breaking point wasn't so bad after all.

'He grabbed me. On the bum. Pretended it was an accident when I turned and looked at him shocked. Then, he went in for the kill. A grope ... you ... know ...' Harriet blushed. 'So I kicked him. Hard. Right in the crotch. It was a knee-jerk reaction really. I didn't mean to rupture him. That was a complete accident. I just wanted it to stop. And to put him in his place.'

'Oh there's always the risk of rupture,' Chloe laughed. 'But you deffo made him stop. I read about it in the local papers. He'll probably never have kids ...'

'Perhaps Chloe should tell us what she did?' Harriet said and she cast the younger woman a snide glance, showing she wasn't so shy and retiring after all. 'I mean, the rest of us have, but she just sits there, laughing and gloating about our misdemeanours.'

'Now, Harriet, we don't shame anyone for not telling their story. Chloe will open up when she feels ready. Just as you have,' Anthony said.

Harriet's face screwed up in fury but a warning glance from Anthony soon stopped her in her tracks.

'Deep breaths,' Anthony said. 'Remember to count back from ten, it'll help you deflate.'

'I'm ready to talk,' Chloe said and she fidgeted in her seat as though she expected to be electrocuted at any moment.

'We'd like to hear your story,' Anthony said.

'It was this girl, she just wound me up. You know? Always making comments. She was late to work every day and I had to cover for her. I worked at a bakery, on the high street. Smithson's. It's a family run business. Do you know it?'

Mrs Badger nodded. 'Nice vanilla slices and egg custards … I go there once a week.'

'Yeah,' said Chloe. 'Proper traditional. Eccles cakes too. I love those. But I can't work there no more. 'Cos of 'er.'

'Don't put the blame elsewhere,' said Anthony. 'Own your anger, that's the only way to get it under control.'

'Yeah. Right. She just got on me nerves though. I were late one day. Weren't even me fault – bloody train strike again! She proper shit-stirred it. Right when the boss was in. And there were nout about 'er being late al'time. So, I get a warning and she's like laughing behind 'er, and. I coulda killed her.'

'What did you do?' asked Devon his eyes were wide with curiosity.

Other people stories were always fascinating to the addicts, Anthony noted. They seemed to get a perverse delight from it. One he didn't quite understand but he suspected that serial killers felt the same when they listen to another killer talking about their kills. This revelation made him feel somewhat uncomfortable.

Chloe looked at Anthony. 'He knows what I did.'

'It's better if you tell the group yourself,' Anthony said. 'That way you acknowledge your addiction.'

'I lost it. On the way 'ome. She got on the same bus as me since I couldn't get the train. So, I followed 'er 'ome. She didn't see me and I well, stole 'er cat. Put it in cat's home as a stray. Then I listened to her whining about the cat being missing. Putting posters up all over the place. It were hilarious.'

'That is mean, but it doesn't sound too bad,' Harriet commented, disappointed.

'Yeah. But then, I tripped her. Down the stairs. It were a bad day and she'd been a bitch fer most o' it. I couldn't help meself.'

'Was she very injured?' Devon asked leaning forward as though the thought thrilled him more than anything in the world.'

'Broken nose/ Lost a few teeth,' Chloe said. 'It improved her stupid face.'

'Now now. Let's have none of that. We need to access sympathy for our victims. It's the only way forward,' Anthony said.

'Sympathy?' said Devon. 'But they all deserved it in their own way.'

'No one deserves to be hit, punched, tripped,' Anthony said. 'No matter what they did in the first place. We must keep control of ourselves. Anger is a bad thing. So is revenge. As I've said many times, the reason you're all here is because you took the law into your own hands and in the end lost control. We are going to change that.'

The group fell quiet, even Chloe stopped sniggering as she took in his firm and direct mantra.

'One question,' Harriet said. 'Chloe, did she ever get her cat back?'

Chloe shrugged. 'Dunno. Not allowed anywhere near her because of the restraining order.'

The group ended on a subdued note and as they all filed away, consolation tea and biscuit drunk and eaten respectively, Anthony was left alone in the village hall to tidy up and contemplate all the revelations that had been made so far. They were a rebellious bunch, and it was going to be difficult to whip them into shape. It was probably the most problematic group he'd had because, they all quite legitimately, had a grievance against the person who they lashed out at. And, it could be argued that that person deserved it. Revenge, however, wasn't the answer: not in a civilised society. Even so, he could see how they would believe the judgement was unfair, but the thing was, they were out of control, and that had to be reined in, no matter what.

Anthony had spent years working with angry people. He'd even overcome his own frustrations along the way. He understood that building of pressure just as much as anyone. But there were better ways to get rid of frustration than merely exploding. He'd perfected the technique. That way of releasing all the pain and so that it didn't leak out at the wrong moments.

Anthony locked up the hall. Then went out into the car park. Only his car remained as all the members had dispersed to their own vehicles, or set off for the bus stop. He wouldn't see them again now for a week, and then, he hoped that the homework exercises and meditation would start to have an impact. Surely they were beginning to see that society would not endure their blatant bad behaviour?

As always after a meeting, Anthony was tense: closer to the edge himself. Anger was an addiction that you could never truly free yourself of, and sometimes there were triggers that could tip you into the void again, but he had strategies. Methods that would help him push down that boiling lava – *a good analogy provided by Harriet*, he thought – and then he could poor the cooling water over those glowing embers, settling himself down again until the next session.

As he drove home, his eyes scanned the streets for what he needed. His wife, Sandy, wouldn't be home when he got there. She always stayed away on the nights he did the group; they'd agreed it was best for both of them that way. But he had to relieve this growing tension and there was only one way he could do that.

He saw the homeless man settling down in the doorway of a long-abandoned shop. Before the big chain supermarkets moved into the area, this had been a thriving hardware store, but now, there was little need for this type of family business. It was a subject that would anger Anthony, if he let it fester enough, which he didn't.

Well, the only way to be calm, was to help someone in need and this man, tonight, would be both his charity case, and his own salvation.

It didn't take long to persuade him to get into the car.

Promise of a good meal, a shower, a bed to sleep in for the night, was often attractive. Of course, he'd have to make sure that anything valuable was locked away, he'd been stung by that before, and he didn't want Sandy upset.

'What do you fancy to eat?' he asked the man now. 'I can stop and get some fish and chips?'

Food agreed, Anthony detoured, then left the man in the car a few blocks down from the chippie. He'd stopped here before, it was a good spot, where few people walked, and the food was always good.

The next morning, Sandy returned around 10 am. By then the used sheets and towels were already washed and in the drier and the house had minimal disruption. Anthony was feeling better too, safe in the knowledge that he'd done some good for a lost soul, at least for one night the man, whose name he'd already forgotten, had had a full stomach. He'd even enjoyed a cold beer before his long sleep.

'Everything, okay?' Sandy asked, relieved to see his relaxed smile.

'All good,' he said.

After that she busied herself in the kitchen. He heard the washer going again later: a long boil wash. No doubt the shower hadn't made his visitor quite clean enough before he hit their spare sheets, but no matter, Sandy was understanding about that sort of thing. She understood that all of this was positive. A kindness.

Anthony had got up early to scrub the bathroom before her return so she didn't have much to complain about on that score either. He was a considerate husband and it was all necessary to keep the peace. Even the strong smell of bleach couldn't ruin his mood that day and Sandy was content, singing to herself as she pottered. He liked to hear her sing, she had a sweet voice and it always meant she was calm, in control, and happy.

Another week passed and Anthony found himself among the group. It was a quieter week. Chloe hadn't turned up, something he'd have to talk to her about. It was, after all, a requirement by the courts that she attended and addressed her bad behaviour. Harriet was subdued, the reverend contrite and Devon was talkative. He knew from his records what Devon had done, but the man had never shared his story before. Anthony listened, he gave advice, and remained, on the surface, calm. But the evening always brought its own trials and Anthony found his mind was distracted. He wasn't concentrating as much on the group as he was feeling that sense of anticipation for later. The relieving of his own symptoms and addictions. The night ahead, if he could find someone to help, would free him up for another week. Addiction, however, was sometimes born of habit, and Anthony was aware that this weekly behaviour was becoming just that. Of course, it would all change when this group finished their pathway and for a while there would be no newcomers and no group to treat, and it would break the cycle again.

The routine was so part of his life that he was craving it now. There'd be a period of withdrawal – cold turkey – a prospect he didn't relish. Sandy would be unhappy during that time as she hated to see him suffer, and though she would do her best to elevate his mood, it wouldn't be enough and he'd always risk losing his own self-control. He didn't want to hurt her, but once or twice, the safe words had fallen on deaf ears, and that was why they decided it was best if he found this sort of R & R elsewhere, where it didn't matter if he went too far.

Now, he was anticipating just that and he wanted the group to finish, drink their tea, eat as many biscuits as they wanted, and go home, feeling they were getting better. It was hard to be upbeat and positive with Devon whining so much about his horrible neighbours and how he'd always be angry until he or they moved.

'You have to remove the triggers,' Anthony said. 'What is it about your neighbour that winds you up so much?'

'His face,' said Devon. 'Though it was the loud music, the barking dogs, and the loudmouth wife who can't seem to speak at normal pitch at first. Then, when I asked them to be quieter, the feud started.'

'Time you put the place up for sale,' Harriet said. 'As Anthony said, you must remove the triggers. It was the best thing for me getting sacked after kicking my boss. Now I work in a peaceful office with other women. No male boss, leching and touching.'

'I wonder if there is something in your childhood,' said the reverend.

'Let's not get into that,' Anthony said. 'That's for private sessions alone, way too personal.'

The three of them looked at him as though he'd lost his mind. After all, the whole nature of the group was personal.

'I think we'll finish early,' Anthony said. 'I'm sorry but I'm not feeling too well.'

They were happy to disperse and none of them commented about Chloe or where she might be. It was always the same in these groups, they soon forgot each other, never taking on the lessons they should learn from the story each of them told. It was a constant source of frustration to Anthony.

He placed the used mugs in the hall kitchen. The cleaner would wash them tomorrow, and Anthony could get away and deal with his own issue before things got out of control. The sense of anticipation came again as he considered his reward for listening to the group. Somehow, that made it all worthwhile.

Later, as he rubbed the dirt from his hands, and patted the topsoil down in the garden, Anthony felt better. The tension was gone again. The pressure had been worse than ever that night, and now he wondered if he'd gone too far and there would be no going back. *But no.*

He was glad they had so much land and no neighbours like Devon to complain about the noise. There'd been a lot of screaming that night and he'd had to gag the homeless girl in the end. He preferred silence when he worked. The stupid creature had thought he wanted to have sex with her! Really, she was filthy and he'd never do that to Sandy! You'd think she'd have been grateful for the food, the bath ... And now the long sleep. She'd never have to worry about sleeping rough again having found a perfect home on this idyllic stretch of land.

He looked now at the newly disturbed soil: seven new spots, representing seven weeks of the course and there were three more to go before he'd have to cope with withdrawal. But he tried not to think of that because it might spoil the moment.

He went back in the house, pulled the spare sheets off the floor, then stuffed them into the washer. *Boil wash*, he reminded himself because dirt and blood didn't come out that easily and Sandy shouldn't have to deal with it on her return.

Anthony switched on the television. There was a news story, about missing young people, runaways, homeless. The statistics on death on the streets were very high. Anthony couldn't understand why anyone would want to live that life; he considered it was why they always went with him. As if they knew he'd help them end to it all. One last meal and a place to rest forever.

He turned the TV off and went to bed. He thought about Sandy. Where she'd be tonight, sleeping in a hotel room alone, avoiding coming home until he'd done his relaxation. She'd be relaxed too when she returned, and the change in regime had saved their marriage because the bondage was clearly not to her taste at all.

A loud knocking at the front door woke Anthony from his death-like sleep. He checked the door camera app and saw that there were several uniformed police and a couple of non-uniformed officers waiting at his door. For a minute he questioned whether he'd cleaned the bathroom sufficiently but remembered his thorough bleaching of the bath and surrounding tiles after disposing of the body. What on earth could be wrong and why were the police here? No one had seen him take the homeless girl, no one ever did.

He pulled on his dressing gown and went downstairs

opening the door. There was a cacophony of sound from outside. Police vehicles as well as a local news van loitering at the bottom of the driveway.

'What's going on?' he yelled.

'Mr Taylor? Anthony Taylor?'

'Yes. What's ...?'

'I'm DCI Harry Banks. We have a warrant to search these premises.'

'What ...? Why?' he asked.

'Can you let us in Mr Taylor? I will explain, but I don't think you want that news crew listening in ...'

Anthony looked passed DCI Banks and noted the news reporter setting up with a camera and microphone. He stepped back and invited the police in.

The game was up and there was no point denying what he'd done. Some would see he'd done a service to the community, taking care of all those angry people, then having to cleanse himself of all of that hate too. It was *quid pro quo* and he'd do it again in a heartbeat.

'We've arrested your wife,' DCI Banks was saying. 'On suspicion of murder.'

'Sandy? There must be some mistake!'

'Mr Taylor, where do you think she was when she was away over night?'

'She ... I ...'

'Sandy has been picking off your patients. From your Anger Management course.'

'Are you insane?' Anthony said.

'Hadn't you noticed that they started to drop off Mr Taylor? From ten, you were down to three,' DCI Banks continued.

'No. They do that. I report their absence to the courts. You can take a horse to water but you can't make them drink. Not all of them can be cured.'

'I'm sorry to tell you this, but your wife was caught. She tried to kill a man named Devon Mitchell. Luckily he was able to overpower her. He called the police. Sandy has already confessed.'

'No. This is impossible. Why would she do that?'

'She said she didn't like what working with these people did to you.'

Anthony sank down into the kitchen chair while around him the team of police surged, searching his home. He couldn't respond, all he could think was how he'd driven sweet submissive Sandy to the brink, making her own anger and aggression materialise. Making her into everything that he was. Of course, she'd been passively facilitating him for years until recently, when she'd begged not to be part of it any longer. Those nights away, were essential for her own mental health, she'd said. He loved his wife so, Anthony couldn't object to that. Not after everything she'd suffered at his own brutal hands.

'Sir,' said an officer appearing at DCI Banks's side.

'What is it constable?' Banks said.

But the constable only pointed. DCI Banks turned and looked through the kitchen window. In the distance he could see the fresh mounds of earth and three more holes in the ground.

'You knew?' said Banks looking with disgust at Anthony.

Anthony didn't correct him. He'd realise soon enough that these weren't his wife's kills, but his own: each one a physical representation of the manifestation of his own fury.

As they cuffed him and read him his rights, Anthony said nothing. He'd need a lawyer and so would Sandy. He could almost see the headlines.

Anger management counsellor's secret burial ground.

He almost relished the idea of everyone knowing. After all, anger was an addiction from which, he'd realised, there really was no cure.

Her Body

Her body was a lovely and bloody tribute; lying like Sleeping Beauty in the casket as though waiting for a prince to steal a kiss he had no permission to take. The coffin was laid out on the patio, underneath a wooden pagoda, that was intertwined with grape vines. It was a desecration. Stunning in its violence. Grotesque in its mockery. Despicable. Horrible. Gorgeous.

Her body was covered with a white dress, stained red – no longer virgin. A long train flowed out under her feet, spilling over the bottom of the coffin, and down the steps: scattered with blood red petals. A bride, in an unholy union with death.

Her body raised an oxymoron of emotions.

The murder was so brutal that on the one hand, DI Gregor Lewinski felt nauseous, on the other he envied the artist behind the murder for his talent. Because, this was art. This display, this pose, this demise. So perfect, so awful, so moving.

His eyes watered and he rubbed the back of his hand across them. Gregor kept his thoughts to himself, knowing his colleagues would never understand: it took a certain kind of mind to appreciate crimes scenes as a form of art.

His boss, DCI Chapel, brought in the forensic team and the small spell that held Gregor broke with the sudden influx of others. They buzzed around the coffin in white crime scene suits and awkward feet covered with shoe protectors, or 'booties' as they liked to call them, careful not to contaminate, to move or change anything at all until they got the all clear.

Her body was photographed and then carefully, and with the deepest respect, bagged and taken away.

Gregor thought the casket looked bereft once she was gone.

'Gregor ...' DCI Chapel said snapping him back to the present. 'Can you go and interview the neighbours, see if they heard or saw anything suspicious?'

Gregor turned away from the scene with obvious reluctance: he hadn't seen enough, even though he'd worked every beat of the murder in his imagination and he'd compare the autopsy report with his mental notes afterwards to see how close he was. The forensic pathologist had given them an estimated time of death based on the degree of rigor mortis, but she would be more precise after the autopsy. For now, they were assuming 18 hours.

'On it,' Gregor said. Then he walked away from the patio, around the side of the house.

At the front he saw them loading her body into the mortuary van. He realised then that he hadn't even looked at her face. Perhaps it was deliberate, less humanising. But the overall impression of loveliness, even in death, would stay with him.

The van pulled away, taking her body with it. She was nothing now, not art, not victim, just a corpse that would soon be defiled again – this time with a scalpel and by someone qualified and permitted to do so.

Gregor turned away.

Next door, he was greeted by a middle-aged woman in tears. The water stretched black mascara down her cheeks and smeared lines through the heavily worn make-up.

'I'm Sara Ingalls,' she told him after he showed his badge.

'Did you know your neighbour well?' Gregor asked.

'Fairly. She taught my son piano,' Sara said as she dabbed her eyes.

Her body had once been a person called Elsbeth Chalmers. A 30 something, ethereal beauty that everyone loved and admired. Single. Living alone. A home owner. More than the remains they'd found. More than a body …

'This is my son, Peter,' Sara said.

Gregor asked the appropriate questions. Peter, was destroyed by Elsbeth's death. Perhaps he'd had a crush on her.

Gregor analysed the boy's bowed head, subdued answers and the sadness and shock he saw in the briefest of seconds when Peter met his eyes. He dismissed him as a suspect there and then. He was just a kid, and there were no crazy vibes coming off him. The only thing he sensed was a traumatised child.

'Why did you go around the back and not ring the doorbell?' Gregor asked.

'I always went around the back,' he said. 'She loved her garden ...'

Gregor's recording device captured everything. Their names, ages, what had happened, what they saw or rather what they didn't see. Would any of it help much in the end? This killer had been around, doing his work for some time. Her body wasn't the first, and Gregor knew she wouldn't be the last.

'Have you looked at the security cameras?' Sara asked. 'I remember when she had those fitted ...'

'We will do,' Gregor said and not for the first time wondered if any of the team had noticed the discreet devices around the property.

He finished his interview, then went back to Elsbeth's house to make sure the recording device was collected for their perusal. It was already unplugged and bagged when he arrived. By then, only a few people remained at the scene, fingerprinting everything to make sure that no corner was missed. He slipped on a pair of gloves and picked up the device.

'I'll deal with this,' he said to the room. None of the team answered.

Outside DCI Chapel nodded at him when he showed the security recorder.

'Get on that ASAP,' Chapel called but there was no need for his instruction, Gregor couldn't wait to open the recording files.

Back at the station, the device was hooked up and the footage uploaded to the secure computer system. After that Gregor began the long hours of wading through the footage. He started at the end and wound backwards. He skipped through the footage to before when the police arrived and began to play it forward at the point when Peter found the body: he saw the shock and he watched as Peter ran home, shouting. Peter's father followed on. Then he rang the police, ambulances ... everyone. He did not touch her body though he remained frozen, staring, for a long time as though he thought she might disappear if he looked away. Or perhaps, Gregor wondered, he saw the beauty of it too.

He wound back farther. Her body had lain under the pagoda for several hours, undisturbed before that. Gregor noted their estimated time was accurate. There was a huge chunk of footage gone between her appearance there and the live Elsbeth moving around, sitting out in her much-loved garden, a glass of lemonade in her hand.

She was pretty but her clothing was conservative. High necked blouse, a skirt well below the knee and a thin knitted cardigan which she had tugged closed and buttoned up. A far cry from the white robe her body had been displayed in.

'There!' Gregor said though no one else was in the room to hear his reactive cry.

There was something to her left, a rustle of leaves, movement in the bushes. Someone was lurking and she turned her head to look that way as though she knew or suspected her killer was there. Then, the immediate jump to the pagoda. Her body. Dead. Blood around her throat still seeping as though it had just been slit, perhaps she was even still vaguely alive even though she didn't move.

Gregor rubbed his eyes as though the water that leaked from them was tears and not from the strain of hours and hours of looking at recordings. There had to be more. Something he could find, perhaps the techies could zoom in on that brief flutter of the leaves and see the culprit?

He went to his computer and sent a note making the request and telling them the date and time to look at. The footage was now on the system and accessible to all who had clearance. It was all down to when they had the chance to look and of course the autopsy report, which Gregor knew, was happening right then.

Days later, the sordid detail of every bit of her death arrived in his inbox. Gregor opened the report and scanned its contents, looking for the facts that would tally with other victims. She'd been washed clean, dressed, and placed in her coffin, and only then was her throat slit. She hadn't been violated. There were no defence wounds. But toxicology revealed that her killer had slipped her flunitrazepam somehow. Different from the other victims … Yet, somehow the same.

Where is the link? Gregor thought.

Gregor picked up the receiver of his desk phone and dialled the number for the forensic team.

The pathologist, Sarah Whitby, answered.

'Did you take any samples from food or drink in the fridge?'

'DCI Chapel said we didn't need to,' she said.

Gregor held back a sigh.

Gregor went back to the house.

The crime scene was still closed and not even the distant relatives that came forward were allowed inside until all avenues had been explored, checked, and double-checked. As a result, nothing had been disturbed since the forensic team had swept through. The once immaculate home had the air of neglect. Print dust was everywhere and everything seemed out of place as though it had been moved, but not exactly returned to where it should be.

Gregor pulled on his gloves and, because he had only one reason to be there, he opened the fridge door and glanced inside at the contents. The jug of homemade lemonade was still there, as he had hoped. He transferred the contents to a sealed container, and labelled it. Then he removed any other open liquids, milk, water, some juice and did the same.

Pathology would look now, at his request. Sometimes

Chapel made snap decisions that made no sense: it wasn't the first time that Gregor had followed up on cases to make sure no stone was unturned. Chapel liked to give orders, but wasn't good when it came to being thorough. Gregor thought he was ultimately lazy.

For good measure, Gregor fingerprinted the jug too, carefully bagging it for future analysis. This time, he would make sure every avenue had been explored.

As he turned to go, Gregor glanced through to the small music room and saw something protruding from the closed top of the white baby grand. He headed into the room, careful not to disturb anything as usual.

The piano was smeared with fingerprint dust, but it appeared that only his eagle eyes had spotted the small corner of a piece of paper.

Gregor lifted the lid and, freed, the paper fluttered down onto the strings coming to rest face down. He reached inside and turned it over. To his surprise he found a sketch. It was a drawing of Elsbeth, lying in the coffin – just as she had been found. There were the three words written below in bold capitals:

A BEAUTIFUL DEATH.

Gregor picked up the drawing and starred at it. Then he took out his phone and took a snap of the image.

Could it be that Elsbeth's killer had left this here? But why, when it could connect him to the crime? He bagged the paper to protect it, then he left the house and locked up.

The paper, the fingerprints he'd lifted, and the liquids were analysed and a few days later, Gregor learned the results.

'Flunitrazepam was in the lemonade too,' he told Chapel. 'But only her prints were on the jug.'

'Well, that tells us nothing,' Chapel sneered. 'The perp wore gloves.'

He wasn't impressed with Gregor's initiative and took every opportunity to show him that it had been a waste of time.

'But there was another set of prints on the sketch. We could run these against the other murders, see if there's a match,' Gregor said.

'If you think it's worth it. But I'm sure there are better ways to spend the budget,' Chapel said.

Gregor fought the urge to deep sigh: all Chapel's arguments were pointless and somewhat petty because it was nothing more than a database search, run by a computer program. No man power involved at all other than setting the search in motion. It cost them nothing and could be essential to the case, which Gregor feared was growing colder by the day. He couldn't understand Chapel's reluctance: it was their duty after all to do due diligence and that meant they had to do everything they could to solve a crime.

Gregor left Chapel's office. Now that he'd reported the extra findings, he'd put in the man hours himself to try and find any connections. To him it wasn't about just ticking boxes though. He wanted to find the killer, and Elsbeth's death had intensified that need even more.

He found himself thinking about her body again. The artistry of it didn't say serial killer. There was no brutality in it at all ... usually they saw an escalation, and often frenzied attacks, especially with killers who used knives. And look at the killer's calling card, a sketch of how she looked, dead. He must have taken the time afterwards to draw it: so secure was he that he wouldn't have been disturbed ... most perps got away as fast as they could.

It was the oddest murder Gregor had ever seen.

Back home, Gregor tried to stop thinking about her body, which had taken on a life and was now called Elsbeth in his mind: he should never have looked at the photos of her before because they only reminded him that she was human. This job was easier sometimes when he forgot that.

He'd had two days off to spend with his seven-year-old son and his ex-wife was due to collect him any moment. Stefan was in his room, collecting his favourite toys to take back to his mother's, and Gregor found himself looking at the sketch again on his phone.

Something wasn't right about all of this, and he didn't know what it was that jarred so much.

The doorbell rang, and he placed his phone down on the kitchen worktop, while he went to the front door.

'Hi,' said Karen. 'Is Stefan ready?'

Gregor always tried to be nice when she turned up. They were divorced, not enemies, and so he invited her in.

'Stefan,' he called up the stairs. 'Your mother's here!'

'How's he been?' she said.

'Great, why?' Gregor asked.

'He's been acting up at school again,' Karen said.

'Come in the kitchen and I'll make coffee,' Gregor said glancing up the stairs because he was conscious that the walls were paper thin and Stefan may hear them talking.

Karen followed him into the kitchen. Gregor put the kettle on and indicated she take a seat at the breakfast bar. As she pulled out the chair, she glanced at Gregor's phone and noticed it wasn't locked, and the snap of a drawing.

'What's that?' she asked.

'Oh! Sorry. Confidential. A work thing.'

Karen frowned as he picked up his phone and locked closed it.

'Stefan … doesn't see any files or …'

'Karen. No! Seriously! I don't bring anything home and he never touches my phone. I'd forgotten to delete this that's all.'

'Okay.' She went quiet for a moment and then, as she sipped the coffee she frowned and looked at Gregor. 'That expression … A beautiful death … reminds me of something.'

'Really? You've heard that before?'

'I think so,' she said.

'Can you remember where?'

Karen frowned again as she concentrated. 'No. But it might come to me.'

Stefan came into the room carrying his tablet and a teddy he refused to leave behind that had to shuffle back and forth through each house. Gregor knew he'd soon grow out of it and so never discouraged his love of the toy. Kids grew up too quickly these days and he wasn't in a hurry to see his son mature faster than he needed to.

'Your case is in the hallway, buddy,' Gregor said. 'Let Mummy finish her coffee then she'll take you home.'

'That's okay,' Karen said swigging it quickly. 'He has a friend sleeping over tonight so we'd better go.'

The house was very quiet when Karen and Stefan left and Gregor felt that tremor of remorse that sometimes snuck in when he was alone. He missed being with Stefan more, but understood that the time they had together was usually more quality as a result. He'd taken his wife and son for granted when they'd been always in his life. The job, as Karen often remarked, was more a marriage to him than theirs was. Now, looking back, he knew it was true. It was true of most detectives and only someone in the force would understand why. Gregor always felt his job was more than that, it was an obsession, a passion, a vocation. Something he couldn't change because it was also a terrible addiction.

He put the coffee cups into his dishwasher, and opened his fridge, pulling out a steak and some salad to make for dinner. He often cooked as he found it relaxing.

He splashed some oil in a frying pan, and seasoned the meat. He was just about to add the steak to the steaming oil when his phone rang. He glanced at the caller ID and realised it was Karen.

He removed the pan from the heat and picked it up.

'Everything okay? Sorry, I just realised we didn't finish our talk … about Stefan …'

'It's not that. He's just trying his luck with a new teacher … It's not serious. But … I just remembered where I saw those words. "A beautiful death" … it was an advert. In a magazine.'

'An advert? For what …?' Gregor asked.

'Artwork I think. A portrait. Where you choose your

ideal death.' Karen said.

'What kind of magazine was that?' Gregor asked.

'I don't know. Something in the hairdressers. I was bored while my colour took ...'

'Okay. Thanks,' Gregor said. 'If you remember which mag it was, that could help me.'

Karen hung up and Gregor turned his stove off. He went upstairs to his home office and switched on the computer. If Karen was right and she'd seen an advert, then she might well have given him a lucky break.

Gregor typed the words 'A beautiful death' and found a whole host of gothic images that related to the subject. The fascination with the subject surprised him, even though he'd drawn comparisons with the way some victims were displayed so artistically himself. It made him realise that his thoughts weren't that unusual after all, though he'd never voiced them to anyone.

But the stuff he found wasn't helpful, nor was it what he was looking for.

Gregor thought for a moment, a web search was only as good as the key words you used. He typed in 'art of my perfect death'. Again, similar things came up. But nothing that related to an article. Then he tried, 'Buy art made personally for my beautiful death'. One more, he struck out. He was running out of ideas on how to spin this and then he thought of 'A beautiful death organisation or company'.

After failing on every search Gregor began to believe that Karen must be mistaken because surely an artist trying to sell their work would have an online presence? He turned off his computer and went downstairs to finish his dinner.

The next day, Gregor still couldn't let it go. The case was getting colder, even the techies hadn't found anything in the enhanced footage, and he felt he had to try any lead he could find. Plus, Karen was always very observant and he knew she had a great memory. He sent her a text asking for the name of the hairdressers she went to. She sent him a quick reply with the name and address. That was when Gregor got his first surprise. The salon was just a few streets from where Elsbeth lived. It was, therefore, possible that she went there for her hair appointments too.

He signed himself out of the station and went to the salon straight away. It was a Tuesday morning, before 9am when he arrived and so there was only a couple of hairdressers there, getting the place ready to open for the day.

Gregor showed his badge and a picture of Elsbeth and the girl on reception recognised her immediately.

'She always has ... sorry had, I saw it in the newspaper ... Tracy,' the girl said, 'She's not in at the moment though. She only works Thursday, Friday and Saturday.'

'Okay, but you knew her too, right?'

'Yes. Only, they don't talk to me like they talk to the stylists,' the girl said. 'It's a very personal service you see ... people almost come in for therapy ...'

'Therapy?' Gregor said.

'Well yes, they tell the stylists so much about their lives ... Helps them get it off their chest. It's part of the job.'

'Did you hear anything while Elsbeth talked to Tracy. Was she depressed? Upset? Scared? Anything at all?'

The girl shook her head. 'She was a quiet one really. I always thought she was a bit lonely though.'

'Why?' asked Gregor.

'She never talked about a partner or dating. Married women are always complaining about their husbands and unmarried ones are always talking about how wonderful their boyfriends are ... or if they are looking ... what type of partner they want.'

'So, you're saying most women aren't happily married?' he asked.

'No ... it's not that. They are just letting off steam. Men do that too I'm sure ... But Elsbeth never talked about a husband or boyfriend or girlfriend for that matter. She didn't say much to be honest.'

'One other thing, can I look through your magazines while I'm here?'

'The magazines? Yeah ... sure ... but ...'

'I can't explain why, police business ... you understand.'

The girl nodded and Gregor picked up the pile of magazines left in a stack on a small coffee table by a bright pink sofa.

'Do you have a back room? Somewhere I can study these?'

'Sure,' said the girl. 'Kitchen. Through that door.'

Gregor took the pile into the back and placed it on the worktop. A few minutes later, one of the stylists came in to make a drink. She offered him a coffee, but he turned it down as he rapidly flicked through the magazines, putting aside any that he'd already looked at.

He found what he was searching for in a copy of a niche magazine called *Goth Girl*. Right in the back, among the classifieds he found a small boxed advert.

> *Design your own death!*
> *Artist realisation.*
> *Email: mybeautifuldeath@outlook.com*

Gregor took a photograph of the advert and the front cover of the magazine.

But he also held on to the magazine as he walked back into the salon.

'Can I keep this?' he asked the receptionist.

'S ... sure,' she said.

Gregor took it and left.

Gregor entered the briefing late much to DCI Chapel's annoyance. The DCI scowled at him as though he'd been away doing anything other than his job.

'Thank you for deigning us with your presence, Gregor, I don't suppose you have anything new to add to the pot, have you?'

Gregor was ready to be put on the spot and so he talked about the drawing, and the connection he'd made with the hairdressers.

'Well done,' Chapel said giving reluctant praise. 'And how does her hairdressers' help us?'

'I do have something more, but need to check it out first,' Gregor said.

Chapel rolled his eyes as if confirming that Gregor's trip out had been a waste of time. Gregor ignored it, he was sure something would come from his investigations. First, he had to find the user of the email address on the advert. Then, he might have the best lead they'd had so far. But how to approach it?

The meeting ended and Gregor went back to his desk. He needed an angle to approach the person first. Perhaps he could say he was referred by Elsbeth Chalmers?

He searched for 'my beautiful death' online, found several gothic and vampire related fan stuff, and wondered if among these, their killer hid.

At this point he was putting two and two together: It was obvious that some psycho with artistic flair was behind the killings. And perhaps, Elsbeth commissioned some art because she was into gothic stuff despite appearances. She may have innocently approached the artist, not knowing that he'd act on the drawing he did of her.

If it wasn't for Chapel keeping a miserly rein on their finances he'd have enlisted the aid of a profiler who could help pin down who and what they were looking for. But for now, and until more pressure was applied by the media, and above Chapel's head, that budget wouldn't be available to them.

At home, that night, using a VPN and an email he created for this purpose, Gregor signed up on a few gothic sites that had artists. His evenings alone were often boring anyway and so he combed the sites, looking for artwork that was like the sketch he'd found of Elsbeth – then he found something: a sleeping beauty picture that looked similar to how Elsbeth's body was laid out. Though it wasn't her. The artist, however, was anonymous. He took a screenshot of the picture and made a record of the site. When he was ready to open-up about his searches he'd get the techies on this to find the ISP details of the person who posted this picture.

Gregor set up another fake outlook email address under the name Carrilyn Roper, and he sent an email to the mybeautifuldeath account, saying Elsbeth had recommended contacting them. Then it was a waiting game. A game that proved to be extremely difficult for Gregor, but he didn't waiver and he didn't badger the recipient, only waited.

It took a week for the reply to arrive. He'd been pulled from the Elsbeth Chalmers case and was now working a more straightforward murder where they'd already arrested a wife for poisoning her husband. These things didn't happen often but when they did, there was a lot of history to unravel and often a dark reason as to why the murder took place. In this case, the woman claimed he was abusing her, but Gregor felt she was lying and he was spending a lot of time looking at phone records to see if she had an accomplice or if she was having an affair.

Chapel had kept control of Elsbeth's case, though he showed no signs of progress at all: as though he never wanted to find the killer. A source of frustration that wound up several of the others working with him, though none of them dared to complain or go against their boss.

Meanwhile, Gregor kept his attention on the new case during the day, but looked over Elsbeth's in the evenings. He still interacted on the gothic sites, all as Carrilyn, which was difficult at first, but he slowly became better at networking as a woman.

What he was doing wasn't sanctioned, but not illegal. He wasn't trying to catfish anyone, just gathering intel that later on he could pass to Chapel and his team.

Gregor received the notification via his phone while he was at work. He looked at the reply, excited, but unable to deal with it until he got home. This was possibly Elsbeth's killer writing to him.

When he got home, he opened the email again.

'The Sleeping Beauty had a beautiful death,' said the sender. 'How do you want yours?'

Gregor frowned at this. Strange wording, and no mention of art.

He replied that he was 'open to suggestions and wanted something creative and beautiful'.

Within minutes the sender replied.

'I'll need a photograph of you, of course,' said the sender. 'And then I'll have ideas and will send you a sketch. I usually send by email, though some want the physical copy.'

'Email will be fine,' replied Gregor and he attached his favourite photograph of his ex-wife Karen.

'I'll be in touch,' was the short reply.

Gregor went to reply again and stopped himself. The sender said he'd 'be in touch'. He'd have to be patient again despite how hard it was. He didn't want to spook the killer.

Three days passed and then he received an email with a rough sketch attached. The artist liked his fairy tales. It was of Karen as Snow White, lying dead with a poisoned apple in her hand.

'If you like this. Tell me where and when,' the sender said. 'And your beautiful death will happen painlessly.'

Gregor read this note in shock. What this implied was that the victim would be complicit in their own murder. They were, effectively, taking out a hit on themselves. Could Elsbeth really have wanted to die? None of the people they'd interviewed ever expressed a suggestion that she was depressed or suicidal, so how was this possible?

Gregor hesitated to reply. He had questions, and the most pressing was the price. But would the killer mention money in an email?

He thought carefully about his reply. It was crucial he did this right. Would Elsbeth have told her friend the price or was that something he needed to ask about. Of course, the cost was irrelevant, he could get the killer to come to his house, trap him and make an arrest without paying a penny probably. But what if he wanted the money upfront?

'How do I reward you for your efforts?' he asked eventually.

The reply was swift.

'£2000 in cash at the scene in a canvas holdall.'

Gregor replied with his address, a date, and a time. He also asked, 'Do I prepare anything?'

'I'll have it all,' said the killer.

Now that the trap was set, Gregor felt nervous. He'd set a sting, without permission, and now it was time to tell Chapel and the team what he'd learned. He expected to be reprimanded for it, but he also knew Chapel would happily take the credit if all went well.

He went into work the next day with his personal laptop, print outs of the emails and screenshots he'd gathered from the various sites that he suspected was also this killer's artwork.

After a long-drawn-out meeting with Chapel, who hit the roof when he heard what Gregor had done, Gregor handed over his findings and the tech department was deployed to unravel the nest surrounding the My Beautiful Death killer.

'My biggest concern is that we don't lose the case against him for entrapment,' Chapel said once he'd calmed down. 'But looking at your responses, you have been very careful and controlled. I think this could work. Even though giving a serial killer your home address was a stupid thing to do, I can also see why you had to respond quickly, before you had time to consider it. Would Karen be willing to be the decoy here, since you sent her photograph to him?'

'Oh no, I need to keep her out of it ...' Gregor said.

'It's just ... the killer will run as soon as you open your front door. Did you also never think, that maybe, once you gave your address, he'd do a recon trip first. Get the lie of the land. I would. If I was him,' Chapel said.

Gregor was shocked that he hadn't thought of that. How imprudent it was. How unprofessional. And yes, he'd given the killer his address, expecting him to just waltz in and be caught, without even thinking that he'd stake out the property first to see who lived there, look for hidden cameras.

'I know you're a good cop,' Chapel continued. 'But this sort of not thinking through of consequences is why I'm a DCI and you are a DI. Policing is teamwork, Gregor. And you can be too maverick in your approach and often forget that. It's the team that wins the day, not a lone vigilante.'

Gregor didn't agree that he'd been a vigilante, and he didn't point out to Chapel that he had given his free time to help with this case. His hard work and diligence wasn't appreciated and all fell on deaf ears anyway. Chapel's ego knew no bounds in truth though, and Gregor chose to believe he was mad at him for not staying clear of the case when he'd been moved off it. It felt personal when he was, and he had been a dog with a bone, not letting it go. He wanted to meet the killer, look him in the eye, and see if he appeared innocuous in his daily life.

'Anyway,' Chapel said. 'We need to at least get an officer who looks like your ex to stay at your place and look like she is the person who sent the email.'

The search for a suitable colleague began, and they found a willing young PC who was hoping to be promoted to homicide. Her name was Di Strawbridge, and she looked a little like Karen, same build, longer hair, which she agreed to cut. Gregor moved her into his house discreetly a week before the sting was supposed to take place. He also told Karen, she had to stay clear, and she and Stefan were not allowed to visit until the whole thing was over.

By then, Chapel had more plain clothes police in the area and his house was under surveillance. If they saw any one out of place, they'd be pulled in and questioned.

'How are the tech team doing on finding the owner of the ISP?' Gregor asked.

'Our perp knew to use a VPN,' Chapel said. 'Of course,

he did! Even you thought of that!'

Gregor didn't respond. But Chapel's constant digs were beginning to wear him down. He felt useless. Stupid. No good at his job. And he seriously began to wonder if he needed a career change.

The day before the killer was supposed to appear. Gregor received another email from him.

The killer warned him that if anyone else was present, the 'beautiful death' would not happen. He also told him to disable any cameras and alarms on the property.

The next day, Gregor made an obvious exit from his home, leaving Di alone, except that Di wasn't alone, several police officers waited inside.

The plan was that Di would bring the killer inside, he'd accept the money, they'd talk about what was going to happen, and it would all be recorded. Then the perp would be arrested.

Chapel insisted on defining all the details. They waited and when an hour over the time passed, they realised the killer had been warned. He was a no show.

'You screwed this up!' Chapel said to Gregor. 'If you'd done this above board from the start, but no! You went out on your own. I think maybe you should consider a change of career, Gregor. Policing isn't for you!'

Gregor fell into a deep depression. The killer had flown, and despite the emails he sent, trying to get his attention again. Nothing worked. They resorted to new contacts, but again, he didn't respond. It was almost as if he knew that it was the police.

After a few months, the blame and accusations stopped. They began to believe that Elsbeth's death would never be solved.

Gregor's depression at the failure grew and he wanted his over active mind to be quiet. There had always been a darkness in him, a tendency to be melancholy, but now he found it harder and harder to shake it. He went home, night after night, alone, stressed, angry, lonely. The idea of an end to it all began to form in his mind and for the first time, he understood why Elsbeth, and perhaps many other victims, had sought their beautiful death.

What more could you do when your career was being stalled by a superior that hated you?

One night, Gregor had had enough. He sent out one last email to the killer. This time, begging for his own end. He didn't expect a reply, but one way or another, he didn't want to go on anymore.

Karen knocked at the door, Stefan was at school, but she was worried about Gregor because he hadn't replied to her last few texts. She knew he got busy with work, but she'd also seen a change in him over the last few months. Though he never told her anything about it, she suspected it was all to do with work and things weren't going well for him.

The house was quiet, no sign of life inside, and Karen looked through the letterbox into the hallway. She could see right down into the kitchen and noticed that the French windows out the back were wide open. Gregor must be outside.

Karen opened the side gate and passed through the small walkway between Gregor's house and the one next door. She opened the back gate and went into the garden.

Gregor wasn't there, she thought he must be hiding from her, but didn't understand why.

She went inside, calling his name. There was no answer. But she'd never been shy about entering personal spaces and so she began to search the house. He had a tendency for depression; she'd always known that, and it had been one of the things that had made their marriage challenging. Even so, she thought those days were behind him once he'd been promoted to DI. Gregor had never had much confidence in his own abilities, it was why he worked so much harder than anyone else.

Karen had expressed her concerns so often. 'You're too hard on yourself,' she'd said. But she couldn't change Gregor's mind set, and had sometimes wondered if it was something born from the childhood he never talked about.

She passed through the hallway and upstairs. At the top she saw that all the doors were closed. She'd been up here, in Stefan's room, but never in Gregor's. That would have been too personal, despite their history, and so she hesitated at the door.

Then, unable to wait any longer, she opened the door.

DCI Chapel did his best to console the hysterical woman as she sobbed on the doorstep.

'He'd gone off work with stress,' Chapel said. 'None of us knew he was depressed.'

'He can't have done that to himself,' Karen said. 'Not Gregor. He was never suicidal.'

Chapel said nothing.

'It was ... so awful, 'Karen continued. 'Seeing him like that, with the tarot card under his feet, showing the hanged man ...'

Chapel passed her over to a female constable and went inside. He'd looked at the body, hanging in the bedroom. The bed was made up with red satin sheets, his face was painted like a joker, and then the card. There was an artistry to it, a kind of poetry. It was, some might think ... beautiful.

Going for Gold

Eleanor Monroe was planning their tenth anniversary party when Nate said he wanted a divorce.

Eleanor was devastated. She'd given Nate most of her youth, and now, just like that, he was done with her.

'Is there someone else?' she'd said through the initial tears.

At first he denied it, but a little bit of investigation was all it took to learn the truth and it was worse than Eleanor could have imagined. Not only was the woman several years younger and more attractive than her, she also ran a successful business.

Eleanor hated her right from the start.

'How long has this been going on?' she asked Nate. 'I deserve the truth.'

'I was going to tell you, but I just wanted the divorce to be clean.'

'It can't be clean. You cheated on me with some bimbo.'

'She's not a bimbo! And this is why I didn't tell you,' Nate said. 'I knew you'd be hateful about her.'

Eleanor's mouth dropped open. This was the worst case of gaslighting Nate had ever done to her, and over the years he'd done plenty, but she'd been a good wife. Loving, caring, and always looked after their home. She didn't even have children because he never wanted any. What more could she have done? Granted, she didn't have a successful career – not like this woman – Victoria – with her chain of fashion shops, but Eleanor did work and contributed to their lifestyle and Nate had no reason to look for sex elsewhere either, she'd never refused him and had believed they had a good sex life. *So why*, she wondered, *had he felt the need to find someone else?*

She did all the usual things, self-blame, looking back to see if there were any signs. But no, Nate had been a good liar, and Eleanor had never suspected. It made her wonder if Victoria was the first or just the last of several affairs throughout their marriage. She didn't put anything past him.

The enormity of her new predicament didn't dawn on her immediately, but as time went on and the situation became clearer she began to fret. This divorce meant changes. The house she'd spent years caring for would have to be sold. And she would only have half of the equity in order to try and set herself up again. She still had her job, but her meagre salary didn't lend itself to getting a solo mortgage, she'd never be able to live to the standard she was used to with Nate.

As this wasn't her fault, her first instinct was to go after everything she could get.

She got advice from a solicitor but soon realised that dragging Nate through a messy divorce wouldn't help anyone. She might be entitled to half his pension, and get more from the sale of the house, but the solicitor's fees would be higher, Eleanor knew that only the lawyers would win in the end. It wasn't worth it and after years of being browbeaten by Nate, she wasn't up to the fight either.

So, she agreed to mediation. And, because she was being reasonable, and Nate, out of guilt, was being fair for a change, the finances and divorce were quickly concluded.

A year later, and now in a two-bedroom house that she owned outright, Eleanor began to feel ready to go out again, get a social life and start meeting potential boyfriends. It had taken months for her to get used to sleeping alone and she still missed Nate, but there were so many silver linings too. It was freeing to be able to do whatever she wanted, eat what she wanted and when she wanted and, also watch the programmes she liked on the TV without feeling any guilt about it. Nate hated most of what she liked and so she'd always given into his tastes and not her own.

While she'd been with Nate, her old friends had drifted away, mainly because she stopped seeing them. Nate didn't like her going out on girls' nights and now, free of him, Eleanor realised just what he'd done to her. Keeping her down all the time, telling her she wasn't worthy. She had believed it, sacrificed so much for the sake of the relationship and for keeping him happy, all for nothing.

She was looking on social media one day and then she saw it. Nate, newly married to Victoria, who was sporting a baby bump! She hadn't meant to spy on them; the pictures came up on her newsfeed as a so-called 'friend' had attended the wedding.

Eleanor sank back into her chair, more mortified than she could possibly imagine. She felt sick. This finally proved that her whole life had been a joke to Nate. She hated him and Victoria even more. It wasn't bad enough that Victoria had stolen her husband, she'd also persuaded him to have children.

At 42, Eleanor felt old, past it, and here was Nate, 45, Victoria, 30, starting a life together and bringing a child into the world. Like any normal *young* couple would.

But of course, Victoria would never be told she couldn't have children, or friends, or gaslighted in any way. Nate would never do that to a woman like her. How could he? She was stronger than Eleanor, and this just proved it.

The whole thing began to grown inside her head. Despite herself she began to stalk Victoria's social media. Instagram was full of pictures of their new home. A six-bedroom mansion, bigger, better than she'd had with Nate, and in an exclusive area that Eleanor would never be able to afford. She found herself looking around at the tiny home she now had. She was bitter and even thought hard about getting revenge, but couldn't imagine how to do it. She was miserable again. There was no way forward, no way to feel better that didn't included seeing them both dead so that she could move on.

One morning, she woke up and knew that things had to change. She didn't like who she was becoming. Hatred was a growing pustule, ready to burst.

'I need to move on,' she told herself.

She began to go by the name Ellie at work and she reverted to her maiden name, making sure that HR knew the change and put this on her records. She changed her passport, her driving licence, bank accounts. Every single legal document she could. She wanted a new start and felt this was the only way to get it.

Five months went by, and she became used to being Ellie. She cut and highlighted her mousy hair, and had it shaped into a neat and professional looking bob. Since the divorce, she'd lost weight. First, it was because of the stress and not eating, then, when people began to comment on how well she looked, Ellie started to take better care of herself. Her colleagues began to say she had a look of the actress, Jodie Whittaker. Ellie liked this and she was looking younger and healthier than she had in years. Maybe she could get out there, meet someone new, get something of a life back that she felt she owned once more.

She watched a show starring the actress on Netflix. Enjoying the fact that so many people thought she now looked like her. The series was called, *Trust Me*, where Whittaker, playing a nurse, pretended to be a doctor, and took on the identity of her former best friend who had moved to New Zealand. The whole story was very implausible, but Ellie enjoyed watching it anyway and after a few days of binging episodes an insane idea came to her. What if she could pretend to be someone else too? After all, in a way she had already reinvented herself.

Then the means for revenge presented itself, as a fantasy, at first. But the more she thought about it, the more she believed it possible. She *was* someone else now, she'd done the hard part already. Eleanor Monroe technically didn't exist anymore. She was now Ellie Sharp. And Ellie Sharp went to the gym, bought younger-looking clothes, and even started getting Botox to erase the small lines and wrinkles from her forehead.

She began watching Victoria's business website, checking the jobs section and then, the right thing came up. They were looking for someone in their head office, someone who knew how to do accounts up to trial balance. Ellie did. She sent in her CV, and with an excellent reference from her current boss, she got an interview – all under her new name and with all the legal documents to back it up.

She knew it was a bold move but she was counting on the fact that Victoria, now heavily pregnant, wouldn't recognise her. Eleanor had never met Victoria. She doubted that Nate had shown her any photos of her and he hadn't taken any with him when he left, even leaving their wedding album behind. Ellie had also made sure that her old social media was full of avatars and nothing else, so even if Victoria was curious about her, which she doubted, then there was nothing to see on there that showed 'Eleanor Monroe'. Ellie couldn't imagine her caring about Nate's ex now that she had him all to herself, and she was sure that not even Nate would recognise her these days either.

'I'm going for gold,' she told herself. *Whatever happens, I'm going to get this job. Learn everything I can about her.*

Then she was going to destroy her.

Ellie had no clue what she would do once she was working inside Victoria's business, but she was winging it. After all she had nothing more to lose.

A week later, Ellie was waiting to see Victoria's HR people, and Victoria came into the waiting room. Ellie smiled at her, putting on her most relaxed and friendly expression. She forced herself to be still and not fidget like she usually did when she was nervous. It was an effort, but somehow, her desire for revenge helped her pull it off.

'Hello,' Victoria said. 'Are you Ellie?'

'Yes,' she said.

'You look familiar, have we met before?' Victoria said.

'No. I'm sure we haven't,' said Ellie.

'I know what it is! You look a lot like that actress, Jodie someone ...'

Ellie's smile widened. 'Whittaker. I get that a lot!'

'That's her! Come through,' Victoria said.

Ellie stood and followed Victoria into an office. The room was typically corporate, tastefully furnished, white, bright, expensive. Victoria went around the desk and sat, indicating Ellie to take the seat opposite.

'Ooh,' said Victoria as she sat down.

'Are you okay?' Ellie asked.

'Yes. It's just this baby. Can't wait for it to happen now.'

'Do you know what you're having?' Ellie asked.

'No. My husband and I wanted a surprise,' Victoria said.

Ellie blinked as Victoria's use of 'husband' caused her significant pain, but she managed to keep her face straight.

'Have you any children?' Victoria asked.

'Unfortunately, no. I'm not married,' Ellie said.

After that the interview went well. Ellie was shown the accounting system, all of which she was familiar with and could speak about at length. When the interview was done, she left her contact details.

As she got into her modest car, Ellie was convinced she'd somehow messed up. Perhaps Victoria had recognised her and she'd taken the whole interview as a joke. She and Nate would even now be laughing at her pathetic attempt to come and work for her.

As she started the engine her phone rang.

'Hi Ellie, it's Susan in HR. I had a call to check a reference from someone called Victoria Monroe.'

'Sorry Susan, I would have warned you, but I've literally just had the interview. I wasn't sure the job was even for me.'

'Well, I confirmed the standard reference, but also gave them a glowing personal one. I suspect they will be making you an offer. They were very impressed with your interview.'

'Oh, thanks Susan! That was very fast! I'll let you know my decision if they do.'

Ellie hung up and within moments, the phone rang again, and as Karen predicted, Ellie was offered the book-keeping job at Victoria's company. She took it immediately.

Six months later Ellie was a valued member of the team. Her salary was better than she'd ever earned at her old job. She enjoyed the busy environment of the office and the new job had some challenges which she relished overcoming too. All in all, she had a great deal of satisfaction working for Victoria's company and for the first time, she was putting in more effort, feeling like she was appreciated, and was good at the job too. It also gave her some perverse satisfaction that she was taking the money from Victoria and she and Nate were now subsidising her lifestyle. Ironic.

Victoria had taken some leave on the birth of her and Nate's baby. It was a girl and they called her Laurell. But Victoria was never going to be a stay-at-home mother and so she returned to work after just a month.

With the rise in pay, Ellie could enjoy some luxuries again. She was even planning a holiday with some friends she'd reconnected with. Life was good. She pushed back the urge for revenge, relishing her new position in life and the fact that it was down to her hard work and not to an unappreciative husband that she had this success.

Ellie didn't see much of Victoria, and Nate never came into the head office. Being recognised was a fear she had when she first embarked on this journey for vengeance, but as time went on, she began to understand that it wasn't going to happen.

Other the next few months, Ellie learnt how Victoria's company worked and was integrated into the group of office workers who dealt with various aspects of the business. All of which she showed interest in. Victoria's operation was fascinating. She was a clever woman, driven and, Ellie had to admit, deserving of the success, even if she was a husband stealer.

Ellie became very torn between her plan and her newfound respect for Victoria. It was hard to dislike someone when they worked so hard and had so much talent and who also treated her employees well.

Her mind changed all the time about what she would do to bring her rival down but as six months became a year, Ellie pushed the idea of payback further and further away until she no longer thought about it every day.

A year after starting the job, Ellie had a review with the head of HR, a girl called Julie Malachy who she'd befriended throughout the months and drank with at the Christmas party.

Julie was fun-loving outside of work but took her job very seriously.

'We've been very happy with you here,' Julie informed her in a solemn tone. 'And that's why, we are offering you a promotion.'

Ellie was shocked. It seemed that her line-manager was leaving, and because Ellie had shown such interest in all aspects of the business, Victoria had suggested her for the role.

It meant another pay rise, and more responsibility, and Julie asked if Ellie was up for this.

Julie was smiling now.

'I'd love to!' said Ellie. 'I can't believe it!'

'Well, Victoria has always recognised flair and she would hate it if you were headhunted. I've always liked how she rewards people for working hard. I wouldn't want to leave here myself.'

'It's a good place to work,' Ellie agreed.

The whole promotion gave Ellie food for thought. She'd come here with other plans in mind. An aim to go for gold and ruin Victoria, yet she had become part of a successful team, and the satisfaction she gained from it couldn't be disputed. She had never felt happier than she did at work. Who needed a man in your life when you had a career, money you earned, and had such satisfaction every day?

That night, when Ellie left work, she had decided to abandon any thought of revenge on Victoria. It was odd, but she now saw her life with Nate as some distant dream, and Victoria had come along and changed her life forever, but now that transformation was for the better. By taking away her security, Victoria had given something to Ellie that she'd never had: drive and a survival instinct that had led her to make a bold decision.

I'm happy, she thought and she couldn't remember feeling like this before in her life. Victoria was the reason for it all. She almost pitied her for being stuck with Nate now, because, Ellie would never give someone like him the time of day again.

Back home, Ellie found a bouquet of flowers waiting for her.

Congratulations on the promotion! The card read. *Glad to have you on our team, Victoria xxx.*

Ellie teared up when she read the card. What other employer would do such a personal thing as this? Was she really valued after all?

Ellie smelled the flowers and then arranged them in a vase. She'd wanted to have retribution, but now, Ellie realised, that it wasn't what she needed any more.

As she looked at the flowers, sitting in pride of place on her coffee table, Ellie knew she'd gone for gold and won even if it wasn't what she'd originally planned. Wasn't that the best payback ever?

But still, part of her wondered, now she had access to every fragment of Victoria's business, if she should still take her retaliation to the next level.

It was tempting. A dilemma she would think on. Scheme a bit more perhaps, while reaping all the benefits that she currently had.

It was a delicious fantasy. One that she may never act on … or maybe she would …

The Curse of Guangxu

The envelope was on the dresser when Sherlock Holmes returned to his room.

The year was 1897 and Holmes was on the last leg of what had been a most satisfying and fascinating tour of China. Having visited several less civilised, even archaic villages, he had planned to round off his trip taking in the delights of Beijing. Once there, Holmes had been amazed at the forward thinking and somewhat modern city which was so far removed from the small shanties he had so far seen, that it made him aware of the poverty suffered by the people who were not fortunate enough to live in the capital. It was something he observed the world over and, on many warm nights pondered on whilst smoking his favourite pipe.

He was much like his old self because of the travel. Slowly his cognitive functions were returning to normal. The torments of Moriarty were ended and the death of his arch enemy, and his own subsequent faked demise – a somewhat knee jerk reaction – was all starting to feel like a distant, insane memory - or worse: an overly dramatised play. In the last week he had begun to consider the possibility of going home again but, when surrounded by the exotic, London seemed to be nothing more than a place that he had once dreamed. He thought of Doctor John Watson sometimes too. His old friend was probably happy with Mary. Married life would suit him, Holmes was certain, but he also believed that Watson would have missed the excitement that their investigative days had brought them. But, perhaps, he would soon respond to the urge to brave the now seemingly alien London streets once more.

Holmes sat down on the edge of the bed and slipped out of his shoes, replacing them with comfortable slippers. Then he removed his overcoat, hung it casually over the back of a chair and pulled on a blue velvet smoking jacket. He picked up his pipe from the bedside table and then his eyes fell on the dresser.

The envelope was an obvious intrusion in the room. He had noticed it immediately but he had not been in the right state of mind to acknowledge its presence. Now Holmes eyed it for a moment, checking for obvious traps, and then picked it up, observing the telegram markings before opening. The envelope was marked with his name as well as specific and carefully penned Chinese lettering, 紅雙喜的酒店 which he recognised as the name of the Inn where he was staying: the Inn of Double Happiness.

'Fascinating,' he murmured.

No one knew that Holmes was in Beijing. No one even knew that he was still alive - or so he thought.

He glanced around the room, eyes scanning the bamboo furniture; the ornate dressing screen that sheltered a tin bath from the rest of the room; the bed that was covered in decadent cushions (which promised more comfort than he had seen throughout his entire journey); and, of course, his trunk stood in the far corner near the balcony window.

He raised the envelope to his nose and sniffed. The scents of ink and bamboo paper filled his nostrils with the subtle fragrance of Jasmine. Holmes focused on the perfume which would have been foreign anywhere else but here in this fascinating world. The smell jarred even so. It felt wrong, inappropriate, though the mystery of why was still a long way from unfolding.

He didn't have an envelope knife and so Holmes picked up the tiny paring knife that had been left beside the full basket of fruit he had requested earlier, and he opened the envelope.

Inside, as expected, was a telegram.

TO: SHERLOCK HOLMES, 紅雙喜的酒店
FROM: SAMUEL JAMES DANBY, 故宮

MY DEAR CHAP HOLMES x HEARD
YOU WERE IN THE CAPITAL x IN
URGENT NEED OF YOUR HELP x I WORK
FOR EMPEROR GUANGXU x HAVE HIS
PERMISSION TO CONTACT YOU x A
GRAVE ILLNESS HAS STRICKEN HIS
BELOVED CONSORT x I AM AT A LOSS x
DOES NOT CONFORM TO ANYTHING I
HAVE SEEN BEFORE x POOR GIRL
SIMPLY FADING AWAY AS THOUGH
SOME EVIL FORCE IS DRAINING HER
LIFE x COME TO THE PALACE YOU WILL
BE WELCOMED x YOUR FRIEND x DR
SAMUEL DANBY x

Holmes read the words carefully; the message was rushed, unlike Henry's usually careful and often more detailed notes, but this was the nature of telegrams. They held such impersonal information and required the sender to write with brevity. Holmes always felt you could not gauge the mood of the sender without the swirl of pen and ink. It was strange that Danby had sent the message this way. If he was working for the emperor, why had he not merely sent a handwritten note around from the palace?

He pondered over the last time he had heard from his old university friend. Danby had been a dedicated man of medicine even then. He recalled how he had chosen to leave England some years ago. Holmes hadn't heard from him since, but had been told that Danby had taken a missionary post. The picture of Danby's life since then began to shape in Holmes's mind. He saw the man, shiny-faced with raw enthusiasm, boarding a ship, doctor's bag in hand.

So, it was to China the man had gone, and he had, it seemed, endeared himself to the emperor. Maybe Danby wasn't naive after all.

Holmes pulled the bell cord beside the window and sat

down at the bamboo writing desk to pen a reply to Danby. He chose to send the letter direct, and not via the telegram office. When the unassuming bellboy arrived at his room, Holmes had already sealed his note ready to send.

A few hours later Holmes opened his door to find a small, thin Chinese man with a long droopy moustache; he was dressed in ornate robes of regal blue and silver, holding a scroll tied with red ribbon.

'Misser Sherlock Holmes?'

'Yes,' said Holmes. 'I am Holmes.'

'I am envoy from Imperial Palace. I come to take you to see Emperor Guangxu. My name is Chang Li.'

'The emperor? I was expecting to hear from my friend, the emperor's physician,' Holmes said. 'Samuel Danby.'

The man nodded, but Holmes noted a slight twitch around the eyes. Holmes narrowed his own gaze to study the man, but the stillness and formality was back in place and his body language was difficult to read. Even so, Holmes knew something was wrong. A tightness around the mouth, an aversion of his gaze.

'Emperor will give you audience now. You come with me,' Chang Li said.

Holmes didn't enjoy being given an imperative and he considered asking Chang Li more questions, but thought it better to hold all his concerns in check. He still doubted himself, not having fully recovered the usual self confidence that had driven him for most of his life.

'Very well. Take me to the palace.'

Holmes removed his smoking jacket and drew on his coat and deerstalker. Then he followed Chang Li out into the street. Two Sedan Chairs, each with four men to carry them, waited outside the inn. Chang Li nodded to the first, and Holmes took his cue, stepping inside. The runners picked him and the Sedan up as though he were of no weight at all and both he and Chang Li were conveyed at speed through the bustling streets of Beijing to the Imperial Palace.

During the journey, Holmes made no attempt to converse with the man in the other chair, even though they were ferried side by side most of the way. Instead, he took the opportunity to examine the city, and observed the change in opulence as they neared the palace. The houses on the streets were bigger, grander, some had expansive gardens surrounding them.

As they arrived at the palace, the large entry gates opened and Holmes and Chang Li were carried inside without hesitation: it was obvious that he was expected. The Sedans were placed down at the bottom of an impressive flight of steps and one of the servants who had conveyed him opened the shallow door beside him. Holmes stepped out.

'This way, Misser Holmes,' Chang Li said. 'The emperor is waiting.'

'Will Doctor Danby be there also?' Holmes asked.

Chang Li made no comment, instead he walked towards the steps and began his ascent into the Imperial Palace.

Holmes took his time climbing the steps and noted the many guards that lined the walls. At the top he glanced around. He was so high up he could see beyond the wall and observed that on one side of the palace was a magnificent moat, which was both functional and beautiful. The splendour of the palace, juxtaposed with the obvious paranoia of the Imperial guard made the hairs on the back of Holmes's neck stand up. He straightened his hat, then walked briskly after Chang Li who had paused to wait for him.

The room was large, tall-ceilinged and was adorned with long flowing, colourful tapestries that hung from the walls. A long carpet led up the centre of the throne room to the focal point: Emperor Guangxu. The emperor wore a long robe of brilliant red highlighted with gold and he was seated at the far end of the magnificent chamber atop a throne that was placed on a platform. There were eight steps leading up to the throne, and the red carpet flowed upwards to end at the emperor's feet. Guangxu sat with all the royal presence one might expect. Beside him was a smaller throne - currently empty - which Holmes knew would sometimes be occupied by the Empress. Other than these two seats the room was devoid of furniture. Those brought before the emperor were not permitted to sit or indeed to expect any comfort whatsoever.

A row of guards stood either side of the room as still as statues, and Chang Li and the Emperor treated them as such. They were meant to be invisible and would only move if they suspected any threat towards the emperor.

'Misser Holmes,' Chang Li said. 'I present his royal highness, Aixin Jueluo Zaitian, eleventh Qing Emperor of China: Emperor Guangxu. Please to bow to Emperor …'

Holmes bowed politely.

'Step forward Mister Holmes,' Guangxu said. 'I have heard much about you. You have travelled a great deal in my country?'

'I have your highness,' Holmes said.

Holmes was impressed by Guangxu's command of the English language. It was flawless and well-studied, impeccable even, not at all the pigeon-speak that his envoy, Chang Li, used.

'I would like you to share your observations with me and tell me what you have seen if you will.'

'Gladly.'

Holmes had heard that Guangxu was extremely well educated. His English was perfect and Holmes told him so.

'An English governess was brought here to work with me. She came originally as a missionary.' Guangxu explained. 'We spoke in nothing but English every day for many years. She taught me a lot about your ways too. It is as much a part of me as my own language.'

They exchanged pleasantries and Holmes was beginning to wonder whether he had been brought here more for Guangxu's intellectual interest than for the serious illness that had been indicated in Danby's letter when Guangxu changed the

116

subject.

'Tell me of my villages,' Guangxu said.

'What would your highness like to hear?'

'How you found my people?'

'There is much poverty. Many suffer in the smaller towns, hunger and thirst are daily torments,' Holmes said with frank openness.

'Thank you, Mister Holmes. You have told me the truth, when none of my subjects will. Walk with me. I need to show you something.'

The emperor stood, and his attendants bowed, and the guards looked at the floor.

'Come.'

The formality of the throne room fell away as Guangxu led Holmes through a screen doorway behind the throne.

'I will speak now in private to Mister Holmes,' Guangxu said when Chang Li began to follow them.

Chang Li's eyes twitched but he bowed his head as Guangxu and Holmes walked away. Holmes had the feeling that Chang Li did not appreciate being left out of the conversation or perhaps he was just concerned about the emperor being alone with a foreigner. It was even conceivable that he, too, was curious about what Holmes knew of China's poor.

'I could see from your letter that you know something of my plight,' Guangxu said, as ahead of them two guards opened an expansive door which was sumptuously decorated with colourful birds and flowers in blue and yellow.

They stepped out into a stunning garden. Holmes paused to take in the two ponds covered with water lilies and separated by a small red bridge. The garden was filled with pink peonies, pale purple Chinese roses and white lotuses. Never had he felt the quixotic more exaggerated than here, where poverty appeared to be another experience that Holmes had only imagined.

A woman walked slowly towards them across the bridge. She was wearing a pale blue long *cheongsam* with silver birds woven into the fabric. Her jet-black hair was piled on top of her head and an ornate headdress was woven into her hair. Silver and blue beads dangled from the front over her face.

As she approached, Holmes could see that she was only young, perhaps in her early twenties. She was not beautiful in the sense that some of the women he had seen here were, but her eyes and lips were accentuated by kohl and rouge, and her skin was powdered to look white; qualities that were admired in this world for some reason he did not entirely understand.

She bowed to Emperor Guangxu.

'Mister Holmes, may I present to you Imperial Noble Consort Jin.'

'Your Highness,' Holmes said bowing.

Consort Jin did not answer and she kept her gaze averted down as she walked away with tiny, precise steps, that Holmes knew were due to the bindings on her feet.

'You understand that she is my ... wife ... of sorts?'

Holmes nodded. He understood the situation perfectly. He had already established that Guangxu had a wife and a mistress. It did not shock him, as he had learnt much about the culture of China on his travels. Guangxu had been a mere child when he came in line for the throne and had not been permitted to rule until he had reached a certain maturity. Even then, he had been refused the privilege of choosing his wife and consort for himself. Holmes noted all of this, compartmentalising it all as possibly relevant information for later, but also made no judgement.

'Consort Jin appears to be in perfect health ...' he noted.

'She is. It is not her that I need you to see.'

Guangxu walked on and Holmes followed, even more intrigued.

They re-entered the house through another small garden.

'I now take you where no man other than myself, Doctor Danby, and my own physician, have ever been. This is the chamber of Consort Zhen.'

Two eunuchs stood before the door of Zhen's chamber. Holmes made no comment about them being 'men'. In Guangxu's eyes they were less than human.

'We have been keeping watch over her, day and night, but nothing we do seems to help the condition,' Guangxu said.

The eunuchs opened the door, then bowed as the Emperor and Holmes entered.

The room was filled with beautiful, vibrant furniture. A dresser with a large, gold-framed oval mirror stood before a window, which had red and gold silk drapes pulled across to keep out the bright sunlight. On the opposite side of the room was a two-seater sofa, again covered with silk. This was red, with gold fire-breathing dragons woven into the complex design. A huge tapestry hung from the wall behind the sofa; it depicted two lovers, standing on a bridge in a garden not dissimilar to the one they had just walked through. There was a silk screen, a further doorway that concealed the sleeping area.

The screen parted and a young girl in a bright blue *cheongsam* bowed to Quangxu and then stepped back. There were other girls in the room, quietly attending the person in the bed. One of the eunuchs clapped his hands and all the women bowed to the emperor and left without him having to say a word.

Holmes could now see a frail young girl in the bed. Her face was whiter than bleached flour. As he approached, Holmes realised that the powdering was an attempt to hide the terrible deterioration of the woman's face. But, even ravaged by sickness, he could tell that Consort Zhen was the most beautiful woman he had ever seen.

'This ... is Consort Zhen ...' Guangxu said, though his explanation was unnecessary as Holmes already knew, but the detective noted the genuine emotion that was evident in the emperor's voice.

Zhen lay with her eyes wide open, staring at the canopy above her. She didn't acknowledge their presence.

'In my culture, an Emperor may not choose his wife nor his concubines. These are chosen on suitability. I was given Consort Jin and Consort Zhen, as well as Empress Xiaodingjing. I do not love my wife, nor Consort Jin. Consort Zhen means more to me than life itself.'

Holmes nodded to show he understood the sentiment,

even though the words of love that Guangxu spoke were as alien to him as Chinese culture that he had encountered on his travels through this vast land.

'How long has she been like this?' Holmes asked.

'One week. We do not know what to do. This affliction struck almost overnight. She became at first lethargic. Then after a day or two of barely eating or drinking she lapsed into this state.'

'May I examine her?'

'Yes,' Guangxu said.

Holmes looked into Zhen's unusually pale eyes; the whites were yellowing, the blue irises - rare though they were in China - were turning white like the cataract-covered gaze of the old. He bent his head to listen to the shallow breathing that rasped through her lips. The vile odour of impending death wafted from her skin. He pressed his fingers to the pulse at her wrist and felt the slow and irregular beat of a labouring heart. Then he lifted the covers to gaze down at her legs. They appeared to be thin, wasted: already the lack of sustenance was having its toll. Holmes noted the bare feet, though and glanced at Guangxu.

'This is most unusual for one of your culture,' Holmes said.

'Zhen wanted to remove the restrictive bindings. She believes we can make a better future for our country. I agreed with her. Her feet had been bound since infancy. Releasing them gave Zhen much pain, but she was determined to set an example for other women of China.'

'I'm impressed with your forward thinking,' Holmes said. 'Now, I must speak to Doctor Danby and hear his diagnoses.'

'*Speak* to Danby? But surely Chang Li told you?' Quangxu said.

'Told me what?'

'Doctor Danby is dead ...'

Danby lay with his arms crossed over his chest. Two gold yuan coins were placed on his eyes. He was wearing his formal dinner suit and black leather shoes, which were polished to a fine sheen.

'When did this happen?' asked Holmes.

Having left the Emperor in Consort Zhen's chamber, Holmes was once again in the company of Chang Li. He was grateful for the placing of Danby in the cold tomb. The body appeared fresh with little or no *rigor mortis* and the heat outside had been unable to speed up the decomposition.

'We did not know if he had any family, Misser Holmes,' Chang Li explained. 'Emperor feel that doctor try very hard to help. He like doctor. He like we inter him in traditional English manner as far as possible in our culture.'

Holmes nodded, but he was impatient for answers. 'I see. So when? A few hours ago, I assume?'

'No, Misser Holmes, doctor die five days ago. He has been here ever since then.'

'*Five days you say?*' Holmes did not point out that the telegram he had received had been sent only that day. 'Does your physician know what Danby died of?' Holmes asked.

Chang Li shook his head. 'It mystery. Like affliction of favourite concubine.'

'But different,' Holmes observed.

He glanced over Danby's body. There was no sign of the ravages that plagued Consort Zhen. Danby's skin appeared strangely healthy. Holmes lifted Danby's arm – the joint bent, the skin felt soft as though the blood still flowed around the body. Danby appeared to be merely asleep. But then, the softening of the limbs was also consistent with a body that was several days' dead.

'Fetch me a small mirror,' Holmes said.

Chang Li was confused for a moment, but then he sent one of the guards to obtain what the detective required. When the guard returned with a small hand mirror, Holmes placed the glass near to Danby's lips. He waited several minutes but the mirror did not mist.

'If only Watson were here ...' But to send for the good doctor would take too long. Besides, Watson, like the rest of the world, still believed that Holmes was dead. For the first time

Holmes felt truly alone.

Holmes pressed his head against Danby's chest. A faint odour wafted up from the body. But it wasn't the smell of death that he detected, it was the faint aroma of jasmine.

'Tell me how you found him,' Holmes demanded. 'Omit nothing.'

'There are some strange circumstances here. The most peculiar of all is that Samuel Danby apparently sent me a telegram from his grave,' Holmes observed. 'Do you know anything of this?'

They were drinking jasmine tea outside in the garden. The smell reminded Holmes of the telegram he had received, and the scent on Danby's body. Consort Jin had poured the tea into the two cups and then she bowed to the emperor and quietly backed away.

'I assumed he had written to you a week ago and that was why you were in Beijing,' Guangxu said.

'I need to get back to my hotel. There are some items there that may help with my investigation.'

'But you must stay here,' Guangxu said. 'We will take care of you and you may have Chang Li to help you with your inquiries.'

'I really would prefer to stay at my hotel at this time.'

'Mister Holmes, I am concerned that these things that have happened ... these afflictions ... have a sinister origin. I would feel happier if you were under palace protection. Doctor Danby did not live in the palace, then ... this terrible thing occurred. My physician is even now concocting a medicine to ward off evil. It is a concern that a curse has been placed on the house of Guangxu.'

'I don't believe in witchcraft,' Holmes said. 'It is my experience that anything unexplained, which may appear supernatural, is usually down to the machinations of man. Evil comes from men.'

'I have been raised with western understanding,' Quangxu said. 'But there are many unexplainable things that happen here.'

'Sometimes we must eliminate the unexplainable in order to find the truth. Is it possible that Consort Zhen has been poisoned?'

'No. Like me, she has a food tester. The eunuch in question has never shown any signs of illness,' Guangxu said.

'Her symptoms do not conform with any poison that I'm aware of either,' Holmes said. 'Arsenic would show in the finger nails. But small doses, such as a food tester may absorb are unlikely to affect the tester at first, especially if the tester is physically larger. This could be the same with any other slow working poison.'

'So, it is possible?'

'Yes.'

Guangxu was quiet and thoughtful. 'But who would poison Zhen?'

'The question you must ask is, who does it hurt to make Zhen ill? And who will gain from her death?'

By the time Holmes was escorted to a room in the palace, all his possessions had been transferred from the Inn.

The room he was allocated was less ornate than other parts of the palace and lacked any personal touches at all. The room held a bed, a writing desk, and an upright chair with a curved back. There was a small dresser made of bamboo but stained red. The room, though sparse, was still far more vivid than anything Holmes would find in London. Behind a parchment screen, which was decorated with birds that resembled peacocks but were painted orange with gaudy plumage, was a ceramic bathtub.

Holmes saw that his trunk had been placed at the foot of the bed, and on top of it was his carpet bag, which contained all he needed to make his ablutions. The carpet bag also featured a secret compartment in which he hid the tools he used for his investigations.

The room was clean. It appeared to have been freshly

prepared with bedding that smelt of the fragrant flowers that filled the private gardens. Perhaps his final agreement to stay had been anticipated?

Holmes opened another screen door to find that he had his own balcony, facing the royal gardens. It was warm but a breeze blew gently into the room.

He sat down to write at the bureau. There was bamboo paper and a sharpened quill, with a small pot of ink. Holmes rarely wrote down his thoughts during an investigation, preferring to think through all problems first but he wanted to make a list of the strange details he was already observing.

He was lost in his thoughts. Thinking of the tale that Chang Li had told him of how Danby had been found.

Danby had stayed in the same Inn that Holmes had occupied and Danby's body had been found on the floor of his room by the hotel owner.

His death appeared to be of natural causes, if the sudden demise of a relatively vital man could ever be called natural.

'The room was tidy, all of doctor's possessions untouched,' Chang Li had explained. 'Inn owner not know what to do, but know Doctor was working with Emperor and he call us. I come and I see nothing wrong in room.'

'No upturned furniture? No windows open?' Holmes had prompted.

'No. Window locked. Door on inside locked. Innkeeper have to use own key to open. Royal physician come and he look at doctor. He say doctor dead. He not understand why.'

Holmes was considering the possibility of giving Danby's body a thorough examination. Though it would be difficult without the help of Watson.

As he began to write some notes on the parchment there was a knock at the door.

'Come in,' Holmes called and a man entered.

He was wearing a simple black long *chang pao*, made of silk, with silver thread sewn around the collarless neckline.

'I am Hui Sen, physician of Emperor Guangxu,' he said.

Holmes observed that Hui Sen was above average height, and his very slender physique made him appear even taller. He, like Chang Li, wore a long moustache that tapered down almost to his chest. He carried with him a leather bag, not dissimilar to the doctor's case that Watson owned.

'Emperor Guangxu request I take you to my room, show you Chinese medicine.'

Holmes stood, and then something small caught his eye. It glittered in the sunlight that came from the balcony and had fallen under the foot of the bed. He placed the quill he was using down on the table.

'I must first get something from my bag,' Holmes said.

He crossed the room and began to rummage in the bag, pulling free a magnifying glass and a small glass phial. He dropped the phial as though by accident. It bounced lightly on the bed and then rolled off the edge. Holmes caught the phial seconds before it hit the floor, in the process he also scooped up the glittering thing he had spotted across the room. He quickly placed both the phial and the item in his pocket. Then he followed Hui Sen out of the room.

A myriad of opulently patterned jars covered a wide centre table in the doctor's room. The room served as both laboratory and sleeping quarters with an area cordoned off with screens.

'You live in the palace?' he asked.

'Sometimes I sleep here when Emperor need me. House is just outside palace walls,' Hui Sen explained.

'What is in the jars?'

'Old medicine, from ancient Chinese recipes.'

Holmes lifted the lid of one of the jars. A waft of damp earth met his nostrils. Another jar yielded the smell of liquorice root. There was an array of herbs and spices and unfamiliar substances. One of the jars contained opium, an aroma that

Holmes was familiar with, but he made no comment. Then he opened a jar that exuded a strong perfume - it smelt of jasmine.

'Tea?' asked Holmes.

'An herb to calm the nerves,' Hui Sen said. 'It contain jasmine and is dispensed in tea. Favourite with Consort Jin.'

Hui Sen was helpful on the surface, but Holmes felt as though he were hiding something. The man was full of superstition and it made the detective wary of the medicinal content of the potions, which seemed little more than old wives' tale medicine. Yet, he had heard from other sources that Chinese medicine had made advances that western doctors could only dream of. There was no evidence of this in Hui Sen's chamber, however. All Holmes saw were the makings of quackery. He was no doctor of course, but Danby was, and Holmes felt certain that Samuel would have seen through Hui Sen far faster than he did himself.

The Chinese physician knew nothing of how to cure Consort Zhen: how could he with only herbs and teas to help exacerbate any symptoms? This explained why Danby had been brought in to help and why Guangxu had insisted that Holmes see Hui Sen's medicine. Guangxu knew that his physician was incompetent, but he obviously did not know what to do about it.

Back in his room and finally alone, Holmes removed the phial and the glittering object he had found earlier on the floor by the bed. Just by the feel of the item he had known it was a ring. Now on close inspection he recognised the gold piece, with a miniature shield, as an alumni award which was given only to the highest achievers at his former university. He had never received one, not expressing much interest in the place after his studies ended. However, Samuel Danby had been the top in his class. Holmes recalled him wearing the ring. The fact that it was here in this room gave Holmes every reason to feel suspicious of Guangxu himself. Hadn't the Emperor said that Danby had not stayed within the walls of the palace? Had he not used this as a reason to justify Holmes's stay, for his own safety?

Holmes examined the ring carefully. He found a purple black stain - a dry powdered substance that was not unlike dried blood in colour and consistency - ingrained in the grooves of the shield. He took a pair of tweezers from his carpet bag, then he scraped off the substance onto the parchment he had been writing on earlier. An overwhelming aroma of jasmine wafted up from the powder with a strong and potent metallic smell that set Holmes's teeth on edge.

Jasmine was the one common element that brought some of the pieces together but Holmes refused to make any deductions. He knew from experience that this would not be the last clue he would find and he never made a habit of drawing conclusions based on first findings.

He sent for Chang Li.

'I wish to talk to the emperor,' he said.

'You have discovered something?'

'If I have then it is for Guangxu's ears only,' Holmes said.

'Emperor is busy,' Chang Li said. 'He in meeting with Empress Dowager Cixi. Cannot be disturbed.'

'Then I will be here when he is free,' Holmes replied.

Chang Li bowed politely and left. After a few moments Holmes decided that he would ask Hui Sen more questions. He left his apartment and walked down the hallway, turned right, and paused. He could hear raised voices. By then he had learnt enough Chinese to recognise a few words.

'Holmes is a problem ...' he translated. He wasn't sure, but he believed this was the voice of Hui Sen.

Then he heard Chang Li's nasally tones as he responded in rapid Mandarin. It was too fast for him to be positive, but he heard Danby's name and a reference to a medicine that would 'confuse' the detective if he 'interfered'. Holmes backed away and hid behind one of the large marble pillars. A few moments later Chang Li hurried past, confirming Holmes's suspicion that he was one of the men in the room.

Chang Li did not see the detective hiding in the corner.

Hui Sen's door was left open. Holmes moved quietly and

peered in through the gap in the hinges. He saw the physician opening a secret panel in the table that held his medicines. He extracted a jar from inside, then, with great care, took out a rusty-looking powder. Another jar was removed from the panel, this one contained dried berries. They were familiar to Holmes, as he had seen them on his tour of Western Asia and knew them to be highly toxic. These were the berries taken from an *Atropa Belladonna* plant. Also known as deadly nightshade.

Holmes watched as Hui Sen mixed a potion together in a mortar. He used a pestle to grind the powder and the berry together. Then he extracted some of the tea-like leaves from the jar in which Holmes had smelt jasmine. Hui Sen boiled water over a small tray, under which candles burnt; he added the hot liquid to the solution and poured the contents into a tea pot. Then he placed the jars back into the secret panel. A few moments later, he took the pot, slipped out of his room via a screen door on the opposite side to the door where Holmes hid, and disappeared into some part of the palace that detective did not know.

Holmes was concerned. Who was the potion for and what was the rust-like dust that he had seen added to it? Surely it had resembled the substance that Holmes had found in Danby's ring. One *Atropa Belladonna* berry was not enough to kill, but it could induce sickness in the person who ate it. Holmes was sure of that at least. He had to find out who the drink was destined for and what Hui Sen was up to.

He entered the room and opened the panel, taking out the jar that contained the powder. He peered inside, then he extracted the phial from his jacket pocket once more, and tipped a small quantity of the red dust into it. He pondered as the metallic smell hit his nostrils once more. Why would it be used in the tea? Was the compound somehow poisonous?

He hurried across to the back of the room and opened the screen gently. He found himself in a back corridor with two directions to go in. He glanced, left, then right. His eyes fell on a small splash of liquid spilt on the floor and so he turned right and followed the corridor down. There he found another screen, which he opened and walked through. This was an empty antichamber of sorts. Holmes looked around. There was yet another screen door. He moved forward and slid this one open also.

He found the physician standing next to a Chinese rose bush in a small walled garden. Hui Sen poured the tea solution into the roots of a plant next to the roses.

'Hui Sen?' said Holmes.

Hui Sen turned to look at Holmes, his eyes widening in surprise. 'What are you doing here, Misser Holmes?'

'I followed you. Can I ask what you are doing?'

'Please you must leave. No one is permitted in Empress Dowager Cixi's garden.'

'I will leave when you explain that concoction.'

As Holmes spoke the plant began to wither.

'Interesting,' he murmured.

Whatever the solution was it was highly toxic to the plant. It shrivelled up and wilted down to the ground, at which point, Hui Sen pulled the plant out. The roots looked burnt and black.

'This is poison for plant that Empress Dowager does not like,' said Hui Sen.

Holmes could not help but wonder what the Empress would use on a person she didn't like, but he made no further comment until they were back in Hui Sen's room.

Hui Sen openly removed the jars from the secret compartment.

'This Cadmium Oxide. In its metallic state it similar to Zinc or Mercury,' Hui Sen explained. 'I use to kill weed.'

'You mixed it with tea …'

'Easy to dissolve and get in soil. And herbs in tea keep good the soil.' Hui Sen said.

Holmes listened but there was still a nagging doubt in the back of his head. This concoction was highly dangerous. What would it do a human who drank it? His mind was still not working as efficiently as it had done in years gone by. He was beginning to wonder if he would ever regain his faculties. He knew he had heard of Cadmium Oxide before, somewhere on his travels in Europe … It was highly poisonous, but for the time being he couldn't quite access the memory of what its effects were on the body, or if there was indeed any cure.

'This is dangerous to humans also ...' he said.

'I only use for plant,' Hui Sen insisted.

Holmes questioned the physician further, but when the physician's story never wavered, he gave up and took his leave to think over everything he had learnt.

'You wished to see me, Mister Holmes,' said the emperor. 'I am sorry I was unavailable earlier, but Chang Li told me as soon as I was free. I am, you see, in the middle of much dispute with the Empress Dowager Cixi. She and I do not always see things in the same light.'

A guard had been waiting to escort him back to Emperor Guangxu when he reached his own rooms. Now Holmes was in the throne room once more. This time he was completely alone with Guangxu. Not even the guards that had formerly lined the walls were present. It was becoming apparent that Guangxu did not know whom he could trust.

'If your highness would like to explain, I would be interested in hearing the nature of the dispute. It may have some bearing on things,' Holmes said.

'Alas the older generation does not see a need to improve. They resent all things Western. I, however, know that we will not survive the future if changes do not occur. The Empress Dowager Cixi has never been quite willing to let go her reign to me. I would like to improve things for my people and I have been working on ways to make reforms. And, I believe I will never be a great ruler if I do not take responsibility for the health of my subjects.'

'Consort Zhen's unbound feet ...' Holmes observed.

'Yes. This is one of the many changes I wish to make. This barbaric ritual of binding must be stopped. Women, I believe, should not be treated as mere pleasure objects. They have minds, and feelings, and a great deal to offer, if only we allow them the freedom to grow.'

'Your highness is indeed very forward thinking. How hard will the Dowager Empress fight to keep things the same?' Holmes asked.

Guangxu turned sad eyes to Holmes. 'I fear she may try very hard. But this is not your concern, or anything to do with the issue at hand. Though I do appreciate having someone impartial to discuss this with. But back to the matter at hand. Consort Zhen has become worse. Her breathing has taken to labouring. Hui Sen thinks she does not have long on this earth. I still fight with the idea that some sorcery is the cause. If there is anything you can tell me to help, now would be a good time.'

Holmes was not ready to tell. There was still too much fog in his mind that wouldn't clear.

'I'm sorry, I'm still not sure I can give you any clear information at this time. I do, however, wish to see Doctor Danby's body once more if I may. I have new information that will point me in the right direction in my search at least.'

'Very well, Mister Holmes. Chang Li will take you there once more. But I do hope you can give me some news soon. I am fast losing hope for Zhen. She has been ... my only ally. My only friend. You understand?'

'If we were in a position to follow the methods devised by Rudolf Carl Virchow for performing an autopsy,' Holmes said, 'I think we would be able to determine that Doctor Danby died because his kidneys suddenly failed.'

'Failed? But how?' asked Guangxu.

'Witchcraft,' said Chang Li.

'Poison,' said Holmes.

'How?' asked Guangxu again.

'See here ...'

On Holmes's instruction two guards had stripped Samuel Danby's body of his funeral vestments, then Holmes had examined the hands, arms, feet, chest and neck of the man.

Now he pointed to a small swelling at the ball of Danby's foot. A tiny pin-prick. He then examined the corpse's stomach and abdomen. There was a darkening of the skin and a significant amount of bloating in this area. Holmes inspected Danby's arms and torso. Previously he had taken the change of Danby's normally pale complexion as being nothing more than a small amount of sunburn caused by the exotic heat, but now he realised – and cursed himself for his poor concentration on the first examination – that this was no sunburn. The colour change was all over the body.

It was then that he requested the presence of the Emperor, Chang Li, and Hui Sen.

He removed the phial that contained the Cadmium Oxide that he had taken from Hui Sen's room. The physician was startled by the sight of the chemical in Holmes's hands but said nothing as the detective held the phial up to the lamplight.

'This is a highly poisonous compound,' Holmes explained. 'A highly concentrated form of this could easily be transferred into a victim through a pin-prick. You can see that Danby has such a mark. He also had the signs of severe renal failure. Darkening of the skin, a bloating around the abdomen, and sudden death, would indicate poisoning. Cadmium Oxide could do this.'

'Who?' asked Guangxu.

'Your physician is the man who holds a supply of this chemical,' Holmes said.

He watched as the guards seized the doctor.

'I did not …' denied Hui Sen.

'What about Zhen?' asked Guangxu.

'Her condition is different and I will need to think on this further. Perhaps a night's sleep will clear my head.'

'This is no game, Misser Holmes,' Chang Li said. 'Emperor Guangxu need to know what wrong with Consort Zhen.'

'I never play games,' Holmes replied sternly. 'A mystery can only be solved when all the facts are present. There is still some information that I need. This requires my full concentration. And a required amount of peace in which to do that.'

'Of course, Mister Holmes must be tired,' said Guangxu. 'The hour is late. We will talk again in the morning.'

Back in his room, Holmes removed Danby's ring from his carpet bag and stared at the red substance in the grooves. He placed it on the dresser and lit his pipe, then he walked around, allowing his shadow to fall on the screen that looked out to the garden. He then lay down on the bed, placing his pipe on a stand beside the oil lamp. After a few moments he extinguished the lamp by blowing on its wick.

He heard a strange hissing noise. The room filled with a familiar aroma and as Holmes lay there, he could smell the familiar and beguiling odour of opium. He took a breath of air and held it as he slipped quietly from the room leaving a strategically placed bulk of pillow and sheets on his bed. He hoped that whoever had piped the drug's intoxicating fumes into the room had been watching his shadow move and would, therefore, be completely fooled into thinking that the detective was still in his bed.

He headed back to the physician's rooms, which now should be empty. There, however, he saw what he had hoped he would. As he hid quietly in the doorway, a small, slender figure moved through the dark room. He waited while the person opened another hidden panel in the doctor's desk.

After observing what they did with the chemical inside, Holmes slipped away. He did not, however, return to his room until dawn when the overdose of opium in gaseous form, which Danby's killer had tried to administer to him, had cleared sufficiently. The one inhalation had been enough to sharpen his focus, though, and Holmes, a long-term user of the drug for just this purpose, was grateful for the way it had cleared his mind. He now saw the answer to the mystery unfolding before him.

He walked into the room at first light. There he saw that his bed had been disturbed. On the pillow where his head would have been if he hadn't left the room secretly, was a small thorn. The thorn pierced the silk pillow case and a rust-red stain besmirched the pale cream. Pulling his tweezers from his bag he picked up the thorn and placed it in another phial where it could do little damage. Then he scrutinised it carefully. The pieces of the puzzle were coming together; this final piece of evidence told him who the killer was, but not all the requisite details of their motivation. Having found the thorn, and seen the perpetrator the night before, Holmes had a very good idea who was involved, but not what could be done about it.

In the light of day, he returned to Hui Sen's room, opened the other secret panel, and removed the jar he found there. He opened the lid. A strong smell of *Prunus dulcis*, otherwise known as almond, assaulted his nose. He was sure now what was afflicting Consort Zhen.

Consort Zhen was sitting up in bed and tentatively eating a thin soup when Emperor Guangxu came into the room. Holmes sat beside her bed, a small smile on his face.

'Zhen!' Guangxu exclaimed. 'You are better. What has happened here? Mr Holmes - do you care to explain?'

'Soon. I think we must wait for Consort Jin, Chang Li and Hui Sen.'

'Hui Sen will be executed,' Guangxu said.

'But of course, he won't,' Holmes laughed. 'All the man is guilty of is a little incompetence. Plus, he did help me catch our killer.'

'Killer? But I thought ...'

Two eunuchs entered the room and glared at Holmes, they were followed by Chang Li and Hui Sen, who was in the company of two of the royal guard. A few moments later Consort Jin was also brought in by another eunuch. She was accompanied by Dowager Empress Cixi. As Jin was timid, Cixi was formidable. Holmes could see the strength of will in the Dowager's stern face and knew that his revelation that day may possibly drive a further wedge between Guangxu and Cixi. Even so, he had to tell the emperor all he knew.

The eunuchs brought in chairs, where Jin and Cixi sat

down. The emperor went over to the bed; Zhen smiled at him.

Holmes took the bowl from Zhen's fingers and watched as the girl, still very sick, slid back under the covers. The mere exertion of sitting and eating had quite exhausted her, but the pallor in her cheeks was far less than it had been. Even her pale blue eyes, which, just the day before had appeared so peculiar, were now looking more normal in appearance.

'There has been a conspiracy,' Holmes began. 'This conspiracy was to silence those closest to you. I can give you the perpetrator your highness, but not the person behind the conspiracy.'

'Give me whatever you have Holmes. Whatever you say this day I will guarantee you safe passage from Beijing. You have restored Zhen; this is all that matters to me.'

'Zhen, is your consort and, as you have indicated, has been your closest ally,' Holmes said.

'Zhen has always spoken up in my support,' Guangxu took the concubine's frail hand in his. 'She believes in the changes I wish to make. She believes this will make China great.'

Cixi shuffled in her seat. She glared at Holmes but he was back in full swing now and could not be intimidated into silence, even by such a redoubtable presence.

'My Emperor is good man,' said Zhen timidly. 'He speak of many things for future of China. Things that I think will make us better people.'

'Quite so,' said Holmes, 'and we will come back to this my dear girl. You must rest, but I want you to hear what has happened to you first.' Holmes stood up from the bed for dramatic effect. 'This poor girl was not bewitched, but poisoned. It was something I suspected all along, but there were some peculiar anomalies that masked the diagnosis. You see I don't believe that the perpetrator planned to kill Consort Zhen, they merely wanted her out of the way for a while.'

'Poison, but *not* to kill her?' Guangxu said.

'Yes. And that was easily done with a small dose of arsenic, every day. Resulting in some of the symptoms that she had, but not causing all. You see your highness, small doses of arsenic can make someone sick, but not kill them. They are also easy to cure. Especially for someone with ancient knowledge of Chinese medicines.'

'Hui Sen!' Consort Jin said.

All turned to her because the outburst was out of character for the plainer, timid concubine.

'No, Consort Jin. Not Hui Sen. I refer to someone with knowledge. Hui Sen does not possess this knowledge. You see he was merely a gardener's son, who was offered a bribe to pose as a physician in the palace, and was promised the knowledge to become what he pretended to be. Hui Sen is only guilty of ambition, and a lot of naivety.'

'What are you saying?' Cixi demanded. 'You Englishmen talk in riddles.'

'If I may speak Emperor?' said Hui Sen and Guangxu nodded his permission. 'What Misser Holmes say is true. I was once a gardener; I love plants and do still care for them. I take care of beautiful garden for Empress Dowager Cixi ... I ...'

At that moment Hui Sen doubled up and would have fallen prostrate on the floor if it had not been for the two guards that flanked him.

'Take him into the other room,' Holmes commented. 'Our poisoner has struck again.'

'No one has access to him since he came in room.' Chang Li pointed out.

'Precisely,' said Holmes. 'Hui Sen was most likely poisoned this morning when given his food in the prison.'

'So many traitors among us!' Guangxu said. 'I will have these murderers executed.'

'There is only one traitor, your highness,' Holmes said. 'Even though I am sure they acted as a marionette for a far more powerful puppet master.'

'I have heard enough of this nonsense,' Cixi said. She stood and left the room. Holmes made no effort to delay her.

'Which leaves us with the puppet,' said Holmes.

Guangxu dropped Zhen's hand and stood up, stepping

forward in amazement. 'Are you saying ...? Cixi ... is the ...? But how ...?'

'We cannot prove this part unfortunately, I can only help you remove those that your enemies control, and help those who are your faithful servants.'

'Mister Holmes, please tell me. Who has betrayed me?'

'Last night someone tried to see to it that I shared the same fate of Doctor Danby. I had, fortunately, anticipated this attempt on my life and took appropriate steps to avoid becoming the next victim to Cadmium Oxide poisoning. I did not expect that the assassin would at first try to confuse me with opium. I am no stranger to its effects, Your Highness, and, therefore, I was able to escape my room long before my potential killer entered it. The singular quality I find with opium is that in small and sensible doses it can be used to sharpen one's mind, not confuse it. Your enemy inadvertently aided my quest. After that I went to Hui Sen's room. I had a feeling that the killer would need to get his supply of poison from the physician's stock. Fortunately, my theory proved correct.

'I saw our killer, even in the dark. There was no mistaking that it was Chang Li.'

The guards seized Chang Li, but Guangxu was too shocked to issue the order for him to be removed. This gave the emperor's envoy a chance to object.

'Misser Holmes is grasping straws. When would I have access to favourite concubine? How could I poison her? No man allowed in here until today.'

'But of course, you didn't. The only person who could have done that was Consort Jin. Who has been jealous of the love that her sister inspires in Emperor Guangxu,' Holmes explained.

Dealing with this issue first, Holmes explained how Jin had used a beauty remedy given to her by the doctor, a solution containing arsenic that was designed to be used to bleach her face and hands. Knowing the effect the poison would have, Jin had been slowly inserting this into Zhen's food.

'What Consort Jin didn't realise, of course, was that Hui Sen was experimenting also with Deadly Nightshade as a beauty aid. Women in Europe already use drops of the plant in liquid form to dilate their pupils: something that is considered seductive I believe. The amount in the solution was small, but it was enough to induce the coma-state that Consort Zhen has been in. And it had also affected her breathing. I suspect that Consort Jin grew afraid once the doctor declared that Zhen was likely to die. She then stopped feeding the potion to her. Am I correct on this?'

Consort Jin was in tears before Holmes finished.

'I only want to make Emperor spend more time with me. I hope he then learn to like me more.'

Guangxu put his head in his hands. No doubt at a loss as to what to do with the girl. Her motives had been jealousy, a state that his love for Zhen had encouraged. He must have realised that he had not spent time with her recently, especially after Zhen became ill.

Consort Jin threw herself onto her knees before him. 'I never mean to hurt, just make sick enough for you to notice me. I would never have wished her death. Please can you and Zhen forgive me?'

Guangxu placed his hand on the girl's prone head. The weight of his position and his responsibility to all in his household gave him reason to forgive, but it would take a long time for Jin to be trusted again. He seemed incapable of speech and so he nodded to Jin's eunuch and the girl was led away.

'Obviously, all it took was a few days of recovery for Consort Zhen's body to start ridding itself of the poison. So, what you see this morning is not a miracle that I created, but a natural recovery now that she is no longer being poisoned.'

'This is all well and good but how did Hui Sen, a common gardener, even know about these potions?' Guangxu asked.

'Chang Li is the man with the knowledge. He was secretly guiding Hui Sen. But he only imparted the very basic of understanding of the compounds to Hui Sen. It became obvious to me when I spent time with your physician that he had no knowledge of real Chinese medicine. He also could not explain to me what effects the compounds he was using had on human or plant life. You see, he did little more than dispense on the advice of Chang Li. This did not stop Hui Sen from believing he understood more than he did. His use of some of these potions has been reckless but I don't believe he intended anything but good.'

Holmes took a seat in the chair formerly occupied by Cixi. There was a strong smell of jasmine left behind from the perfume of the Empress Dowager.

'I deny all charges,' said Chang Li. 'What proof does foreigner have to support words?'

'The proof of my own eyes, Chang Li. I saw you mixing the Cadmium Oxide last night. You daubed it on a plant you were carrying. A rose bush.' Holmes reached into his pocket and retrieved the phial containing the thorn. 'This was on my pillow this morning and you shot it there through a reed of bamboo. I suggest you search him.'

The guards searched Chang Li and found a small reed secreted in a pocket of his robe.

'And as you see, your highness,' Holmes said pointing to the end of the reed. 'There is a small red stain. This is the same substance that you will find on my pillow.'

Chang Li was taken away by the guards then. He could no longer deny his part in the death of Danby and the attempted murder of Holmes.

'But why has he done this? Other than Zhen, I trusted no one above Chang Li,' Guangxu said.

'I think that is something that you and Empress Dowager Cixi will have to discuss. But I suspect that this is all to do with the plans you have to reform your country.'

'We will torture this information from him,' Guangxu said.

'Of course, there is still one mystery that has not been solved,' Holmes said. 'Who sent me the telegram after Danby's death? I was given many red-herrings on this score. I even briefly considered the Empress Dowager Cixi as being the sender.'

Guangxu smiled, and then Holmes knew: Guangxu had used his presence to help thwart Cixi's potential coup. It had been the emperor himself who had arranged the telegram. It explained the stilted and abrupt tone that the detective had always been suspicious of. He should have realised all along that only Guangxu had the appropriate knowledge of the English language in order to execute such a ruse.

'Doctor Danby talked of you many times,' Guangxu said, confirming in the only way he could that Holmes's hypothesis was correct even though neither of them voiced what that assumption was.

Nevertheless, the glance that Holmes gave the emperor and the glint in the eye that Holmes received in return revealed that a secret understanding had passed between them.

With the mystery solved, Holmes took his leave of Beijing, taking with him Samuel Danby's ring with the intention of returning it to his family, if - and this was a thought that crept in even closer to his thoughts now - he should ever return to London.

Some months later Holmes heard of Guangxu's plans for a 'One-hundred-day reform' but the emperor's ideals were never achieved. It seemed that by the time Chang Li reached the dungeon he had already swallowed enough arsenic to silence him forever. It was never proven who had killed him, but for the sake of preventing further unrest, Guangxu declared it suicide. Thus, Empress Dowager Cixi remained free to lead a coup which ended the efforts of the Qing Dynasty's eleventh emperor. Holmes later heard of Guangxu's death at the hands of his own guard and the unfortunate demise of the outspoken concubine, Consort Zhen.

The Wind in Her Hair

The wind blew through the narrow alley, tugging at Veronica's raven-black hair as she hurried along the deserted street. Her high heels clicked on the pavement, a rhythmic echo in the quiet night that made the backstreet seem darker and more dangerous. Veronica was the embodiment of allure, with an air of mystery that drew men to her like moths to the proverbial flame and she'd been making a living from their attentions for over a year now via a social media platform called *OnlyFans*.

All it took was a little persuasion, some flirting, a lot of smiles and the writing of some sensual poetry, for which she had a great deal of talent. They paid a monthly subscription into her account and for this she spoke to them in private chats, shared images of her gothic, scantily-clad body, and relished their comments and praise, answering every single one of them personally and privately: gushing about their kindness.

She saw it as a business: a way of making the life she wanted for herself. For this reason, she also had a moral code and rules that each of her patrons had to adhere to. No full nudity or pornographic videos. Instead, she shared videos wishing them happy birthday and congratulations on new jobs. It was all personal, designed to make each of them feel like she thought about them as much as they thought about her. The truth was, she only thought of the money they paid and if any of them couldn't pay, they were cut from her inner circle, blocked, and abandoned as soon as the latest donation didn't appear.

But the usual men, that showered her with expensive gifts, whose money paid her bills, keeping her in a more than comfortable position, had begun to bore Veronica. That night, at the risk of losing a few of the needier patrons, she had turned off her phone. She was searching for something new, something unpredictable, something risky.

She was on her way to meet a man she had been talking to for some weeks online and his messages had intrigued her. He wasn't like the others, there were no monthly payments or donations, though he did throw her the occasional compliment, and because of this, she had been more receptive to an actual meeting, rather than private messages and facetime calls. Something she didn't offer to just any of her followers. She didn't want to ever give them the impression that she was a prostitute as Veronica prided herself on that not being the case – unlike some of the women on the same site. She was about companionship and being on a pedestal, unreachable, but enjoying their eyes on her. The men liked that too. A form of voyeurism. Look but you can *never* touch.

As Veronica reached the designated meeting spot, a dimly lit café nestled between two abandoned buildings, she shuddered. The place was devoid of life, the only sign of activity was the flickering neon sign that read 'Temptations'.

She paused for a second, weighing up the chance she was taking. Why had he chosen this place, if not for its isolation? What was she doing here? But she knew the answer to these questions: curiosity. Plus, she'd always been attracted to men who were indifferent to her. They were a challenge and those hardest won, often paid the most in the end.

She pushed open the heavy wooden door and stepped inside, her eyes scanning the room. There were very few customers at this time of night and so her eyes fell on the one man sitting alone in a corner booth. He had long black hair and a cynical smile and she recognised him from the one picture he'd sent her.

Looking up from the coffee mug he was nursing he saw her in the doorway and motioned for her to join him. His eyes filled with a predatory hunger that made her feel naked and exposed. She shuddered again, recognising a delicious sexuality emanating from him, that some primal instinct inside her responded to. Even so, Veronica hesitated, her instincts warning her of danger, but her curiosity got the better of her.

Besides, he'd seen her now and there was no going back. Not without appearing foolish.

She walked over, her hips swaying, and sat down across from him.

'Darius, I presume?' Veronica said and she raised her eyebrow as though she found him and the café amusing and not at all sinister. Playing the part of her online persona somehow made her feel less nervous. She was in control here, just as she always was. It was her decision and hers alone to come and meet him after all.

'And you must be Veronica. I guessed you use filters on your photographs but still, they don't do the real you justice,' he said.

Veronica was taken aback by this somewhat backhanded compliment. Who was this man that he thought he could talk to her any way he wanted? Even though inside she objected to his attitude, she didn't stand up for herself. She felt instead a sick pleasure in being subdued by him. Cowed even. Something that a strong woman should never enjoy.

'Darkness flows through both of our veins,' he told her.

'I don't know what you mean?' Veronica said.

Then, he told her how much he loved the macabre and was fascinated with death.

'I'm intrigued by killers,' he said, and watch a lot of true crime programmes.'

'Why?' she asked.

'I want to understand them. What makes them tick.'

Veronica was both repulsed and drawn to him as he talked. There was something lurking behind his eyes, an open roiling darkness that threatened to consume her. She found herself looking away from him, trying to break the spell she was under. She knew his sort, narcissistic, manipulative, compelling.

As the night wore on, the café emptied, and the two of them were the only customers left. Veronica didn't notice they were alone at first, and when she did, she began to feel uncomfortable.

Sensing her nervousness, Darius leaned in closer, his voice barely a whisper. 'Veronica, there's something I must confess. I am not who I claimed to be.'

'Who are you, then?'

A smile played on Darius's lips. 'Do you really want to know?'

Veronica sat back in her chair and looked at her red painted stiletto nails. She feigned boredom. 'You're just like everyone else,' she said. 'You want my attention. And I'll admit, for a while you had it. But this is where your mystery ends.'

She began to stand, but Darius reached out with unexpected speed and grabbed her arm. His fingers dug in her wrist. Veronica's blood turned to ice as she realized the gravity of the situation. But still, there was a thrill that passed through her, a desire to be owned: something she'd never experienced before. Was Darius the one who could control her?

'You've read about me,' he said. 'I'm the *OnlyFans* killer.'

'The *OnlyFans* killer,' Veronica repeated.

For months the newspapers had been full of stories of the macabre deaths of people who frequented *OnlyFans*. Someone had been picking them off ... killing them in a variety of interesting and imaginative ways. Veronica had seen a downtick in her own engagement figures as a result, but nothing too serious.

She looked into his eyes, yanked her arm free, and rubbed her wrist. Then, Veronica laughed at his preposterous revelation.

'You're stupid if you think I believe that!' she said.

'You're alone with me now,' he continued despite her ridicule.

'You have no idea who you're dealing with,' Veronica said.

'Oh, I'm aware of who you are, Veronica. You're a woman who uses men. But, this time, the tables have turned. You are alone here,' he repeated. 'And I'm going to enjoy you, in a way that all those other fools that pay you, never will.'

Veronica could see the insanity in his eyes and it quashed

the perverse desire to be dominated that had originally surfaced. Her instinct for survival returned. She had to act. She glanced around the café. Where was the waitress that had been serving earlier, as well as the customers that had been there when she came in? It was as though they were all complicit in Darius's endeavours.

She reached for her handbag as it sat on the bench beside her. Without taking her eyes from Darius, she opened the bag and grasped the handle of a small switchblade she carried for protection. Slowly, she slid it out, concealing it in her palm.

She pushed back her chair and leapt to her feet as Darius stood, his movements languorous, as though he knew she could not escape.

Veronica backed away, but he was around the table and grabbing her arm once more, even as she tried to flee.

The blade felt warm in her palm and she pressed the switch, letting out the razor-sharp blade. Reacting without thinking, Veronica slashed the blade between them. It connected with Darius's hand, slicing into the palm with a sickening sliver that made her think of a steak knife cutting through animal flesh.

He recoiled in pain, a mixture of surprise and anger etched on his face. But the hesitation was only for a second, and as only the insane can do, Darius threw himself at Veronica, knocking the knife from her fingers as he bore down on her.

Their bodies locked in a deadly dance. Veronica was slammed into a table, her back screamed in pain. But she couldn't let him overwhelm her: her life depended on it and she wasn't ready to die yet.

The sound of their struggle echoed through the empty café, a symphony of violence and desperation. The wind outside howled in response, as if mirroring the intensity of their fight. Veronica fought back, even as she cried out, desperate for someone to come to her aid. But no one did. She'd been abandoned to the mercy of someone she suspected had been stalking her for a while. The thought made her fight harder but her strength was failing, and Darius was so much bigger and stronger than her.

And then, the worst happened. Darius hit out, a hard blow landed on her temple and Veronica's legs gave under her. She fell hard, down onto the dirty tiles. Falling with a crack as her head connected with ceramic. Darkness took away all pain as she was swept into oblivion.

Veronica became aware of her surroundings first by the sound of a steady drip from a tap nearby. Her eyes opened. It was dark and she had no idea of knowing where she was. She was no longer in the café, at least not the front of it, but instead found herself on a metal surface. Her fingers explored the metal and she realised it was the stainless worktops used in a professional kitchen.

Her eyes began to adjust, but her vision was blurred and her head hurt. She could feel the sticky dampness of blood where her head had hit the tiles. She probably had a concussion.

Veronica moved slightly, stretching, and testing her limbs. She was not restrained and Darius was nowhere to be seen. Had he been interrupted before her could kill her? Or was he watching her now, waiting to pounce again?

Veronica's heart raced; her body was covered in a sheen of sweat. With a swift movement she sat up and jumped down from the work top. A bout of dizziness hit her and she swayed, holding onto the counter until the sensation passed.

Where was Darius and what was he planning to do with her?

A moment later she was blindsided. She felt the air move a split second before her own knife was used to slash her arm. Veronica yelped in pain, but became alert in that moment. A surge of adrenaline coursed through her blood, granting her newfound strength. Her eyes adjusted to the gloom. She turned to face Darius as he emerged from the darkest corner of the kitchen. He was playing with her, but Veronica was not without skills. She seized the opportunity, delivering a swift kick to the Darius's chest, sending him crashing backward, the switchblade skittered from his fingers, coming to rest at Veronica's feet.

As Darius sprawled on the floor, winded, Veronica stood over him. The adrenaline pushed her to a primal ferocity: it was him, or her. She knew this was her chance to end the madness once and for all. She bent down, and without looking away from Darius, searched the ground with her fingers until they found, and gripped the blade. Then she advanced on her victim, while his lungs gasped hard to regain his breath and strength.

'Wait ...' he said. 'I'm not the killer ... I just wanted to teach you a lesson ...'

For a moment Veronica paused.

'I know,' she said. 'Because I am the *OnlyFans* killer.'

With one swift motion, Veronica plunged the switchblade into Darius's heart with the skill of someone who knew exactly how to kill.

The life drained from his eyes as his body went limp. It was swift and merciful, unlike her usual kills, but she couldn't risk Darius getting the better of her again.

The wind outside continued to howl, as if mourning the loss of Darius. Veronica stared down at the lifeless body before her, contemplating the dark path that had led her to this moment. An act of jealousy against another more popular influencer and Veronica had developed a taste for death.

From that day forward, Veronica had become a predator. She used her charms and intellect to lure them into her web before delivering her own brand of justice, whether they deserved it or not.

She washed her switchblade under the dripping tap and stowed it in her pocket. Then she thoroughly cleaned the worktop, removing all signs of her presence.

Then she turned her attention to the body ... another victim of the *OnlyFans* killer ...

It took an hour or so, but she positioned the body at a table in the café. Sitting with a knife and fork in his hands. In front of him on the table was a feast.

In a drinking glass was his own blood; on a side plate

were slices of his own brain, carefully filleted; on the main plate was his heart, accompanied with his eyeballs, a slice of his liver, and a section of intestine.

For afters was his tongue, marinating in bile from his stomach.

Veronica inspected her tableaux, pleased with the results. That would give the papers something to talk about. Then she returned to her original table and retrieved her handbag. There was nothing inside to identify her with, but she never took chances.

She slipped the knife back inside, made a final check that nothing incriminating had been left, and exited the café.

Outside the wind blew through her hair as though it were the questing fingers of the dead. Veronica laughed and pulled up the hood of her coat before walking away into the darkness.

Why?

I grew up in a very different world to the average person. As a viscount and son of an Earl, I would one day inherit my father's title. In our world this means land, money and an estate that had been in the family for centuries. It also equalled loneliness because I was an only child, always surrounded by adults who chose to remind me who and what I would one day become but didn't understand how to bring this knowledge down to a child's level.

During term times, my parents sent me away to a boy's boarding school. It was the same place my father had gone, and his father before him and was a family tradition. My parents were always at one with tradition and there was never any thought at any time that they would have done anything but send me away.

Things changed when Art Wendle, our chauffeur, brought his young daughter to live with us because her mother died. She was called Melanie and she was six years old at the time. I was eight but had a very old head on my shoulders because of my interactions with the adults on the estate. Even so, Melanie and I struck up an immediate friendship because we were the only children who lived there.

Melanie went to a local school, and lived in the servants' quarters with her father. Up until then, times spent at home were boring compared to school but we saw each other in the holidays and, after a while, I began to look forward to going home more than I used to.

I envied Melanie in a way. She had more freedom than I did. No one was ever concerned where she was or what she was doing. My mother treated her like she was my pet-friend: a miracle solution to her refusal to have any more children. And, in truth, it wasn't lonely on the estate with Melanie there. She was funny, natural, and entertaining.

Once I heard my parents talk about this. In those days, they subscribed to the 'children should be seen and not heard' philosophy. I was well conditioned to being silent around them, and they, in turn, often forgot my presence and treated me as though I couldn't hear their conversations.

I learnt a lot about their cold relationship, especially Mother's lack of empathy, from those conversations. I often wondered why they had even married in the first place. But as time went on I realised this had more to do with Mother's money and father's title than any real affection between them. Theirs was an alliance – two great empires pulling together to sustain the equilibrium. I understood what that meant, but not the attitudes behind this staid and archaic sentiment. I lived in a world where little had changed over the centuries. Opinions of a bygone age still presided. But I was young, hopeful, and wanted to change things in the future. I listened at school, but I also listened to the world around me, and observed the natural loving relationship that Melanie had with her father. A relationship I craved to have with mine but which I knew, could never exist.

When I was home, Melanie and I were mostly AWOL somewhere on the estate, or I ate in the servant's quarters with her. This gave me a strong sense of normality, something that the huge dining hall where my parents ate, never did. I felt part of her family more than my own, and I was happy. My parents didn't seem to mind, if they noticed my absence. I was being kept 'busy' and not bothering them so it was good for everyone.

That's how we grew up in that house together. Melanie was allowed anywhere because, like me, she'd learned to go unnoticed. My parents indulged her. I think my mother, on some level, even liked her. She was my friend. Playmate. A surrogate sister.

Then, when I came back the summer of my second year at university, Melanie had just finished college. I'd been away, having a whale of a time, enjoying more freedom than I'd ever had, and I had barely thought about her or the estate. I'd been planning a trip to Europe that summer, but the two friends I'd been going with cried off. I decided it wouldn't be much fun going alone so I went home instead.

Melanie and I had drifted apart as we'd gone our separate ways after I'd left school, and childhood friendships had begun to change, as though we both knew that they couldn't go on in the same way. We were both adults now, I'd turned 20, Melanie's 18th birthday had happened a few weeks before the end of my semester. I hadn't even thought to send her a card, even though I'd spent many birthdays in her company in the past. But she had her own friends now, slowly built up from the local school and college she'd attended.

But I knew she'd done well in her exams, and she'd got into Cambridge because Mother had mentioned it, and so Melanie would be joining me there as a freshman in autumn. Even so, I didn't think about our friendship continuing. I had my own peers, and Melanie would have to build new friendships too. We were at different places in our education and our age gape, though small when we were young, now seemed so much further apart.

But that summer, I saw Melanie in a different light. She wanted to be called 'Mel' now, and it was difficult because I'd never abbreviated her name, just as she'd never shortened mine. I was always Jonathan, never Jon.

She was friendly, casual, when we came into contact in the main house hallway. I had a little jolt when I saw her, grown up as if in the blink of an eye, while my attention was elsewhere. She was very attractive. Prettier than I'd ever realised, and I wondered if I'd been blind or stupid before, or whether she had just blossomed throughout the last year that I hadn't seen her.

'How was Cambridge?' she asked unaware of my interest in her beyond our once easy friendship.

I told her a little about it, knowing she would be looking forward to going there soon too. I assumed she had a scholarship as I couldn't imagine Art being able to pay for it and so I asked her about it.

'A combination. I didn't manage to get a scholarship, but

Dad saved up a fund for my education. He was very frugal. I'm getting some student loans and hopefully will find a job in Cambridge to help,' she told me.

I felt bad then. All I had to do was concentrate on my education and on enjoying the experience of university. I knew that Mel wouldn't get to do that. She'd always be studying or working in some bar somewhere, or worse, waitressing, in order to get through and make ends meet. It was the first time I truly understood the difference between us. But it made Mel more interesting to me. She would triumph, she already had with better grades than I, or any of my peers, had achieved despite our opportunities. What could she do if she was given even greater chances?

Art had been a loyal and trustworthy employee for years. Surely my parents could help Mel out now? I decided to speak to them.

'We should pay for her, you mean?' asked my father when I proposed the idea. 'Why would we do that?'

'To help her,' I said. 'She's been here for years. A friend to me … Art has been a good employee …'

'Jonathan,' Mother interjected. 'What's this about? I hope you aren't getting *feelings* for the girl. I mean, we let you run around with her for entertainment, but that is as far as it can go. She's *not* your sort. We could never condone … a relationship of the romantic kind.'

I began to look at Mel through Mother's eyes and was appalled. Mother was wrong, and her snobbery annoyed me. Mel was a beautiful soul, and always had been. I didn't understand why they couldn't see that. But Mother's attitude made me realise that I was right about how they'd treated Mel over the years. They'd used her to keep me from bothering them. It was hateful and it made me angry.

Even so, I persuaded Dad to provide a fund to help Mel in her first year at Cambridge behind Mother's back because I knew how to manipulate him better than her.

'She's a smart girl and deserves a chance,' I pointed out. 'It's the philanthropic thing to do.'

Father liked to be thought of as caring and so my little management of the situation worked. I didn't tell him that, selfishly, it would mean Mel would have more time at university now, not just to work, but to spend time with me.

And so, it began. Before I'd left for university two years earlier, Father had given me the 'wild oats' talk with a great deal of emphasis about spreading them with care. He didn't want, he said, 'a bastard grandchild'.

'Father. This is too embarrassing even for you,' I'd pointed out. 'I've known about sex since I was seven and how to avoid pregnancies for a long time.'

'Quite so,' Father said. Then he coughed and looked around his study in embarrassment. I couldn't believe he and mother had produced me. I felt so different from them both, so removed emotionally and intellectually.

I got out of that conversation as soon as I could. He was such a fuddy sometimes. Awkward, red-faced, fumbling around subjects that embarrassed him: a man so privileged he'd never needed to expand his mind and become aware of the way normal people lived.

I made a point of not spending much obvious time with Mel that summer. We'd both agreed that it was for the best, and so we met in secret after everyone had gone to bed, and I'd bring some wine from the wine cellar, and Mel would sometimes bring vodka. I tried to keep seeing her as a friend, but the curve of her breasts in a tight-fitting tee-shirt, and the swell of her tiny hips in her jeans, just made it impossible for me to not be attracted to her. But best of all, Mel was still the funny, warm and natural girl she'd always been and her company made me happy.

I didn't make any move on her for all sorts of reasons. Mostly, despite being hugely attracted to her, I felt it was not appropriate. She was younger than me, clearly still … innocent and I felt, as the older of the two of us I had to be the sensible one and respect necessary boundaries.

One night, we were drinking on the balcony of the second-floor ballroom. The room was barely used these days, and Mel and I had often played there growing up. It was a warm night and we'd drunk too much. Mel decided it was time to go to bed and as she stood, she stumbled. I caught her. We looked into each other's eyes. Then, half expecting her to object or laugh at me, I kissed her.

She didn't push me away. She didn't laugh. Instead, Mel kissed me back. It was the most perfect kiss I'd even had. Then as we drew apart, I saw the serious look in her eyes and I knew that all along, she'd had the same feelings for me, that I had for her. But, I'm sure she felt as shy and overwhelmed as I did, because she left me then, going back to the servant's quarters, making as little noise as possible.

We didn't mention it, or meet alone again before we went to Cambridge. It wasn't that I was avoiding her, or she me – it was because we both knew this was serious and the risk of being found out would have massive implications on what happened next. We needed no interference, wanted to make our decisions.

A week later, we went off to Cambridge, and I told Mel to travel with me, especially as her father, Art, was driving me anyway.

Mel was staying on campus for the first year, as freshers usually did, while I was sharing a flat in Cambridge with a couple of other male students, who I'd been friends with for years. So, we went our separate ways, laptops, and cases of clothing and personal effects in hand. I didn't see her then for a few weeks.

But it was like we were magnets, drawn to each other, and it wasn't long before we were dating, and Mel was spending more time in the flat, than in the accommodation on campus.

It was as though I'd planned it, and maybe on some subconscious level I had. There'd been no lover before me for Mel, but I'd had a couple of girlfriends and on campus hookups over the last two years. I didn't feel the urge to do that again, now that Mel and I were an item.

She fitted in well with my peers too. Having lived with

us for all these years, she spoke with the same accent as myself, and so everyone just took her for one of us.

'We have to keep "us" secret when we go back home,' she told me more than once though. And she wouldn't let me post any pictures of us together on social media. I wanted to come out about it. Not really caring what my parents thought.

'Why?' I asked.

'Don't be naïve,' she said. 'Your mother will be furious.'

Maybe I was naïve, but part of me thought my parents would approve, once they knew we were happy together. Why would they have a problem with that?

I planned to stay on at Cambridge for a further two years and get my master's degree and by then, Mel would be graduating. In her second year, we'd decided we'd rent a place together. After we qualified, we'd both be ready to go out into the world, qualifications in hand, and I was sure that Mother's resentment would disappear after that. How could she really object to Mel when she made me so happy and she was such a capable, brilliant, and hardworking girl? I convinced myself that Mother and Father would see that we were meant for each other.

That was because I'd fallen completely and utterly in love with her and just couldn't see anything negative about our situation. Mel was everything to me. She was also a great influence and I worked harder on my course because of her encouragement, unlike my freeloading peers, who happily spent their parents' money and did as little as they could in order to pass their exams.

That year was a blur though, and my parents were the last thing on my mind and so, when we both travelled home again, together, but pretended not to be in a relationship, I was mulling over telling them the truth anyway. I could see our future together so clearly and I knew I wanted to marry Mel in a few years, when we were both established.

We arrived back at the estate and went our separate ways. Mel was back in her father's quarters, me into the house. I already knew I'd not, only passed my degree, but would be graduating with a first. Mel in turn had flown through her first year, and we both planned to celebrate when we met up again in our secret place on the second floor. Even being apart from her for a few hours, felt like torture. All I wanted was to tell them about us, have it out in the open. Maybe even move her into the main house, in my room, because we were so used to living together by then anyway. But I knew Mother would take some convincing and so I went along with the plan that Mel had proposed. We'd one day share our happiness, but for now, we needed to pretend we were still just friends.

Later that night, Mel snuck into the house again and we were cuddling up on the sofa in my room. It was odd to be here, and be together, and I couldn't bear the thought of Mel leaving and not sleeping beside me. We hadn't slept apart since a month after we'd both gone to Cambridge. So, I asked her to stay.

'You can sneak out at about six before your dad wakes, and Mother and Father are never up that early,' I told her.

Then we made love. Afterwards, Mel agreed to stay. Like me, she felt the wrench of separation would be too much.

We carried on like this for most of the summer, keeping our relationship secret from the entire household. The sneaking around was sort of fun, too. It spiced things up a bit, not that we needed it to. Mel told me she went back to her room early and then messed up her sheets, pretending she'd slept there. As an adult in the household, I wasn't woken by staff, but always made sure to straighten Mel's side of the bed just in case. But for the fact that we didn't share meals we might have well been living together as we had in Cambridge.

Throughout the summer, we both went out on dates away from the house on occasion. Mel would say she was going out with friends and I'd do the same, so it wasn't that hard for Mother to start getting suspicious.

She called me into Father's study a week before Mel and I were due to go back to Cambridge.

'I know what's happening, Jonathan,' she said. 'And you need to end it, or I will.'

I denied it, of course. But Mother wasn't stupid. I told

Mel we had to cool things down so that we wouldn't get caught. It was a massive worry for me. Mother, when she set her mind against something, had never been swayed, and the timing of getting her on side had to be right.

I decided to talk to Father in the end and found him alone out in the garden.

'I need to talk to you ...'

'Mother already did,' he said. 'And Jonathan, you have to end things with Melanie. I'm happy for you to do that, back in Cambridge so that it doesn't get awkward here. I've spoken to Art and he agrees that this *unwise* ... relationship ... has to stop.'

'No ... Father ... you don't understand ... I love Mel. And she loves me.'

Father shook his head, 'Mother recognises a gold digger when she sees it.'

'No,' I said again. 'It isn't like that. What is wrong with you?'

'I'll make you a deal,' he said. 'If this is going to be too difficult for you to end, take a gap year, go travelling to broaden your education. I'll continue to pay for Melanie's education while you're away, if the two of you don't get in touch and this thing ends today.'

I stared at him, shocked that he could possibly say such a thing.

'But you like Mel ...' I reminded him.

'I like her well enough as the chauffeur's daughter,' he said. 'But she's not daughter-in-law material Jonathan and you know it. This is an infatuation. It'll pass as soon as she's out of sight. Europe has many beautiful girls to spend time with.'

'No. I won't end things with her. I love her. You and Mother will just have to deal with it.'

I walked away then, went back to my room, and began packing. Mel and I would go back to Cambridge early. The flat was already paid for anyway for the year and if my parents continued to be difficult, then, both of us would get jobs this year. We didn't need them.

I sent Mel a text, telling her what had happened and warning her that Art knew about us too. She didn't reply immediately and then she said. 'Dad is getting the car. Get your stuff and meet him downstairs.'

I was thrilled. We were going to do this. My parents had to learn they couldn't tell me what to do with my life.

Downstairs, Art took my bags and put them in the boot. He opened the back door of the limo and I got inside.

'How long will Mel be?' I asked as Art got into the driving seat.

The doors locked. 'She's not coming,' Art told me, and then he started to drive away.

'Stop immediately!' I said.

'I'm sorry, Jonathan. This is for the good of all. Your parents have instructed that you are to get on a plane. You're off to Europe and an escort will be meeting you at the airport. I have tickets and your passport ready.'

'You have no right to do this! What about Mel?'

Art didn't answer, but he glanced in the rearview mirror and so I turned around and I saw Mel running out of the house and after the limo as it sped away. She stopped in the driveway: she was crying. Then I saw Mother come out, take her by the arm and practically manhandle her back inside the house.

'How can you do this to her?' I said.

Art met my eyes in the rearview mirror. 'We aren't the same as you. I wouldn't want Melanie to be put through it. You should have known better, even if she didn't.'

I realised then that Art had his own prejudices, just like my parents. I was as much on the wrong side of the tracks for his daughter as she was for me in my parents' mind. But they were wrong. All wrong. We could make it work.

I was met at the airport by a team of bodyguards who escorted me through passport control and onto a private plane to Paris. All the time I was thinking about my escape, but I knew it was pointless. By now, Mel would have been whisked away from the estate. One of the bodyguards who I soon nick-named Minion 1, gave me a new mobile phone. There was only one number in it and that was Mother's. I rang her and ranted my fury at what she'd done.

'Jonathan. Melanie is gone. She won't be at Cambridge. You must take this year out to mull over your insane behaviour. We cannot have the future Earl marrying a chauffeur's daughter, no matter how pretty and intelligent she is.'

'You had no right!' I said. 'Taking Mel from her dream degree. She worked hard for Cambridge. Why can't you see how good she was for me?'

Mother hung up without a word.

'You've got a clean slate now,' Minion 1 said. 'A whole phone to fill again with future conquests. I'd love to be in your shoes.'

I glared at him but didn't answer. He knew nothing about me. I'd never give Mel up. Even if it took years and years to find her again.

I was told that my Cambridge Masters had been deferred for a year. They wanted to ensure my absence and stupidly my mother believed that I would forget Mel during that time. But despite being her son, I wasn't that shallow. There was a hole in my heart that only Mel could fill.

I travelled the world to 'broaden my education'. I saw it all: the wonders, the cities, the seediest places. My parents paid: a reward for letting her go.

I thought about Mel all the time.

Alone in Europe, I saw her shape in anonymous crowds. I heard her voice in the space between slumber and consciousness. Sometimes I found her smile in a painting; her description became that of a heroine in a book. I saw her face everywhere.

I began to feel feverish, sick: the tenuous grasp I had on my reality fragmented.

All the time I was asking *why*?

They didn't mind when we were young and Mel was an innocent companion. They feared I'd be isolated, lonely, weird. She made me normal. She gave me the love I needed. The love

I'd never had from either of my parents.

I grew to hate them both.

Sometimes Mother sent me texts, accusing Mel and Art of duplicity. But neither of them had showed any signs of the vile things she suspected them of: the planned deceit; the hooking me in to rob me of my fortune. And worst of all, the scheme to elevate Mel to a position in the world that her heritage gave no access to. Mother's words … not mine …

I didn't believe her, of course. Mother was the worst snob and Mel, my sweet innocent girl, had given me nothing but love. I wasn't like them anymore, and they knew it. Mother could never allow me to be anything other than what was expected of me.

In Amsterdam I missed Mel's hand holding mine. I walked the streets, the glaring red light district – blind to the women flaunting themselves in huge shop windows. I ate at Dutch pâtisseries and thought about Mel's favourite foods. I drank too much to drown out the emptiness. I couldn't let go, no matter how hard the minions tried to make me forget in their attempted radicalisation, or how many suitable women they paraded before my eyes.

Then, six months in, I saw her face splashed over the front of a broadsheet. Mel had disappeared.

I almost boarded a plane back, but mother's minions wouldn't let me go home and the only transport I was allowed would take me to another country not to England. They wanted me kept out of it, never to return because the risks were too high.

In Germany, I thought I saw her looking out of the window of a departing train. The minions said it was impossible, and I knew then, they'd sent her somewhere far from me and our paths would never cross again if my parents had anything to say about it. It was better to believe this than the alternative: that missing meant dead.

Would Art have really been involved in that? I couldn't imagine it. But he'd been so cold that day when he followed my mother's instructions and deposited me at the airport.

After a time, things quietened down. Mel's disappearance

stopped being reported and speculated on in the press. I had never been mentioned in any of the stories and I knew then, somehow, *they* were keeping me in the clear.

I wondered if Mel's father still worked for us considering the situation. He can't have been happy, despite his complicit behaviour: his daughter was gone too, out of reach – maybe she would never be returned. All because they thought we had no right to love each other.

It was the slowest year, but after it passed, they let me return as they promised they would. I was angry still, but had learnt to hide it from my wardens. The minions, five in all, remained nameless to me. I'd never sought their company, knowing they were always there regardless. It was time to go back to university, take up the master's degree.

A new chauffeur picked me up. It spoke volumes: Art was gone despite his loyalty. No one mentioned him, or Mel.

I went to my room when I got back and discovered it had been decorated. They'd gone through all my things and anything related to Mel had been removed. It was the biggest violation. My anger grew.

Mel, I thought, *where are you?*

Now I was home I had access to my laptop again and so I took to social media, searching for Mel or Art or anyone related to them, but Mel's socials had no new posts from her, merely ones from concerned friends who feared she was dead.

As a last thought, I opened my emails and downloaded them, wading through a backlog of unopened messages and there I found news of her. An email from Art.

'They betrayed us all,' it said. 'I have news of Mel, but you won't like what they did to her.'

Art left a telephone number. I called it and on the third ring he answered.

'Where is she?' I asked.

What they'd done was worse than I could have imagined other than murder: Mel had been sectioned. Abandoned and alone, not believed by doctors and pumped full of drugs, she'd been in a very fragile state when Art, with the aid of a private investigator, finally found her. He'd had to prove he was her father before they released Mel into his custody. And, after months of refusing to believe her, Art pursued a court case against the private facility, which settled out of court for a tidy sum. Since then, he'd been living with Mel, keeping a low profile.

Without saying a word to my parents, I got into one of the family cars and drove off the estate to a secret location to meet up with Art.

They were hiding in Scotland in a small cottage just outside of Edinburgh. I drove all the way without stopping for fear of Mother's minions catching up with me before I saw Mel again.

Throughout the journey the phone they'd given me kept ringing, until, aggravated by it, I threw it from the car window. When I reached Edinburgh, I abandoned the car and took a taxi to the house Art was in. Stopping briefly to buy a simple cheap phone to use to let him know I was close now.

The taxi pulled up to the cottage and Art immediately opened the door, and stood on the threshold for me.

I leapt out, almost running to him.

'Where is she?' I said.

'Inside, but be warned, she's delicate. Not herself.'

I pushed passed Art and ran inside, stumbling down the small hallway towards the open door at the back of the house. Mel was sitting on a small, old-fashioned chair with a blanket over her knees. She was overly thin and fragile, as Art had warned. But her smile when she saw me, made up for everything.

'Marry me,' I said falling to my knees to hug her.

It didn't take long for her to agree.

I soon learnt that you can't just elope to Gretna Green anymore and with Art's help I arranged the wedding for the nearest possible date – 29 days was the legal requirement – and Mel, Art and I remained off grid, waiting for that time to pass.

In the meantime, my parents were probably scouring the country for us. I considered flying to another place where the waiting time was shorter, but Mel needed this time to regain some weight and help her recover both her mental and physical strength. I could only imagine what she'd been through all this time.

'They may cut me off,' I told Art.

I was fearful to use my credit cards or withdraw money locally as it would help them find me.

'Don't worry,' he said. 'The lawsuit I filed gave us plenty to lie low with for as long as possible.'

'Why did you change your mind and stop helping them?' I asked him.

'When they wouldn't tell me where Mel was. It was one thing intervening, but making my daughter vanish and then finding out what they'd done, ended any loyalty I had to them.'

I understood. They'd betrayed me too. And worse, Mel didn't deserve what they'd done to her. This beautiful, innocent love of my life, deserved only the best.

Mel and I quickly reclaimed our relationship and though she'd been cautious at first about getting married against my parent's wishes, she soon came around to it. Art didn't object when we started sharing a bed again in the cottage, after all I was soon going to be his son-in-law.

'Jonathan,' Art told me a few days before the wedding. 'I hired a PI to keep them off the scent. But your parents are trying very hard to find you. We think they got wind of the wedding at the registrar, so I've changed the venue, and now it's taking place at a hotel, in a private closed room. Not far from the registrar's office, but they've been paid well to keep the secret.'

I was glad that he was on the ball. Then, Art did something very smart, he got his PI to leak another venue, privately hired on the same day and time. Nothing was going to stop our wedding from happening.

The day came, and Mel was looking lovely in a long empire-line dress, that she said had belonged to her mother, and Art drove us to the new venue.

The registrar was there, and after we confirmed our paperwork and were asked those final questions the wedding proceeded without a hitch.

Afterwards, Art had hired a limo in which he drove us to a hotel for the night.

Mel had recovered well in the last month, and Art said it was all down to me being there.

'I can't think of a better son-in-law,' he said before leaving us for the night.

We had the wedding night that we both wanted most. Quiet, with champagne brought to the room as well as room service food. Nothing mattered but us, being together, and married at last. There was nothing my parents could do now.

The next day, Art collected us in the same limo and we began our journey back to my parent's house to confront them with both our marriage and to threaten them with exposure for their deceit and the awful thing they'd done to Mel.

Art had spent the months searching for Mel to work out exactly what we had to do in order to punish my parents and to ensure that they wouldn't interfere in our future happiness. Now that we were married, there wasn't much they could do but accept the situation. We'd leak some pictures to the press too, to make sure everyone knew, especially to the society pages. There would be a momentary scandal, but as the future Earl, I knew that this would soon be forgotten by my parent's friends and relations. It was too late for them to do anything now anyway.

We reached the estate by nightfall, where minion 1 was on the gate. I opened the window of the limo and glared at him.

'I'm here to see my parents,' I said.

'We've been looking for you,' he answered. Then he opened the gates and Art drove the limo inside and directly up to the front entrance. He parked up, all three of us got out; equals now, not chauffeur and his daughter with the son of the Earl, but man, wife, and father-in-law.

As we walked into the house, we were confronted by Mother and Father at the foot of the stairs. Father looked at us: me holding Mel's hand and Art standing beside us. His face went bright red.

'we're married and there's nothing you can do to change that,' I said, defiant in my rage for all they'd done to us.

Father began to speak, but the redness in his cheeks intensified and then he clutched his chest, fell to the ground and despite the efforts of a quickly summoned paramedic, died soon after from a severe heart attack.

The doctor's warned that Father's condition might be hereditary and had been dormant for some time. I was told I should have regular checks as I got older to try and prevent the same thing happening to me. But I was only in my 20s and I believed I didn't have too much to worry about, at least for now.

A year passed and Mother's fury abated. Father's death had subdued her, along with Mel's pregnancy and the news that she was carrying a boy.

As the only son, I inherited Father's title, and the idea of a future, legitimate Earl, soon to be born into our world silenced the arguments once and for all.

Once the baby was born, Mother became more pliant. She was even civil to Mel. At that point I was pleased that we'd found common ground. And Mel grew into her role of Countess and lady of the estate far better than I expected she would. Mother had graciously retired from the role, despite our expectations that she'd be awkward.

It was then, with the greatest surprise that one morning Mother was found dead in her bed. Beside her was a note, and a bottle of something lethally poisonous that she'd taken.

'Why would she do that?' I asked, shocked. 'Everything was fine!'

We called in the authorities.

We were questioned for weeks after her body was taken away, but all evidence pointed to her suicide. I suppose, after all she'd done to prevent my marriage to Mel, followed by the death of father, it wasn't really that much of a surprise that she'd felt depressed after all.

The coroner's office gave a verdict of 'suicide' and we tried to move on from it.

But I found it difficult to take Mother's death. It seemed

so out of place that she would kill herself. So irregular. She'd been strong, even when she conceded defeat.

With the death of my second parent, I was sad about the last two years and what had happened. The only light was Mel and my son, Jonathan, who was named after me.

But I told Mel I was upset, and down, and more than a little confused. After all we never kept anything from each other and I knew by sharing how I felt she would be my rock.

'That's not surprising,' Mel said. 'They both put us through so much, and now they are gone. And so suddenly. It is sad. And it didn't have to be this way.'

She poured me a glass of Father's favourite brandy and stroked my hair. I sipped the drink, savouring it and wondered why I hadn't thought to touch this bottle since he'd died. It really was good stuff. But I hadn't seen the decanter around either.

When the heart-attack began to bite, I realised what she'd done.

'Why?' I asked as my last breath squeezed from my lips.

'We have a future Earl now,' she said. 'And this was always the plan. And ... I couldn't have a depressed whinger around any longer. It's not good for my son.'

Trophy Wife

The rain hammered the soft top of the old MG convertible as I dragged the body out of the passenger seat, heaving it to the edge of the cliff a step and a tug at a time. The body was heavier in death than the man had been in life, but stubbornness and determination won out and I pushed him over the edge and his corpse tumbled like a broken marionette – heftier still as gravity took hold.

I was trembling as I climbed back into the car. Sodden. Cold. I blinked the rain out of my eyes and stared out over the precipice thinking about how my life had taken such an unexpected turn.

Three Years Earlier

'What's your name?' The man took the unoccupied seat on the train opposite mine.

I was in first class, a table seat by the window. I was alone and so he assumed he could impose himself on me. It was the start and the end – I just didn't know it then.

I glared at him over my laptop, showing my disapproval of his unwanted interruption.

'I'm Cillian,' he said, flashing me what I soon learnt was his trademark grin. He was pleasing to the eye; and things would have been less comfortable if he hadn't been.

The steward came and offered us drinks. Cillian ordered wine for us both, he was confident, even though I continued to blank him.

But I was curious and so I took the drink but made him work for details about me right up until the last moment and the train was pulling into Kings Cross Station. Then, I gave him my business card which read 'Melissa Marshall' along with my phone number and email address.

I hadn't even left the station before I received a text inviting me to dinner that night.

I didn't reply for three days. But I admired his boldness in a way. This was the last time I was stubborn over anything with him.

It was clear from the start that Cillian was a narcissist and so I fed him the lines that made him think me weak and controllable: 'My last boyfriend cheated on me'; 'I lack confidence'; perhaps it was all because of my 'dodgy childhood'. I wanted him to feel that I was ripe for the picking and he fed me the appropriate reassuring words that promised me a safe and happy life in his hands.

Six months down the line he proposed. It was the 'right time,' he said.

I'd let him make love to me the week before for the first time. He thought me predictable, moral, and coupled with my attractive looks, a safe bet for a wife. That and the fact that I'd been damaged by a previous relationship that made me cautious, and grateful and so, so desperate for stability. He promised me security in hushed tones under the sheets even while I shivered under him, a paragon of nervous virtuosity – false – but he liked to believe me a virgin right up until our first coupling as though anything that had happened before him simply wasn't important.

After that, he claimed he was 'the making of me' and I took on the role of being 'reinvented' and became the bride-to-be that revelled in the lush cash he flashed to prove he was in control of our mutual destiny. He even chose and paid for my wedding dress, booked the venue without my consultation, and gave me the list of those to invite. He never asked for my opinion on any of it, nor for a list of friends and relatives I might also want there. It was all about him by then and I was submerged in his sole view of the world. The co-star of his story. I must be grateful he spotted me. Pursued me. Owned me.

I knew all along how to play him.

The wedding was faultless and so were the guests: they were puppets who danced as he pulled the strings. I watched how he controlled and manipulated them all – even his boss – into believing he was the man of the moment. One to watch. Perfect. And now he had a wife who was under his sway just as much as everyone else was. Cillian was on a roll.

We went on an expensive honeymoon: a trip to Dubai followed by a long, leisurely cruise around the Bahamas. When we got home, I found a letter from my old boss accepting my resignation. He hadn't asked me if I wanted to be a housewife, but had merely sent the email from my account, giving notice on my behalf. Though it took me by surprise, I didn't object. It was … predictable behaviour for someone like him and therefore should have been expected. I promised myself after that he wouldn't catch me out again. I had to be even more careful.

I took to the role of trophy wife like the proverbial duck to water, living in the house he'd chosen and bought before we met, overseeing renovations he'd decided we needed: all his choice. I only voiced a positive opinion, expressing how his taste in everything pleased me. How I'd never have thought of this colour or that. Even though his style appeared to me excessive and ostentatious and was always, without doubt, about how others would perceive and admire him and not about making me happy.

He was like a child sometimes, all wide eyed and excited with his control of the new money he'd worked hard to earn – all fruits of his labour: just as I was. Proof of his self-worth.

On occasion when I tried to buy my own clothes, he never liked them. They were too short, too long, too tarty, or not sexy enough. I gave up after the fourth round of returns and let him choose for me from then on. It was simply easier that way. It wasn't long before all the clothing, jewellery, and shoes I'd owned when we met disappeared from my lavish walk-in wardrobe. I never saw him throw them out, but noticed one day that they'd gone.

He was cash rich but I had to ask for every penny. He'd check my credit card bills in detail to make sure I hadn't bought anything that was not pre-approved. He even took to looking at my mobile phone bills – scrutinising any numbers he didn't recognise, questioning me about them. He stopped doing this when he learnt I was an open book. All calls were explainable, most of them were to him, or for him, as I fulfilled the errands he left me to do during the day.

When I gained a few pounds, he bought me a gym membership and checked up that I was using it on set days to keep myself 'nice' for him.

I knew what I was. I knew my place. I was complicit after all: I was in it for the long haul, no matter how much it took. There's always a price to pay and I kept my goal in view as I thought about the day when it would all be about me: the widow after the fatal accident that would take him from me all too soon.

Even though I didn't fall for any of the lifestyle he permitted me, I allowed him to manipulate it and me. And he never suspected that he was a mark, like any other, as I cultivated him, playing him even as he thought he was holding all the cards. I still had the aces up my sleeve.

I thought that maybe we'd have the 2.4 children before I had him where I wanted – all of which would happen when he said it was time. I must never push the issue or suggest it. By then, I would be such a dutiful wife he'd never expect me to question him. And I wouldn't have, but for the emails he received on his personal laptop that signposted the first problem: some of the business trips he went on were a lie. He was so sure of me; he didn't even bother putting a password on his machine for he didn't know I had it in me to be nosey.

Of course, I'd paid attention all along, despite my apparent complacency. I wasn't the laid back, silent, calm partner he thought he possessed. I had bank accounts he didn't know about, resources to draw on anytime I wanted. Even though he thought he kept me in a place of controlled destitution that made me completely reliant on him.

Once I saw the emails, I realised that there was another woman in his life, but I couldn't involve a private investigator to find out who she was. That would allow another person knowing that our marriage wasn't perfect, after all. And to the outside world it had to appear as though it was, if my goal was to be reached.

I told white lies in place of whole truths with the same straight and honest face. Distracted by the texts he was now receiving on his phone from his new flame, he barely looked in my direction.

I wondered about stopping taking the contraceptive pills he got for me, but he'd taken to checking them every day – something he'd never done before. For some reason it was now important to him that I *didn't* get pregnant. It could only mean one thing: soon I'd be usurped in his affections if indeed I hadn't been already.

This changed *everything*.

I crashed the timeline of my once long-term plan. I had to step things up.

I don't know why I cared, but I also needed to know who this new woman was.

I pulled some old clothing from my storage unit – something Cillian had never known about. He didn't recognise me in these dowdy slobs as I followed him to work for a week. He was so sure of me; I could have been in plain sight and he wouldn't have seen me.

The secretary he'd hired recently was an effervescent blonde with legs up to her armpits, but Cillian was never going to be so obvious, and a woman like that wouldn't *need* him and would be too hard to control. I dismissed her as the guilty party almost immediately.

I mapped his days, learned his habits, and then discovered the little coffee shop he liked to visit during his lunch break. Odd, as he often ate at his desk. It was glaringly obvious that this new habit had nothing to do with coffee.

Her name was Sophie. She was one of the baristas.

I guess she'd been hard to win at first because it was Cillian's *modus operandi* to go after someone who appeared to be impossible to land. But now she was putty in his hands, laughing at his corny jokes, grinning back at that flawless, confident smile. She was wearing a diamond tennis bracelet, almost identical to one he'd bought me after the first time we slept together. Would there soon be an engagement ring on her finger too? I wondered what he planned to do to disentangle himself from me.

Before he went back to work, I saw them exchange a kiss at the door. When he'd gone, I went into the shop and bought a latte. She served me. The coffee was good, but I wondered how she would feel about never working here again once Cillian decided she had to quit. It was like waiting for a car crash that you knew was going to happen. Would she walk into this not knowing what he planned? Or was she, too, in it for the duration?

She wasn't as well turned out as I was. Very girl next door, simple even. There was so little sophistication that I couldn't really see the appeal, knowing what Cillian liked. But then, I recalled his words to me of reinvention and I saw Cillian again with fresh eyes. Eyes that someone like her might have. Maybe she realised he had money. Maybe she even knew he was married. Maybe she didn't; after all there was no sign of recognition on her part when she served me: I was just another customer.

A divorce would cost him dearly, but if he'd fallen for this girl, would he really mind? I decided I wasn't ready to let her take over my life, not after all I'd put into it. Cillian wasn't easy to please, even when I made it appear effortless.

I went home with a plan forming. Something I perhaps should have considered sooner. It really was time to move forward and end this silly game, once and for all.

Soon after dinner, Cillian fell asleep on the sofa. His phone still casually held in his hand, as though he waited for Sophie to message him. I took it from his fingers, he murmured but didn't wake. I'd spiked his wine with sleeping tablets to make sure.

He had Sophie listed under a work colleague's name, but the texts they exchanged were anything but professional. He'd taken to sending pictures of himself – nothing indecent, that wasn't his style – but selfies in his office; in the coffee shop with her behind him; in our bed as though he'd just woken up. I tried to recall when this one might have been taken as my side was neat and empty, and looked as though it had never been occupied.

I discovered he had an Instagram account full of pictures like this. She was following him, and he was following back. There were no photos of 'us'. All of which confirmed that I was his secret from her. *Dirty* almost. A mistake he'd made, and had yet to correct.

I forwarded everything I could find over to a phone that Cillian didn't know I had. Then I deleted all my activity from his history. I dropped his phone to the floor by the sofa, then nudged him awake.

'Darling? Are you all right? Should I help you go to bed? You've been working so very hard …'

After that, I gave up following him and started following her.

Sophie lived in a small, rented, studio apartment in Putney. To the casual eye she was ordinary. When she wasn't seeing Cillian or working in the coffee shop, she stayed in, alone in her apartment. Cillian never went there.

I became fascinated with Sophie. I wanted to know more about her. Where she came from, who she really was. I did an internet search and found nothing other than the Instagram account I'd already seen and Cillian would eventually boycott if he made her his. On the surface, there were no friends, no family and no one other than my husband in her life. She was a ghost – just like I was when Cillian met me.

I couldn't recall him ever asking me about family, or friends: Cillian had treated me as though no world before him ever existed.

I zoomed in on the photo he had of her on his phone, making coffee in the background. Was this taken when he first set his sights on her or as a way for them to be innocently in a photograph together? She was facing him. Her expression one of concentration as she placed a tall latte glass down before another customer.

I did a search for her image online. Nothing came up. I was

more curious about her than ever. Almost everyone has some social media presence. Except me, and this was a deliberate choice, which made me suspicious of Sophie.

I looked again at the images that showed on her Instagram: cups of coffee; inspirational banners about lifestyle; an occasional cat picture reshared from somewhere else.

Who was she?

He wrapped up his next trip away as business but I knew this wasn't true. I ironed his shirts, packed his case carefully and watched him climb into the taxi before I looked at his emails.

The booking was a five-star hotel in Dover. I knew there was no reason workwise for Cillian to be going there. Knowing where he was going negated the issue of following him or Sophie.

In my mind's eye, I imagined the two of them meeting at the train station. It would be first class all the way, Cillian never did standard. I saw Sophie, wide eyed, excited, in love, as she smiled at him over the table. Cillian would be on the side facing travel. Sophie would be content to travel backwards but even then, the start of his control would set in.

My body trembled at the thought of them together. In a hotel room. I had to stop this: I wouldn't give up my place that easily in Cillian's life. Not until I was ready.

The MG had been static for several years in a garage in Richmond, but I had a portable battery to get the engine started. As the car had been left in storage, it wasn't taxed any more, and any MOT long since expired. I didn't want the complication of being stopped by the police because of a casual scan of the plates and so I removed them and put on a set I'd copied from another MG of the same colour I'd discovered a picture of online for this purpose.

As the battery charged, I cleaned the car, removing all trace of its dusty home and the spiders that had taken up residence around the side mirrors. When the car was working, and clean. I got in and drove it away.

My route to Dover was already planned.

When people aren't expecting to see you, they don't see you. It was something I learned some years ago, before my Cillian days. Unobtrusive, uninteresting, in plain sight, I watched Cillian and Sophie in the hotel restaurant.

He was fixated on her at all times, and her response to this was modest and sweet as she blushed a little with his somewhat full-on attention. Cillian had never been like this with me. He'd appeared to be less confident and self-assured with her. This wasn't a side of him I'd seen before and it worried me more than if he'd been doing his usual behaviour – showy and pushy, flashing cash around like it didn't matter. No. Cillian was not like this with Sophie. In fact, he was avoiding bringing attention to them at every opportunity. But why then bring her to such a public hotel? I was never more uncertain of his intentions towards her than now.

When they retired for the night, they had separate rooms. This really surprised me. And not adjoining either. Cillian's booking was only for the weekend. And when Sunday came, he left, giving Sophie a small kiss goodbye in reception. Sophie, it seemed, was booked into the hotel longer. A taxi waited outside for Cillian, and as it drove away, my phone pinged. I looked at it to find a text message from Cillian saying he would be home that day.

I was in a quandary, I had to get back before he did, or he'd question where I'd been.

I sent him a reply to give myself more breathing time.

'What time should I expect you?' I asked.

His reply told me he had some work-related meetings first and would be home for dinner. I took this to mean he was going into the office first.

I left the MG in the hotel car park and caught a taxi to Dover Priory train station. Once near, I booked myself on the next train, after Cillian's, and sat in a local coffee shop following the progress of Cillian's train on the app. When the train had departed the station, I stood up and walked towards the door of the coffee shop and then I saw Cillian, striding confidently down the street. He'd obviously not got the train. He had changed his clothing, he was wearing black jeans and a black polo shirt, with a dirty looking anorak. He'd covered his hair with a woollen hat, something I'd never seen him wear. But there was no mistaking his walk despite this somewhat bizarre disguise. Confused, but curious, I followed him all the way back to the hotel.

Cillian followed Sophie at a safe distance as she left the hotel. As I shadowed him, I was nervous but intrigued. She appeared not to know he was there, and if she turned, Cillian ducked out of sight, making sure she didn't see him. It was the oddest game of cat and mouse and so closely reflected my own course of tracking him that I began to wonder if they both knew I had been at the hotel after all and if this was some form of trap.

I dropped back from my pursuit and observed Cillian as Sophie entered a bakery shop. He waited for her, picking a location to observe from, without being seen, or so he thought because his focus was taken up by her. I knew then he had no clue anyone was watching him.

Sophie left the bakery clutching a paper bag with something hot inside which I suspected was a pasty. Cillian never allowed me to eat junk food like this and I saw the set of his shoulders as Sophie opened the bag and tucked into whatever it contained. He nodded, as though he were confirming something to himself that he already knew about the woman. But I couldn't see his face and therefore wasn't able to read what he was thinking. He took out his phone from his jeans pocket and sent a text. Sophie halted and reached inside her jacket pocket as her phone pinged in response. She read the text, stowed the phone away, and then took another bite from her pasty.

While I was distracted by Sophie, Cillian walked away in the opposite direction. I didn't follow him.

I made my way back to the hotel, Sophie a few feet ahead of

me. On the walk back I received another text from Cillian, this one telling me he wouldn't be home that night after all. Whatever he'd observed on his stalking of Sophie it had changed things. This, at least, meant I no longer had to rush back either. Using an old card that I kept active, I booked a room in the hotel for the night. The card, like the deeds on the MG, were not in the name I currently used and were not registered to my current address. Though if I were looking for grounds for divorcing Cillian, my presence at the hotel could be fully justified. I still wasn't sure where this whole adventure was going or what I'd do if he decided to leave me for Sophie.

That evening, Sophie ate alone in the hotel dining room then went to bed early. I didn't catch sight of Cillian all evening and eventually I went upstairs to my room and, removing the brunette wig and clear spectacles I'd been wearing all day, I went to bed too.

I got up early the next day, determined to drive the MG back to London and get home in advance of Cillian's expected return. I'd heard nothing from him the previous evening, which wasn't unusual when he was on a supposed business trip. But, despite the uncertainty of the future, I'd slept well and felt refreshed, even though a modicum of anxiety returned on walking.

I put the wig and glasses back on and took my small overnight bag, leaving the hotel room. As I entered the lift, I heard a piercing scream that seemed to come from the floor above. Knowing I didn't want to get caught up in anything, I exited the lift, left the hotel, and got into the car where I waited. A short time later, a police car and an ambulance arrived. I turned the key in the engine and pulled the MG out of the car park, leaving Dover behind me. Whatever had happened it was nothing to do with me and my fake plates and ID might not bear up to too much scrutiny.

Cillian returned home for dinner that night and he appeared to be calm and happy. I asked him politely about his trip and his eyes glowed as he lied to me about a 'deal' he'd made, and how this might lead to a promotion. That night he didn't look at his phone once. I knew then something had changed. Had he realised that Sophie wasn't for him after all and ended it?

'Maybe we need to start a family soon,' he said after dinner.

I didn't comment, but gave him the smile I'd cultivated which gave him my agreement without me saying a word. I let him make love to me and then lay still as he fell asleep soon after.

He'd left his phone charging in the kitchen and I couldn't help wondering what had happened with Sophie. His attitude had changed, the darkness I'd sensed lurking like a poisonous parasite in every word he'd uttered to me in the past few weeks had now washed away. The evening was a normal one for us. Normal because I showed no sign of rebellion, or made any effort to refuse anything he wanted, but Cillian was relaxed again.

I slid from the bed, already forming the excuse I'd give if he woke, but he didn't stir.

In the kitchen, I found his phone. He'd left it switched on, and I scrolled through it looking for signs of the texts, but they'd all been deleted along with the contact number he'd had for Sophie.

I returned to the bedroom and found Cillian sleeping soundly, as if he had no cares or worries.

The next day, I heard about Sophie's death on the news – her body was found in that same hotel in Dover by a housekeeper. She'd been strangled.

Cillian mentioned us having children again a few nights later. By then he was acting perfectly 'pre-Sophie' normal. If he knew she was dead, he didn't appear to be upset by the prospect.

A few months later, Cillian started something with another girl. I didn't take kindly to this. There was a nervous energy growing inside him and I became aware of it sooner. His pattern of behaviour reverted back to the 'Sophie days' but this time it was obvious to me.

I'd failed to get pregnant, despite our attempts – Cillian didn't know that I was, secretly, still taking my contraceptive pills having obtained my own supply. I had changed my mind about a lot of things since Sophie, and now I watched Cillian harder than he watched me.

When the 'business trips' began again, I didn't bother to follow him, or try to learn who the girl was. It would probably burn out anyway. But then, I saw him with her: a Sophie lookalike, wishy-washy, girl next door, and I was betting she had no life beyond Cillian either.

She was called Chloe.

When I saw her photograph appear on the news a few weeks later I knew that Chloe had again been strangled because she failed to live up to Cillian's expectations of her ... whatever they may be.

I didn't need another girl to die to prove to me that the time to end things with Cillian was rapidly approaching. I continued as a dutiful wife while making plans. When I felt that steady nervous darkness edging back into his behaviour, I acted on it.

Now the rain hammered the soft top of the old MG convertible as I sat and looked out over the sea.

Pills crushed into wine and a long drop over the cliff when Cillian took his next business trip. That finished the disaster that was our marriage. And the girl that waited for him in that five-star hotel would never know what a lucky escape she'd had. Though I always would.

I started the engine and turned the car away from the cliff edge. I was a long way from home, but I had an iron clad alibi in place. It wasn't the ending I'd originally planned for him, and it had come sooner than the long-term plan I'd mapped out when I first chose him as my mark. It was funny how things turned out.

TROPHY WIFE

I had a lovely house, all the money I needed … I was free once more.

Until I decided to play the game again.

Being a trophy wife is not so bad sometimes … but I wanted to relish my freedom for a while longer …

All Summer Long

The summer of 1990 began to drag almost as soon as Eddie left Sixth Form college. All his friends had gone away or had plans for most of the holidays and Eddie was left behind like the biggest Billy no-mates. To stop him moping, his mother insisted he spend the days with his grandparents while she was working and to 'keep him out of trouble'. Not that he was the sort to do anything wrong, but his parents were a bit old school about 'idle hands' and so Eddie had no choice.

His grandmother used him constantly; dragging him shopping so he could carry the bags back in a two-mile trek from the shops. He couldn't understand why she didn't use a supermarket like every other normal person or take the car they hardly used. Eddie had been taking driving lessons himself, but his dad wouldn't let him drive his car even though his test was weeks' away. He hoped that by being a good grandson, his Grandad would see fit to put him on his insurance at least. A car, when he started university, would come in very handy.

At the end of every week, for all the jobs he did, Eddie received an allowance from his grandmother. It was only five pounds, much less than he'd get if he'd found a summer job instead, but he put the money away in his university account and didn't complain: his grandparents were paying towards his education and so it didn't seem right to ask for more.

Eddie knew he was lucky because most of his year group couldn't even afford to do college, let alone university. But the holidays were boring for him, and he couldn't wait to get on the campus and be free to do what he wanted without his parents and grandparents watching his every move. It was almost as if they were afraid to let him be young!

About halfway through the summer things improved: he met Jess.

She was working at the grocery shop his gran liked to visit, packing bags and sometimes on the till. Eddie guessed they were the same age, and he soon developed a crush on her that he kept to himself. Jess was out of his league, but sometimes she'd smile at him and occasionally, he thought he saw her wink when Gran was being particularly difficult about the sprouts she wanted. At those times, Jess would throw in a few extras after they were weighed. She soon became her gran's favourite server and she was disappointed whenever they went in and Jess wasn't there. But Gran wasn't as upset by Jess's absences as Eddie was. Just seeing her broke up the long days and after that they flew by, too fast now, as Eddie began to regret his decision to live away from home after all, because he might not see Jess again.

With just two weeks of the holidays left, Eddie came to his Gran's house determined to make a move and speak to Jess if he saw her that day. But his Gran was out of sorts when he arrived.

'What's up Gran?' Eddie asked.

'My sciatica has flared up,' she said. 'I just can't do that walk today. Will you go without me if I give you a list?'

Eddie said he would and was pleased when the list included a necessary visit to the grocers. Two miles there and two miles back would be worth it if Jess was around. Maybe he'd pluck up the courage to ask her out too.

Eddie took the list and made the trip in record time without Gran slowing him down but he was disappointed when he went inside the greengrocers, because Jess was nowhere to be seen.

After collecting the shopping, Eddie picked up the bags and began his walk home. Slower now that he was laden. He couldn't help feeling fed up as well, because no Jess, and all that effort.

A car pulled up at the kerb beside him. He glanced at the orange Skoda and saw Jess at the wheel.

Jess wound the window down. 'Need a lift?'

She had never spoken to him before and Eddie wasn't

quite sure what to say for a moment, but the bags were heavy and he did want a lift, so he climbed in the passenger seat and put them down in the footwell.

'Thanks,' he said. Then he gave her his gran's address.

'Oh, so you can speak!' Jess said. 'But I guess you don't get chance to get a word in, do you?'

Eddie flushed. His gran was very vocal and he really didn't speak much around her, but the reason he was silent with Jess was that he really didn't know what to say.

'Yeah. She talks a lot,' he agreed. 'I switch off most of the time.'

'Oldies, hey? Sometimes you wonder if they were ever young. My mum is always saying she's on her last legs. I'm never growing old ...'

Eddie laughed even though he knew that no one avoided getting old in the end.

Jess took a packet of cigarettes from the glove box and offered Eddie one. He didn't smoke but didn't want to look like a wimp so he took one. Jess lit hers from the cigarette lighter, then after a few puffs, pressed the tip of hers against the one for Eddie, she drew in a sharp lungful, then passed the now lit Marlborough to Eddie.

Eddie took a drag and immediately started coughing.

'Whoops! You don't smoke do you? You should have said.'

Jess took the cigarette back.

'It's not for everyone. Don't be embarrassed. I'm a very live and let live person. My Mum says I should have been a hippy but that era, sadly, is long gone.'

Eddie didn't know what to say. Jess was very mature. She appeared to be more knowledgeable about the world than someone her age usually was.

She rolled down her own window, threw the lit cigarette out on the street, and then continued smoking her own. At no point did she make a move to drive him home, the car just sat at the roadside where she'd picked him up.

'What are you doing after summer,' Eddie asked. 'Uni?'

'Nope,' Jess said. 'You?'

Eddie nodded. He hurriedly added that he was the first in his family to go.

'So, you're clever then?' Jess asked.

Eddie blushed. 'I worked at it I guess. My grandparents wanted me to go.'

'And whatever grannie wants, grannie gets?' Jess observed.

Eddie laughed at that. It was true that his gran was a force of nature.

'So what will you be doing?' Jess asked.

'English,' said Eddie. 'Then possibly go into teaching.'

'Wow,' said Jess. 'You're a swot!'

Jess stubbed her cigarette out in the ashtray, then she let the handbrake off and with a glance over her shoulder, she pulled the car out and began to drive him home.

An awkward silence fell between them and Eddie thought that by being a 'swot' he had ruined any chance he had with Jess. He imagined that at school she had been one of the popular girls who smoked behind the bike sheds and let one of the older boys kiss her in exchange for a cig, but at the thought of this, Eddie felt a surge of jealousy.

'What will you do then?' he asked suddenly. 'With your life?'

Jess glanced at him, then turned her eyes back to the road.

'I've got a game plan,' she said. 'But for now, I'm working at the grocers and I'm happy there.'

'My gran loves you,' Eddie said.

'All the oldies do, especially when I slip them some extra veg. They charge too much for it at that place anyway.'

Jess glanced at him again and this time there was no doubt that the wink was for him.

As they reached his gran's house, Eddie picked up the bags.

'What you doing later?' Jess asked.

'Later?'

'Yeah. Tonight. Want to go to the pub?'

Eddie was eighteen but he hadn't been inside a pub, nor had he ever wanted to. Jess's invitation changed that. He wanted to see her again and a date, even at the local pub, was fine by him.

They arranged a time and place to meet. Jess had suggested inside the pub, but Eddie knew a girl shouldn't go there alone, his dad would never forgive him if he let her do that, and so he said he'd pick her up at her house.

Armed with her address, Eddie took the shopping into his gran's kitchen. Gran gave him his allowance and he put it in his jacket pocket. Normally on a Friday, Eddie would take the money to the building society and put it in his account, but he'd need something that night for drinks and so he kept it.

When he got home, he looked in his wardrobe at his disappointingly square shirts and old jeans. He'd never faced the dilemma of what to wear before and realised his friends from college would laugh if they saw him now, stressing over it like a girl. He opted for a plain white shirt and his newest jeans, then pulled on his grubby trainers, all the time wondering what other people wore to go to the pub.

He reached Jess's street early and hung out at the end of the road so as not to seem too eager. Then, on the dot of seven pm he walked up to her door and knocked.

He heard someone remove the chain and took a breath, half expecting to be greeted by one of her parents, but Jess opened the door and then Eddie discovered he had dressed right for the pub because, other than more makeup than she wore in the day, she was casual too.

There was an awkward moment in which Eddie didn't know whether to shake hands or hug Jess, in the end he did neither. He stepped back and waited while she locked up.

'No one home?' he asked.

'Huh?'

'Your parents?'

'No. They don't live here,' Jess said.

Eddie had even more respect for Jess on hearing this.

She'd left home already and so young. But she was supporting herself and it made him think about the news report he'd seen about young entrepreneurs who were making something of themselves and had massive disposable income. But surely Jess couldn't be one of those, not working part time at a shop?

The pub was in walking distance of Jess's house and Eddie thought he was entering an alien world when he walked in for the first time. The place reeked of beer and cigarette smoke. Within seconds, Eddie could smell it all over his own clothes and in his hair, but Jess seemed oblivious as she made her way to the bar.

'What you having?' he asked.

Jess asked for a pint of lager. And Eddie followed suit, then paid. Once they had the drinks, Jess led them to the least crowded part of the pub where they found a table and sat down. He sipped the drink and found it repellent, but didn't let it show because Jess swigged hers with confidence.

'Hey! Over here,' Jess called out and Eddie followed her gaze to see who she was waving at.

He saw a tall muscular guy approaching wearing a leather biker's jacket. He was carrying a pint in his hand and he came and sat down opposite the two of them, placing his glass on the small round table.

'Who's your friend?' he asked.

'This is Eddie,' Jess said.

'Right. Eddie. Welcome to the fold. I'm Daz.'

Eddie was confused about Daz's appearance but didn't say anything. Daz didn't offer his hand to shake and so Eddie didn't either. He was a little put out though, as he thought he had a date with Jess and hadn't expected anyone else to join them.

Within a few minutes more people gathered around the table, drinking, laughing. Eddie was introduced to them but found it hard to keep up with who was who. As the pub got fuller and louder, Eddie asked Jess how she knew Daz.

'He's a mate. We've hung out for years. He's a good guy, don't let the muscles and the jacket worry you.'

Eddie nodded, taking in Jess's words. He couldn't deny that Daz's presence made him feel a bit uneasy, he wasn't his sort for sure, but he trusted Jess's judgment. After all, she seemed to know him and any unease about the man was probably down to jealousy on his part.

As the night wore on, Eddie found himself caught up in the lively atmosphere of the pub. The drinks flowed, laughter filled the air, and the initial awkwardness he had felt faded away. He even began to enjoy the taste of the beer. He was having fun and he liked Jess's gang more than he expected to. It filled the void of his own absent friends and the summer holidays didn't seem so bad after all.

Jess and Daz regaled the group with stories of their adventures, which were a combination of farcical capers and moments tinged with danger and excitement. Daz hinted at his brush with the law in the past. All of it ended with Jess and Daz miraculously getting out of these scrapes unhindered. It was risky, but funny, the way they talked.

Eddie listened intently, hanging onto their every word. It was a glimpse into a world he had never experienced before, a world of freedom and rebellion that beckoned him.

Eddie became more relaxed, the alcohol having its effect on his inhibitions. He found himself laughing more freely, joining in the banter, and even taking a few sips from a shared bottle of whiskey that Daz had brought along. The night was turning out to be more fun than he had imagined.

Then, last orders were called, and the gang began to disperse. Soon, Eddie found himself alone again with Jess.

'Same time tomorrow?' she said, kissing him on the cheek after he walked her home.

Eddie flushed and gave an awkward nod. 'See you tomorrow.'

He rushed away, walking home on none too steady feet. Then, he let himself in and slipped into his room before his parents saw how drunk he was.

The next day, Eddie felt rough. The alcohol had affected his sleep. He had a headache and for the first time understood what a hangover was. It was Saturday and both his parents were home. They tried to persuade him to come shopping with them, but Eddie was sick of grocery shopping and had no intention of doing that all weekend too. He lay in bed, bemoaning his sore head to himself, and when his parents left, he went downstairs and took some paracetamol to help with the pain.

After more sleep, he felt a bit better. He was looking forward to seeing Jess later and to hearing more stories from Daz if he was there too, but he realised he'd used up all of the five pounds he'd had with him, and so he went out to the building society and drew out some more money.

Then, he went out to meet Jess, this time in the pub because Eddie now realised what an antiquated notion he'd had about women going there alone. All because it was his dad's view, and it bore no resemblance to the modern world where anyone could be anything and do anything if they wanted to.

Daz was on good form and already in the pub when Eddie arrived. He was talking about a 'hypothetical' break-in that he'd always wanted to commit.

'You know … like you break into an empty house, eat their food, watch their telly, then bugger off when the owners get back.'

'Not steal or damage anything?' Eddie asked.

'No. I'm not a criminal. It's for laughs, mate. A dare even. Haven't you ever wanted to do something bad, that you have no chance of being caught doing? Just for the rush.'

Eddie had never thought of taking part in anything risky. He'd always been honest and well-behaved. And a little nervous of the police whenever he was around them, feeling guilty, even when he hadn't done anything wrong. It was irrational, but he couldn't help it. But the idea of Daz's plan seemed like a lark and the thought of taking a chance, doing something risky, gave Eddie a small surge of excitement.

Daz painted a picture of adventure, and freedom, enticing Eddie with the prospect of breaking free from the monotony of his existence. Of having a moment of daring and outrageous behaviour before he had to settle back down and study towards a serious career.

'You're only young once ...' Daz said and the thought resonated with Eddie, especially as his parents and grandparents seemed so old and boring, as if they'd never done anything the least bit outrageous. Never even been young since they didn't seem to understand the concept.

Eddie's heart raced with a mix of excitement and apprehension. The idea of committing a crime was far from his comfort zone. Yet, the allure of the unknown, coupled with Jess's presence and the desire to prove himself, tempted him to consider Daz's proposal.

The three of them plotted the details of the break-in, each member assigned a specific role. Eddie found himself swept up in the adrenaline-fuelled fervour of the planning process. Partly believing they'd never do it, and talking about it was just a game. He was dazzled by the notion, and as Jess said, it would be an opportunity for them to escape their mundane lives for a while.

'And no one will get hurt ...' she pointed out.

A week later, Eddie found himself driving Jess's Skoda. He didn't tell her that he hadn't taken his test yet. It didn't matter in the scheme of things, especially as they were going to break into some random person's house that night which was far worse than him driving without a licence.

'So, these people are away?' Eddie asked.

'Yeah,' said Jess. 'Gone to Tenerife.'

'Alright for some,' Daz said from the back seat. 'Must be loaded.'

'Yeah but we aren't stealing anything, are we?' Eddie said.

'Well ... some food and beer ...' Daz said.

'You aren't getting cold feet are you?' Jess asked glancing at him. She was in the passenger seat.

Eddie shook his head. 'Course not.'

But he was nervous and apprehensive. He'd never broken the law before, but although he knew it was wrong, Daz's suggestion still felt like a harmless game. He was going to do it, no matter what, but he couldn't be a wimp in front of Jess.

'Down there,' Jess said.

Eddie turned the car down the dark back alley and pulled in beside a row of dustbins, neatly lined up with their metal lids firmly in place. He switched off the engine and turned the lights off.

'Now what?' he asked.

'We're going in through the back door,' Daz said. 'Leave it to me. I know what to do.'

They got out of the car, and Daz opened the boot, taking out a gym bag, from which he extracted a crowbar. At some point he'd pulled on a pair of gloves and so had Jess. Eddie wondered if he should have brought some with him too, but decided he'd be careful not to touch anything in the house. He didn't know a lot about police techniques when it came to break-ins but he was sure they would sweep for fingerprints at the very least.

'This way,' said Jess.

A few feet from the car, and halfway down the alley, Jess approached a gate. She reached over the top and drew back a bolt. There was barely a sound as she pushed open the gate and they all entered the back garden of the property.

'Lock it, will you,' Jess said to Eddie and as he was the last in. He closed and locked the gate behind them.

They crossed a perfectly mowed lawn in the dark and reached the back door. By then, Daz had taken the crowbar to the lock, it cracked open just as Jess and Eddie reached him. He opened the door and went inside.

'Come on,' Jess said in a whisper. 'Easy that, wasn't it?'

Eddie's heart thumped so hard in his chest he was certain that she must be able to hear it. Though nervous, he followed her into the kitchen. Daz was already making his way through the house, as though searching for something.

'Now what?' Eddie asked.

'Now we make ourselves at home,' Jess said. 'Go look in the fridge.'

Eddie used his sleeve to open the fridge door. Jess was

beside him, looking in. She reached for a can of beer and cracked it open, handing it to Eddie.

'Drink up!' she said.

Eddie raised the can to his lips, taking a big swig. Over the past couple of weeks, he'd grown used to the taste of beer and he was glad to chug some down now to take the edge of his nerves. Jess took another and opened it, drinking it down as fast as she could. She appeared to be nervous too, and this made Eddie feel less stupid.

'Come on,' Jess said, grabbing his arm. 'Let's go check out the house.'

Putting down the beer can, Eddie let her lead him through the downstairs rooms. She didn't turn any lights on, as though she already knew where she was going.

'Have you been here before?' Eddie whispered.

Jess gave a quiet chuckle.

'Living room is in there. Go and close the curtains then turn the tv on, but no lights!' Jess instructed.

'Where are you going?' he asked.

'To get some snacks. That's what we're here for, right? Break-in, raid their fridge and watch their telly.'

Eddie nodded. He did as she asked, then he took a seat on the sofa and reached for the remote control for the huge, fancy television in the corner of the room.

There was a loud thump above his head. Eddie leapt from his seat and headed towards the door just as Jess came back in with a bowl filled with crisps and another beer, already open.

'I heard something,' he said.

'It's just Daz pissing about upstairs. He's nosy, likes to look in drawers and cupboards. You know ... to see if they have sex toys.' Jess laughed.

Eddie was shocked by Jess's comments as he'd never heard a girl come out with such a thing before, but it also implied that she and Daz had done this sort of thing before – something they'd both failed to reveal when Daz first suggested it to Eddie. Even so, he didn't say anything. Instead, he sat back down on the sofa and Jess placed the bowl and the opened beer down on the coffee table in front of him.

Another thump from above set Eddie's nerves on edge.

'He's not stealing anything, is he?'

'Nah. Chill. He'll be down soon. There's a late-night film I wanted to watch. Channel three.'

Eddie picked up the remote and switched the television on. The room was illuminated by the glow from the screen. He found the channel and Jess sank down on the sofa beside him. She reached for the can of beer then passed it to Eddie. Without thinking he took a big swig, then he offered it to Jess.

'You have it,' she said. 'Enjoy the crisps too.'

Eddie took a handful without thinking. He munched the crisps, dropping crumbs all over the couch while Jess crossed her legs and became engrossed in the film. Before he knew it the beer was gone and Jess picked up the can and took it away, bringing him another.

'So how long do we stay here?' Eddie asked.

'Until Daz is finished … In fact, I'll go and check on him.'

'Yeah. Maybe we should leave soon,' Eddie said, then stifled a big yawn. His nerves were calm now, aided by the beer and he was so chilled out that he was no longer worried. There was no real harm done, after all. And the rush, as Daz and Jess had said, was worth it. Now that the adrenaline had gone he felt tired. In fact, the whole thing was starting to bore him.

Jess left the room as Eddie closed his eyes; a cat nap while she fetched Daz was all he needed.

Eddie came out of his stupor as someone pushed open the living room door.

'In here …' shouted a male voice.

He struggled to open his eyes and then found himself face to face with two police officers.

'Don't move, son,' said one of them.

Eddie's limbs were sluggish, he wondered how much beer he'd consumed. It had never made him feel like this before. He lifted his heavy arm, his fingers felt wet and sticky and something lay across his thighs.

'What ...?' Eddie glanced down and saw the crowbar on his knee. His jeans were stained by something that covered it. It slowly dawned on him that the red substance was blood.

'What happened?' he said.

The coffee table was covered in a white powder.

'Was it for drug money?' asked the other police officer.

'What?'

'Did you kill them for drugs?'

Eddie sat upright at these words. 'Kill who?' he asked.

'He's shit-faced and out of it,' the first officer said.

They reached for him then. The crowbar fell to the floor smearing red onto the taupe-coloured carpet. Eddie noticed his shoes were already covered with it. He didn't resist as they tugged him to his feet.

Eddie said nothing as they handcuffed him, but as they pulled him through the house, Eddie saw a photograph on the wall of a couple and a young woman: Jess.

'I don't understand,' Eddie said.

'Edward Beacham, we're arresting you for murder and attempted murder,' the first officer said. Then he read him his rights.

'Do you understand?' the officer asked.

'Where's Jess?'

'In the ambulance,' said the officer. 'Thankfully she escaped and raised the alarm.'

Eddie saw the ambulance parked outside, Jess lying inside on the trolley, being treated.

'Who did that to her? What happened?' he said.

'You'll remember once you come down from your trip.'

The police bundled him into the back of the car and took him back to the station. Eddie was bemused as they dragged him through the corridors and deposited him in an interview room alone. He stared at his reflection in the mirror that covered one of the walls. He'd seen somewhere that these mirrors were two-way and he found himself wondering if he was being observed while he tried to make sense of what had happened the night before. The last thing he remembered was falling asleep while waiting for Jess and Daz.

Two plain clothes officers, one female, one male, and a male PC came into the room. The PC stood by the door as the man and woman sat down opposite him.

Eddie had lost track of how long he'd been there by then.

'Edward,' said the woman.

'Eddie,' he corrected.

'Eddie. I'm DI Debra Stringer and this is DCI Paul Philips. We need to know what happened last night and it will go better for you if you volunteer the information.'

'I don't know what happened last night,' he told them.

'There are two dead bodies and an injured young woman, so you'd better start remembering,' said Philips.

'Daz ... ' he said. 'It must have been Daz. It was all his idea to break in and watch their telly. But he went upstairs instead ...'

'Look son, Jessica Wells, says you broke in and killed her parents. Then, when she walked in on you, you threatened her, made her sit next to you, while you ate crisps and drank beer. When she tried to escape, you hit her with the crowbar as well. She was unconscious for a while, and that's when you fell asleep. She came round, saw her chance, and ran to a neighbour's house to get help.'

'No! That's not true! Jess is my *friend*. Why would I do that?'

'You fancied her and she turned you down ...' said Stringer.

'No ... well yes, I like her, but she invited me out,' Eddie said. 'It was Daz who came up with the idea to break into a house. It was a sort of dare ... and Jess picked the house ...'

'Pull the other one,' said Philips. 'Don't think for one minute that we'd believe that distraught young woman encouraged you. Why would she break into her own house? Face it. You're a weirdo. She wasn't into you.'

Tears streamed down Eddie's face as he denied everything. Why would Jess lie to him like that?

'Ask Daz ...' he said.

'Daz who?' asked Stringer.

'I don't know his last name. A friend of Jess's … It was his idea …'

'Lock him up,' said Philips to the constable. 'A few hours in a cell might loosen his mouth.'

Eighteen months later, Eddie stood in a court room and received his sentence. Despite everything he told them, the evidence was stacked against him. His mother cried when he was found guilty, but even she hadn't believed that he was innocent. It didn't look good that he'd suddenly started drawing money from his university fund, all of which, the prosecution claimed, was spent on drugs, and not in his endeavours to impress Jess.

Jess was the biggest shock of all: lying on the witness stand like that. And denying knowing anyone called Daz and despite the barrister's best efforts, no one had come forward to support his story about Daz either.

Eddie had filled in the blanks since: Jess had drugged him, making sure he fell asleep. Daz must have killed her parents and the two of them had framed Eddie. It didn't take a genius to work it out. It was obvious.

As they led him away, Eddie plotted his revenge. They'd said he tried to kill Jess, something he'd have been incapable of doing at the time, but now all he could think about was really taking that crowbar to her and bringing it down on her head until her brains leaked out. The thought gave him a perverse satisfaction. But it would be a long time before he could act on it. He'd been given a lengthy sentence, made longer because he'd refused to confess and the judge said he showed 'no remorse'.

Eddie had regrets of course, and the main one, that he'd been stupid enough to fall for Jess in the first place. Now his life was in tatters, and his parents were heartbroken. His dear old gran had died while he was on remand, and Eddie was sure stress was a factor. So many victims and all he wanted to know was why? Why did Jess want her parents dead so badly that she set him up?

Jess watched them take Eddie away through a door at the back of the courtroom.

'Justice is served,' said the man at her side.

Jess looked at her new husband, Phil. They'd had a quiet wedding just a few weeks before the trial began. She'd met him when he was processing her insurance claim: her parents had made sure they left her well provided for.

Once Daz had taken care of her parents and helped her frame Eddie, Jess had made sure he was out of the picture too. She'd been working on Daz for twelve months before they decided they needed another patsy and Jess had chosen Eddie.

Daz had thought she loved him. But Jess wasn't sure what love was, even though she could play the part well enough.

While he'd been upstairs dealing with her parents, Jess had cut the brake cables on the motorbike Daz'd left around the corner to make his exit on. The 'accident' happened soon after he left the crime scene. He hadn't been carrying any ID and so he was just some John Doe whose body no one ever claimed or identified.

Jess had chosen well, Daz had been just some kid who'd grown up in foster care, but was then living alone. No family. No real friends. He'd been perfect.

As Phil took her hand and they left the court together, Jess marvelled at how well the 'game plan' had turned out. If only Eddie had realised that he would be part of her future security when he asked her about her plans?

No matter.

Phil was fully insured too, should she ever tire of him …

But for now, Jess had enough money and she wouldn't risk drawing attention to herself … at least not until the dust had settled. She had her life all mapped out. Travel, beautiful clothing, and a husband who earned a great salary. Everything a psychopath could ever want.

Slash

'The mind is its own place, and in itself, can make a
Heaven of Hell, a hell of Heaven.'
- John Milton

'And it's a wrap,' said the director.

Lucia Santana walked off the set. Another Italian/American horror film down and she was still nowhere near as popular as her co-star Franco Benicia. She wondered again how she had been talked into doing this film. It had been the worst script Lucia had ever had to work with. Written and directed (and produced and edited and scored ... he even probably painted the sets!) by the same man – never a good thing – but the money offered had been respectable enough and she just couldn't turn it down with no other work in the offing. These films, dire though they were, had a huge following. Years after the *Giallo* period, Lucio Fulchi and Dario Argento had followed in the footsteps of other ground-breaking Italian creators but even as the horror genre was diminishing the independent film industry was still trying to recreate their works. Hadn't Franco found international fame from doing them? That kind of success could get her out of Europe, and hopefully into better roles in the United Kingdom.

'Lucia?' Franco said behind her. 'Want to come for a drink in my dressing room? Now that we've finished? We deserve to celebrate.'

Lucia looked over her shoulder and smiled but her eyes remained cold. She had no intention of being alone with Franco, his reputation for not accepting 'no' was well known, and she wouldn't be another notch in his bedpost.

'My boyfriend is waiting for me,' she said softening her rejection. An out and out refusal had seen his last co-star thrown off set never to work again. Lucia wanted more opportunities and no enemies and so she tread very carefully with both the director and male lead.

Franco shrugged, 'Another time then?'

'Of course!' Lucia said. 'Great working with you!'

She hurried away. Aware of his eyes on her back, she found herself wondering if his stare was poisonous. She didn't look back for her own peace of mind.

In her dressing room, Lucia cast off her character's blood-stained clothing. All that effort to make it look as though she really stuck a knife in the heart of her on-film attacker and the whole thing was blown out of proportion with the excessive amount of *faux* blood used. The clothing was soaked and so was her skin beneath, which was stained so red that even Argento would have admired the effort it took to get off afterwards. Lucia took a shower and scrubbed her skin until she was no longer sure whether the pink stains were just from her efforts or still the remains of the obnoxious sticky concoction.

She stepped out of the shower, a flash of the horror and gore she'd witnessed rushed behind her eyes. Lucia found herself swaying. Sometimes in this world it was hard to separate life from the art.

Lucia pulled on a glittery gold jacket over her bra. She had decided not to go to the afterparty Not with the letchy director and Franco both there. It was bad enough avoiding one of them, let alone both when they were drinking and on their worst behaviour. Let them have the lesser stars for their sexual fodder. She was beyond that now, hadn't she already paid her dues? So, Lucia had arranged to meet friends, there was no boyfriend on the horizon and there only ever was when she needed an alibi. Lucia's own preference was one that was deemed unacceptable in a beautiful Italian actress – not if she wanted to sustain any kind of credibility anyway: she liked women. Men did nothing for her.

The phone on her dressing table rang as she buttoned up her double-breasted jacket and tugged the shoulder pads neatly in place. She ignored the ringing for a moment, tempted to disregard whoever was calling. She was tired and ready for some much-deserved Champagne but the caller was persistent and she felt compelled to answer. She picked up the receiver.

'*Si?*'

'Lucia? It's Manny. How did the shoot go?'

Lucia deep signed. Manny Fishburne, her American agent, was about to get the full blast of Lucia's wrath. If only he'd told her the truth, she'd have been prepared to fend off the two creeps so much better.

'The director *and* the leading man – you know exactly how it went Manny!' she said.

Manny took a long slow drag of something, a cigarette or maybe a joint, Lucia didn't know which as his breath hissed out and she imagined the released smoke floating over the mouthpiece.

'What? At the same time? Did you—?'

'No. I did not! What do you take me for?' Lucia said. 'I don't do casting couch; you need to protect me better.'

'Yeah. Well. No harm then,' Manny said. 'I knew you could handle yourself.'

'I shouldn't have to deal with this at my level,' Lucia said. She pouted but then realised that such a physical gesture would be lost as Manny couldn't see her.

'Every woman has to deal with this shit, whatever level,' Manny said. 'You think Sophia Lauren hasn't had her fill? Name anyone you think hasn't and I bet I have a story to prove you wrong.'

'It's not right.'

'It ain't. But it's the industry you signed up for.'

Lucia fell silent. She wanted to lose it with Manny. Yell. Scream. Threaten to sack him. But she knew what he'd say. 'Lucia have you taken those pills I gave you? You know you have to keep calm …' Why did she even bother trying to talk about the issue with a man? He'd never understand, nor would he help her. Things had to change. She couldn't do this again, and maybe Manny wasn't the right manager for her anyway. Despite all his empty promises, she was still no closer to the British or American studios.

'So – how did the filming go?' Manny asked again.

'Fine,' she said but the full force of her disappointment hung between them like the smoke from the dry ice the director had insisted on using in almost every shot of this awful film.

'Good. 'Cos I got an opportunity for ya,' Manny said.

'Another B movie?' she asked.

'No. Something way better. I got you an audition in London. All expenses paid.'

The plane took off and Lucia picked up her Campari and lemonade. She was struggling to believe all that had happened in the last 24 hours. Manny had sprung it, despite all her doubts. There she was, flying first class to London from Rome. He hadn't told her much about the job – the script would be given to her when she arrived. It wasn't the lead, he'd explained, but this was a stepping stone in the right direction. And the director had seen and admired her in other roles.

Lucia was nervous, knowing so little, but Manny had assured her that the producers weren't going to compromise her, and they thought highly of her. The comparison made her think again of unhappy times when things had gone wrong. She sometimes felt *damaged* by it. Especially at the beginning, when her father had managed her. Those days … the decisions he made on her behalf …

Lucia's mind closed this thought down as fast as it came. No, she wouldn't remember that now, and though it was hard to trust that things wouldn't go wrong again, it was easier to believe she was cared about when she found herself here, in first class.

Later, when she collected her luggage and swept easily through passport control, Lucia found a man waiting outside in the arrivals' hall, holding a plaque with her name printed in expensive-looking gold lettering.

'I'm Carl, your chauffeur, Ms Santana,' he said. 'I've been instructed to take you to your hotel.'

Lucia tried to hide her excitement at having her own

chauffeur – surely only the big-name stars were treated this way? How many times had she struggled to the studios on public transport at stupidly early times in order to be made up and on set just as the director strolled in?

After that the London trip was a whirlwind. She was whisked off to a beautiful hotel and given a stunning suite all to herself.

As Carl deposited her luggage in the room, he informed her there was a dinner reservation in the hotel restaurant. Lucia was worried this was some kind of ploy by the director or producer, it was all too good to be true. But when she arrived downstairs, fashionably late by 15 minutes, she found a whole table full of people, including the leading lady, a famous face she was very familiar with. Lucia had spent her whole career trying to follow in her footsteps.

'Carlita St Clair …?' she said.

'*Si*. Come and sit beside me. We Italian sisters need to stick together!'

Lucia couldn't believe the welcome she was receiving.

'Benjamin, the director, has told me all about you. You have done so well to catch his eye,' Carlita said.

Lucia's ego was duly boosted and from then on she would have done anything at all to keep in Carlita's good graces and to impress her. But it wasn't necessary, Carlita was easy company and so relaxed with the other actors, and she introduced Lucia to them as though the younger actress was her own protégé.

'Where is the director?' Lucia asked.

'He never joins in with these dinners,' Carlita explained. 'He thinks it's unprofessional.'

'You've worked with him before?'

'Many times,' Carlita said.

'And he isn't … he doesn't …?'

'Oh goodness no! We're in London now, you don't need to worry about being molested by some *strisciamento*.'

Lucia's eyes were round and shining as she enjoyed the delicious dinner and the expensive wine: all of it paid for by the studio. Lucia was incredibly happy for the first time since she had stepped foot onto a set. Manny had really done her a great turn this time. Yes. He was, at last, worth the percentage she paid him, and maybe wasn't so bad after all.

After dinner the talent all dutifully went off to their own rooms. If there was anything between any of them, Lucia didn't see it. She was so unused to this civilized behaviour that it all felt like a dream, or a well-constructed script to lull her into a false sense of security.

Her phone was ringing as she reached her room. Lucia hurried inside and answered to find Manny on the other end of the line – calling long distance from Los Angeles.

'You having a good time?' he asked.

Lucia thought this a strange thing to say but soon poured out all that had happened.

'Good,' said Manny. 'These are good people. Listen ... they want to shoot with you tomorrow. I didn't tell you you'd got the job already on your own credit. Thought you'd be nervous.'

'Tomorrow? Shooting the film? But I haven't seen a script.'

'It'll be adlib. Kind of a warm up for the real thing.'

'Oh, so this is an audition then,' Lucia said disappointed.

'No. You're in. This is the real deal and you're filming and getting paid from tomorrow.'

Manny told her how much. A week's salary was more than she'd earned for the whole of the last film. Lucia had to sit down.

'You're taking your pills, aren't you?' Manny asked.

'Of course,' Lucia said.

When she hung up, she lay back on the bed, wondering about how wonderful this all was. She was finally going places. So, what if she wasn't the lead. Carlita's draw would help bring Lucia to British screens and fandom more than anything and anyone else had so far.

'I'm on my way ...' she thought.

Lucia left the make-up department wearing a smart skirt suit, flat shoes, and simple make-up. Her normally luscious black hair was swept up and away from her face and tied back in a severe knot at the nape of her neck. As a finishing touch the make-up artist, Ally, had given her a pair of clear glasses.

'What am I? A librarian?' Lucia asked.

'No. A normal woman, a teacher maybe or an office worker,' Ally smiled. 'It'll all become clear.'

She still hadn't seen a script but she felt oddly comfortable in the dowdy clothing. This was going to be a serious role. At last! She might even win an Oscar for it ... *No*, she corrected herself, it was a British film so more likely a BAFTA ...

But any accolade would be amazing. She didn't care at all. All she wanted was her name on those credits and the recognition she deserved.

Lucia walked onto the set and found herself in an office situation.

'I'm Ben,' said a voice behind her.

Lucia turned and saw the director for the first time.

Ben was holding out his hand. Lucia took it and they shook.

'We are going to do some ... role play here ...' Ben explained. 'You are a secretary and you work for this man. His name is Victor. Your character is slightly infatuated with Victor. But he's not what he seems.'

Lucia took a step back, her eyes swept over the set. The camera man and the sound technician were conversing in the corner, and Ally from make-up was waiting at the door to touch up her hair and make-up as necessary.

'I ...' Lucia said.

'What's wrong?' asked Ben.

'Is this ... is this a ... *porn* film?'

Ben laughed. 'Oh no. Goodness no! Think of it as a love story that has gone wrong. You see your character is in love with Victor, but he is in a relationship with Lauren – Carlita is playing her. You're jealous. This is unrequited, you see?'

Lucia gave an awkward laugh. 'I'm sorry. I've just been put in awkward positions before ...'

'I'm more into method acting. You know, you submerge yourself into the role and give me what you feel the character would do in a situation. Then, we'll go over the script and talk about how to bring these feelings and emotions into it.'

'Yes. Of course!' Lucia said.

Her face broke into a smile brought on by her relief that she had not been duped again. All sorts of murderous thoughts had gone through her head as she briefly considered what she would do to Manny if he'd set her up.

Even so, her heart was still palpitating as she took up her position after brief instruction from Ben.

They ran smoothly through a scene then, walking through what action should take place for the camera as Lucia met her co-star for the first time, an unknown actor, but striking to look at. She barely heard his real name as she sank herself down into the illusion that he was Victor and she was Diana, his secretary. Ben even referred to her as Diana after that, and so did the crew as they set the scene around her and Victor.

For the first time in her career, Lucia began to genuinely find the actor on set with her attractive. Even as thoughts that he was out of her league pushed into her subconscious. She barely noticed how well the costume she was wearing made her feel she was Diana and all that was boring and dowdy about her came out of her mouth.

'Action!'

Lucia walked onto the set carrying a coffee mug for her boss. Victor didn't look up as she placed the cup down on his desk before him.

'If that's all?' she asked.

Victor nodded.

'Cut!' said Ben. 'Did we get all that?' he asked the cameraman.

Lucia looked up and over the set, she felt as though she was staring out from the screen of a television looking back at the audience. How strange this method acting was. How surreal. She almost didn't want to return to her normal self.

'Take a break,' Ben told her. 'But stay in character both of you please. Everyone, this is Victor and Diana for the rest of the day.'

'Would you like a drink, Diana?' said a voice beside Lucia. She saw then an elderly woman standing beside a trolley on wheels on which was placed several cups of coffee and some fruit snacks.

Lucia was about to say she preferred her coffee black but then she considered how 'Diana' would drink it. Diana would have cream. And perhaps she'd have sugar too.

The catering woman obliged. Lucia felt pleased with herself. She was sure she was going to learn so much from working on this film and Ben's suggestion of method acting was a good one. Hadn't actors like Dustin Hoffman made a career out of 'becoming' a character? It was rumoured he'd lived as a woman for his role in *Tootsie* and the film industry grapevine said his best role was yet to come. Lucia wanted that same success and recognition for her talent too, because she'd known all along she was destined for more than those awful slasher films.

'New scene,' Ben said. 'Diana. This is the morning after. Victor got you drunk the night before and used you for a one-night-stand. But you woke up thinking this meant he loved you. Then, you find him with Lauren. You see him propose to her. How do you feel? What do you do?'

Ben walked away and left Lucia to think about all he'd said. What would Diana feel? She'd be hurt. She'd cry!

They played the scene out with Victor and Diana. The tears were easy but Ben called a halt to the filming halfway through what Lucia felt was a breakthrough performance.

'I don't believe it because you don't believe it,' Ben told her. 'I want to see what Diana feels and I want to see what Diana does. This man used her. Is she going to let him get away with that?'

Lucia took up her mark and the scene began again. Victor alone in his office smiled as she came in, but it wasn't a warm smile. It was the smile that said 'I used you and I don't care'. Lucia felt that primitive hatred she had for men like Victor and she did feel the stirrings of Diana's emotions shifting inside her. It wasn't just her usual analysis of what she thought the director wanted, but something else, as though she could connect with

this poor boring girl who had given away her most precious gift.
'Cut!' said Ben. 'That's enough for today. Diana – go back
to your hotel – think about things. Victor, come with me, I need
to talk through what I want from you.'

Lucia was tired after filming but she was also elated. To
not have to scream like a banshee. To not be running around a
set, pretending to be chased. To not be covered in blood ...

Only a few of the actors attended the dinner that evening, even
Carlita had called off, claiming to be learning her lines. Lucia
envied her for having a script. Improvisation was so much
harder when you had so little direction. Transforming into
someone else in such a short time was also not easy.

As the few actors around that evening dispersed to the
hotel bar, Lucia found herself alone with Victor.

'I'm sorry,' she said. 'I forgot your real name with all this
method work today.'

'That's okay. Call me Victor, it will only help for
tomorrow.'

Lucia nodded but her confidence had slipped back with
her failure so far to satisfy Ben's demands that she 'become'
Diana.

'Cheer up,' Victor said. 'It will all fall into place.'

'I don't know,' Lucia said. 'It's not how I usually work.'

'Then let's rehearse a little more, Diana ...' Victor
suggested.

Victor ordered two large brandies and against her better
judgement Lucia let him accompany her to her suite so that they
could rehearse in private. Lucia sat down on the sofa while
Victor placed one of the glasses of brandy in front of her.

'I was new to method acting too,' Victor said. 'But I've
been working with Ben for a while now. I'm better for his
instruction. And I promise it will get easier. In a way, you just
have to lose yourself into the character. It frees you from your
usual inhibitions.'

Then Victor began to talk to Lucia as though she was his

secretary. They played out the role of her bringing him coffee, the coffee of course was the brandy, and then Victor invited Lucia to drink with him. As Victor pressed the glass into her hand, Lucia thought, *why not?* For once she would try to be free. No one would know about it, after all. It would all remain between her and Victor and she could bring the experience to the table during filming the next day. After all, maybe some things were worth sacrificing for your art.

When she woke a few hours later, Lucia reached out her hand to Victor's side of the bed. She felt the warm spot that he had recently vacated and a strange disappointment came over her that he hadn't remained for the night. She latched on to the emotion, knowing full well that this is what Diana would feel, and she turned over, swallowing the hurt and then anger and blending it with Diana's character. Who was she anyway? A drab spinster that someone like Victor could never love. Yet there had been tenderness in the act that suggested otherwise. Lucia told herself she was Diana and she closed her eyes and forced sleep. But her sleep wasn't restful, haunted as she was with memories of the past. She'd done things she'd rather forget. And her father ...

The next morning Diana woke. She was groggy and irritable. She recalled her tormented dreams following her encounter with her boss, Victor. *Oh no!* She hadn't really slept with him, had she? Her judgement had been so impaired by the alcohol and she'd had this stupid dream that they were both actors, playing their parts in a film. She wished.

Diana stumbled out of bed and into the shower, throwing on her drab work clothes as she glanced at her cheap watch. In the bathroom she found a pill bottle with the name Lucia Santana on the side. Confused, she dropped the pills into the bin.

She was late, but surely Victor wouldn't comment on that

fact. Not after last night?

She felt a little nauseous. How much did they actually drink? How had it even come about? Oh yes, Victor's girlfriend, Lauren, had dumped him. Then he'd invited Diana to have a drink. There was always hard liquor in Victor's desk but he'd never asked Diana to share it with him before.

When she walked into the office, Diana felt embarrassed. She could see Victor, standing by the door and he was talking to someone else who was in his room, but who Diana couldn't see. She decided taking his morning coffee in would be a good excuse to face him for the first time, especially as he wasn't alone. There could be no awkward exchange of words. And although Diana suspected Victor might regret their encounter, she wanted to hold onto the fact that he might feel otherwise. For, as long as he never told her there was nothing between them, then she could hope there was.

The coffee was steaming in her hand. As she passed her desk, Diana saw the pile of letters waiting for her to take into Victor's office for his attention. She picked up the envelopes and walked towards Victor's door.

There she saw Victor sink to one knee; a small box sat on his open palm as he held it out.

Diana paused. Her heart missed an excited beat and then a long-nailed hand reached out and took the ring from the box. There was a squeal of delight as Diana pushed the door open and saw Lauren, sliding the ring onto her finger. A perfect fit.

'Leave it on the desk,' Victor said barely looking Diana's way and dismissing her as if she were nothing.

He threw his arms around Lauren, picked her off the ground and swung her around. They danced around the room oblivious of Diana still standing in the doorway.

A range of emotion swept over Diana. Tears of anguish began to fall and then she saw Victor for what he was. A brutal selfish man who had used her to take his mind off Lauren. How stupid she'd been. How ridiculous were her dreams of them being actors, thrown together for the first time? Diana didn't even like men that way ... But she had been blind to his deceit, desperate for his lurid attention anyway.

Her eyes fell on the sharp letter opener that Victor always kept on his desk and then to the cup of scalding black coffee in her hand. She threw the coffee at Lauren, the black liquid connected with her beautiful face, burning her cheeks in an instant. Lauren screamed and before either she or Victor could react, Diana picked up the letter opener and plunged it into Victor's faithless heart.

There was more screaming and chaos around her. Diana found herself pulled away, even as she yanked out the knife and aimed another strike at Victor.

'My god! What's happened?' shouted Ally running from her post by the door to the office set.

'She's lost her mind!' Ben said.

Victor stood by the table still, blood pooling over his crisp white shirt, even as someone threw water over Lauren's red and blotchy face.

'Get an ambulance!' yelled Ben.

The sound engineer and cameraman held onto the writhing body of Lucia as she screamed and spat and foamed at the mouth.

'It's only acting!' Ben yelled in her face. He ran his hands through his hair and then as Victor stumbled against the desk, he hurried forward to catch him.

But Lucia's aim had hit true, up and under the ribs with the practiced skill of an actress who had spent too many years working on *giallo* movies and had somehow absorbed how a killer would really strike.

Victor's heart stopped long before the ambulance arrived.

'This is your fault, Ben,' Lauren wailed as the ambulance crew looked at her burns and Victor's body was taken away in a black body bag. 'You told him to sleep with her.'

Ben sank down into the chair behind Victor's office

desk. His head fell into his hands. 'It was all for the art. I didn't know she'd really *become* Diana!'

In a padded cell, Diana, formerly Lucia Santana rocked back and forth. She knew her lover, Victor, was dead and that Lauren was probably scarred for life. But it wasn't her fault. It had all started with her father ... For a moment she recalled the dark and how, in the middle of the night, she'd feared the covers being lifted She shook her head pushing back all recollection down into the deepest recesses of her broken mind. Now she was Diana, she could truly forget about *him*, and think only that she got her revenge on the man that used her. A crime fitting of a Hollywood star, and one whose name would go down in history for taking 'method' as far as she could.

The Wives

'This meeting is adjourned,' Stephanie said and she picked up her agenda sheet and shuffled the papers as a final sign that it was time to go home.

Stephanie was a smart, sophisticated, and very attractive woman in her late 30s. The leader of the group, and founder of the charity that was dedicated to helping local causes. Stephanie was hardworking, enthusiastic and driven.

'Good meeting,' Carol-Anne said. 'Fancy going for a drink before going home?'

All the women around the table nodded, they weren't yet ready to go home, but felt their good deeds for the day needed rewarding.

Gemma Rawlings was new to the club. She'd joined when they approached her a month ago and doing something moral in the light of her circumstances felt great.

'Can I just say, a heart-felt thanks to everyone who voted me in,' Gemma said. 'I'm so thrilled to be here. And I think helping the orphanage get their playground resurfaced is a great cause.'

'Oh, there's many great causes we'll help over the years, Gemma. It will make everything we do so worthwhile,' Stephanie said.

Stephanie put the papers away in her briefcase and stood. The other women followed suit and filed out of the meeting room behind her and into the hotel bar.

'No shop talk now,' Stephanie reminded them all as they each ordered a drink. 'Happy to talk about kids and family though – and everyday life.'

'Of course,' said Carol-Anne who was recognised by the group as Stephanie's second. They'd created the charity initially and it had grown over the years to seven committee members now that Gemma was in, all doing everything they could to improve the world around them. Or at least within the scope of their community. Though Stephanie had hopes for more, wider reaching projects. It was still early days though and the women all understood that. Probably their numbers would have to grow in order to truly expand.

'Gemma, tell us about you,' Stephanie said.

'Oh! Well. I don't have any kids,' she said.

'Not yet, anyway,' said Marg, the oldest of the group in her late 50s.

'No. I don't think I want any ... not now I know ...' Gemma began.

'No shop talk!' Stephanie said.

'Sorry. Yes. Anyway. I'm not the maternal type,' Gemma concluded.

'I have three children,' Marg said. 'All grown up now. Two girls and one boy. My son, Jeremy is the youngest and he went to university last month.'

'What are your daughters doing?' asked Gemma.

'Jenny works in advertising, and Regina is married. We are expecting our first grandchild soon.'

'Congratulations,' Gemma said.

'I have a newborn,' Carol-Anne said. 'I know. I'm a mature first-time mum, but like you, I wasn't sure for a while. Stephanie helped, and so did Marg, to get over that silly hurdle.'

'You think it's a hurdle?' Stephanie said. 'I don't see why it is. You either agree to have kids with your partner or you don't. It can be part of the deal ... but here I go, breaking my own rules. No shop talk!'

Stephanie looked around the bar. It was not very busy and no one was near their group that could eavesdrop.

'We can't talk here. As I've told you. Never in public,' she reminded them.

'Gemma, do you have a day job?' asked Carlie who so far had been quiet all evening.

Carlie was brunette, petit and had this aura of 'victim'

around her, Gemma noted. Not all the women were strong in this group, despite their protestations.

'Yes. I work in an office. I'm a secretary, that's how I met my wife. She was the PA to the CEO and I was working under her. She's moved on now, promotion and then headhunted for a better job. She's doing so well! But sometimes the pressure ...'

Stephanie gave Gemma a look that cut her off mid-flow.

'But of course,' Carlie said. 'The pressure is a major factor with a highflyer. Like our partners. And we all do everything we can to support them at home.'

Carol-Anne nodded. 'Let's go and sit over there,' she suggested. 'It's away from the bar ... and maybe we should talk a little about pressure?'

Stephanie rolled her eyes.

The group followed Carol-Anne now and they pulled two tables together and huddled around them. Stephanie sat facing the room so that she could watch out, make sure they weren't overheard.

'We perhaps should have remained in the meeting room,' she said.

'Maybe, but it's a bit more relaxing in here,' Carlie said.

'That's what I'm worried about. People start running their mouth off and we all get in trouble,' Stephanie said. 'But, okay. If this is how it is tonight. What we do is all about helping each other too.'

'We've talked about this,' Marg said. 'We are all okay. We know the score.'

Florinda and Cassie, who sat with their backs to the room both spoke at the same time. They were twins, married to twin brothers.

'It helps to talk,' they both said.

The women all looked around the table at each other. They were nervous, twitchy, and all seemed desperate to communicate their feelings.

'The blood,' said Carlie. 'I find washing his clothes so stressful sometimes. I know one day it's what they'll question me on the most. Were there signs? Didn't I see blood. I'm certain my machine will be full of DNA that will convict us both.'

Stephanie stared at her. Then she pouted. 'I don't think we should be so detailed ... And besides. You'll only have that if you're careless and don't protect your family. Talking like this is ... dangerous. We should stop now.'

'Why?' asked Gemma. She glanced around. 'No one can hear us.'

They looked around again. A group of whispering women, Gemma observed, looked guilty by their fear of conversing.

'The trophies concern me the most,' said Marg. 'I worry that the children will find them. After we're gone. I've talked to him about it. But he won't give them up. He spends hours looking at them.'

'What does he take?' asked Gemma.

Marg pursed her lips. 'Teeth. I know, it's weird. I told him once, he's like the tooth fairy ...' She gave a bitter laugh. 'He didn't find it funny, so I never mentioned it again ...'

'Anyone else have trophies to worry about?' asked Gemma.

'Underwear,' Florinda said.

'Shoes,' said Cassie.

'Jewellery,' said Carol-Anne. 'He gives the pieces to his mother and I see her wearing them. Which he enjoys a great deal! I can't look at her when she's wearing a dead girl's earrings. Sometimes I think she knows what he does and secretly relishes it. What about you, Gemma? Trophies?'

'None,' Gemma said.

'Jon takes pictures,' Stephanie said being drawn out despite herself. 'When the pressure is building, he spends time looking at them.'

'Digital pictures? Like with his phone?' asked Gemma.

'Mostly. But he used to like Polaroids when he first started. He keeps them in a box. In his office. Locked up in the safe. I know things are bad when he gets those out ...'

'Do you ever look in the box?' Gemma asked.

'Oh no. I couldn't! He wouldn't like it, and well ... I don't want to see anything more ...' Stephanie said.

'You saw something?' Carol-Anne said. 'You never told me.'

'It was in the early days. When he wasn't as ... *neat* ... and he brought the man home ... Jon is a bit like a cat sometimes. He likes to play with them before he ...' she glanced around the room again, aware that she was talking too much. 'He used to share too much about them to me too. But I asked him to stop. It's part of our deal now. I don't ask, he doesn't tell me. Then, I don't *know* anything. And I support him in every way I can to make sure he doesn't ... let the pressure build too much.'

'Is it always men he takes?' asked Gemma.

Stephanie nodded. 'I don't ask what he does with them. But the first one. Oh my god. He ... no. You don't need those images ladies. It's bad enough I have them.'

'I'm sorry,' said Gemma.

The group stared at Stephanie now. It was the most she'd ever told them and they didn't know why, despite her own rules, the torrent was pouring out, as though her pressure had reached its exploding point too. Like her husband Jon's often did. He, was probably the worst of the spouses. Even though Marg's had been going the longest.

'What about you, Marg,' Gemma asked. 'The pressure, the tells? When do they manifest?'

'Peter is an opportunist. There isn't an instant I can pinpoint. He sees the moment and seizes it. The teeth thing ... I've never asked, but sometimes I have nightmares about how he extracts them. After an "incident" though, he's always calmer in himself. *Better.* He's always been a great father, but sometimes I wonder about the kids. Do they sense it? Is that why they all left home as soon as they could?'

'I worry about that too,' said Florinda. 'Little Jamie. My son. He's such a beautiful child but sometimes he has that dark look in his eyes. Just like his father. They say nature can be a cause ...'

'You can do everything possible to keep him on the

straight and narrow ...' Brenda spoke up. 'But as you know, my son ... If I didn't help him. He'd be worse. I've always thought he'd be one of those mass shooters given the chance. The little bit he does take, stops that happening. I see it as the lesser of the two evils, let him release the tension or see him go completely off the rails.'

'What is his deal?' asked Gemma.

'It was random once. He would just get it on him and do something. No MO, but I helped him by giving him a cause. A strategy that we can both live with. He takes the homeless. And druggies. The dregs of society that no one cares about or will miss. It's why he hasn't really made the papers.'

The ladies fell quiet as this sunk in but none of them pointed the finger at Brenda. They were all facilitators and the guilt ran through them all.

'Why do we do it?' asked Cassie as though voicing all their thoughts.

'Love,' said Marg.

'Fear,' said Stephanie and Carlie. They glanced at each other as though they'd just had a moment of mutual understanding.

'For the children,' Florinda said. 'They couldn't lose their father. They can't find out ... what he is.'

'My father was one,' said Gemma. 'I guess I found that in my wife too. That *rage*. My mother never stopped him, she knew. She must have. I think she was one of us but without the support. I guess I didn't know any better and was attracted to Silvia because I could sense what she was.'

She let her comment sink in and the ladies at the table looked stunned by the implication that they had chosen partners based on this awful attraction they had to evil.

'What do you mean?' asked Carlie eventually.

'We're conditioned, aren't we? To do what they want. Live how they need us to. We do what they say because we fear the consequences of not going along.'

Stephanie sniffed. A single tear crept down her cheek before she dashed it away. 'They'd kill us,' she said. 'We all know that. We have no choice.'

'Living like this is killing us,' said Gemma. 'Don't you realise that?'

'But it's why we do the good things. Raise money for charity. Help the needy ...' Stephanie said.

'It's why we started the charity,' Carol-Anne confirmed.

'It makes you feel better?' Gemma asked. 'All of you?'

Florinda, Cassie, Brenda, Marg, Carlie, Stephanie and Carol-Anne now turned their eyes on Gemma.

'Yes. Well, it's supposed to,' Stephanie said. 'What else can we do?'

'Don't you want a life?' Gemma said. 'Don't you want to break free?'

'It's time we went home,' Stephanie said. 'This has gone too far tonight. We shouldn't ... we ... *mustn't* talk like this! Gemma, if you're to be one of us, you have to stop being so ... open ... and, you need to curb your curiosity. Curiosity kills.'

She stood up, smoothing a hand over her perfect hair as though she were ruffled somehow. 'Goodnight, ladies.'

Stephanie walked away leaving the others behind.

'I should go too,' Carol-Anne said.

'Why not have another drink,' Gemma said. 'My shout.'

Carol-Anne glanced at the door and at Stephanie's back. Stephanie didn't look around. Carol-Anne sank back into her chair.

'All right,' she said. 'I'll have a cocktail.'

'Me too,' said the others.

Gemma went to the bar and ordered a couple of margarita jugs.

'We should celebrate, when we can,' Gemma said when she returned. 'After all, one day each of our spouses and ...' she glanced at Brenda, 'sons ... will be caught.'

'What do you mean?' asked Florinda and Cassie in unison.

'Despite our support ... they are all serial killers. They'll make mistakes. It's inevitable,' Gemma said.

A waitress arrived with the jugs and glasses and Gemma

dutifully poured the margaritas. When the waitress was out of earshot, Gemma whispered, 'We need an exit strategy.'

The women collectively leaned forward to hear her. She knew she had them.

'Let's be honest, none of us would have chosen this life. We were dealt a crap hand,' Gemma continued.

'True,' said Brenda. 'All I wanted was a normal kid. Then he started killing the local cats. It was so hard to cover up. I had to move house three times in one year.'

The women sympathised with her. They felt it too; though theirs were spouse troubles, ultimately they were all in the same boat.

'Little Jamie might stand a chance if his father wasn't around,' Cassie pointed out to Florinda. 'He's a bad influence. His view on life ... those sexist comments he's always making. Same with my husband. He wanted us to have kids at the same time. I never told you this, I was taking the pill. I didn't want a child. I didn't want the extra ... worry. Nurture ... that was the problem with those two. Their father. What a pig he is ... they have no respect for women at all because of him.'

'And our nurture too,' said Florinda. 'Our mum was so controlling. We weren't allowed to do anything. She was always claiming there were paedos on every corner. Then, we met the boys. We walked right into it. All that romantic shit they spouted. Double wedding. Happy ever after dah-di-dah-di-dah ... Cassie and I might as well have had a target painted on our foreheads.'

Cassie nodded. 'I've never admitted it before, but they made us complicit on our joint wedding night. James and Charlie went out to "blow off steam". We didn't know what that meant. Then they came back to us. And it was obvious what they'd done. What do you do in a situation like that? Newly married. Your husbands have just murdered a girl. We were both so sheltered before then.'

'We found ourselves in a horror story,' Florinda continued. 'I cried all night. But he was so sweet to me. So gentle. He promised he'd never hurt me. And Charlie was saying all the same stuff to Cassie. But they wanted it out there. Kept calling us the *Four Musketeers*. They made us part of it, even though we didn't want to be.'

'All of us are,' said Marg, 'there's no denying that.'

'So. What did you mean, Gemma? About exit strategy?' Carlie asked.

Gemma leaned forward.

'Maybe we need to turn them all in.'

'No!' gasped Carol-Anne. 'We can't!'

The other women looked mortified.

'He's my son,' said Brenda. 'I swore on the day he was born I'd always be there for him.'

'He's also a serial killer,' said Gemma. 'You can stop him, Brenda even if you can't protect him anymore. Maybe that is "being there" for him.'

'Wait. What about your wife. You haven't told us about her,' Florinda says.

'She hates men,' Gemma said. 'She hasn't told me why. And as you all know; they don't like being questioned on their … habits …'

The women fell quiet again. They looked at Gemma. To them she was radical – a leader – someone to look up to because she was also saying something brave. Something they all wanted to hear, wanted to be like. Gemma, despite her circumstances, was heroic just speaking her thoughts because it was dangerous.

'If we were to agree, how would we go about it?' asked Florinda.

'We'd need guidelines. An agreement. A plan,' said Cassie.

'Yes. We would. I do have an idea. But I need a promise first …'

All the women nodded.

'Promise we won't tell Stephanie. She'll never go for it and … it'll put us all in danger if you do.'

'Agreed,' they all said but Carol-Anne looked doubtful.

'We've been friends for years,' she said. 'Our own

support group. She deserves to break free too.'

'I see that, but in her own way, Stephanie is the worst of us. She's a dictator. She's just enforced the rules our spouses gave her. Do we really think that a little bit of charity work cleans away the guilt?'

Brenda shook her head. 'I first got involved for those reasons, but then didn't feel so alone anymore. Stephanie found me, though. I would never have looked for her. Or any others in my situation.'

'Yes. About that,' Gemma said. 'How did she find us all?'

Florinda and Cassie looked at each other.

'Well, it was ... I don't really know. I was invited to join the committee,' Carlie said.

'Was that the same for all of you?' Gemma asked.

They all nodded.

'Me too. I think I know why ... Our partners and sons, know each other,' Gemma suggested. 'Maybe they have their own little meet ups and charity evenings.'

'No,' said Marg. 'Not possible. My Eric doesn't work with anyone. I know that.'

'No?' Gemma shrugged. 'Just a thought. But maybe we need to be a bit more observant for a while. See if they are somehow connected?'

'What difference does it make if they are?' asked Carol-Anne.

'The difference is that you, me, all of us was targeted and drawn together by Stephanie. Whose idea do you think that was? Hers? Or her *husband's*? What better way to make sure we always keep our mouths shut, than have us together with women like us. Wives like us. We're all under the thumb. We are all helping them do what they do. We are all damning our future for them.'

Brenda swigged down her margherita and reached for the jug to top it up. Carlie began to chew her nails. Florinda and Cassie held hands to give each other mutual support. Marg fidgeted and finally Carol-Anne stood up.

'I'm not comfortable with this anymore. But don't worry,

I'll keep my promise. Secrets are something I'm good at.'

'And then there were five,' Gemma said as Carol-Anne walked away.

After that, all the women rapidly excused themselves. It was early days; Gemma would work on them more over the coming months. Rome wasn't built in a day, after all.

'So, how was it?' asked Lesley, when Gemma came home. She wrapped her arms around her and kissed her.

'Stephanie excused herself quickly after the meeting. I had a drink with the others.'

'And?' asked Lesley.

'It's early days. I need to develop friendships with them. Trust. But it was a good idea to send me there. I think some of them are salvageable.'

'They believe you?' Lesley said.

Gemma nodded.

'Good. All we need is one of them to speak up. The rest will or won't follow, but we'll get those bastards.'

'What about you?' said Gemma.

'It's going well. The group think I'm one of them now after we manipulated the headlines. It's not easy though. Knowing who and what they are.'

'Do they share stories?' Gemma asked.

'They didn't at first, but I heard some horrible stuff tonight from Jon. It's a pity I couldn't risk wearing a wire.'

Lesley stretched.

'I'm so tired. This is so draining.'

'I understand, Babe,' Gemma said. 'Let me run you a bath.'

Later, when Lesley stopped breathing, Gemma cleared up the splashed water from the floor. She'd put up a good fight, but Gemma had the upper hand by being above and able to put her whole weight behind holding Lesley under the water.

She dried her hands, then picked up her phone and dialled a number.

'Jon?' she said.

'Gemma. What news do you have for me?'

'Lesley is dead.'

'Okay. Bold move. Did she find out who you really were?' Jon asked.

'No, but the expression in her face told me she was working it out in those last few seconds. I fucking hate lesbians and I didn't need her anymore.'

'What about the committee meeting tonight?' Jon said.

'I don't think you have anything to worry about with the wives and mother. They pretty much ran away at the mere suggestion of turning you guys in.'

'Good to know. I didn't feel like killing Steph. Not yet anyway. She's useful.'

Gemma hung up.

She emptied the bath, then set to with chopping up Lesley's body. Tomorrow she'd call into the police station and report her missing. Her colleagues would think her cover blown, never knowing that her own partner had been roped in to help and that she had befriended the very killers Lesley was trying to bring down.

She hadn't lied to Lesley; the women of the committee were a work in progress and it would take time. But she'd persuade them to come forward. Or most of them, and the rest would go down soon with their husbands anyway. She wasn't into sharing the territory even if those other weaklings were. This was her town. The long game was always worth working, no matter what the cost, and when they were all safely locked up, Gemma would begin her own reign of terror and no partner, or fellow killer would be in on her life.

Making sure she'd never get caught.

About the Author

USA Today bestselling author Samantha Lee Howe began her professional writing career in 2007 and has been working as a freelance writer for small, medium and large publishers ever since.

Samantha's breakaway debut psychological thriller, *The Stranger In Our Bed*, was released in February 2020 with Harper Collins' imprint, One More Chapter. The book rapidly became a *USA Today* bestseller.

In June 2020, Samantha signed a three-book deal with One More Chapter for her explosive spy thriller trilogy: *The House of Killers* (Book 1 *The House of Killers*), *Kill Or Die* (Book 2) and *Kill A Spy* (Book 3); all were released in 2021. Pitched as *Killing Eve* meets Jason Bourne the series is a nerve shredding, enemies to lovers tale that is simmering with obsession and espionage.

In August 2020, Samantha signed a deal with production company Buffalo Dragon for the option and screenplay for *The Stranger In Our Bed*. The feature film went into production in November 2020 and premiered on Showtime in the USA on 1 July 2022. The film has been sold to USA, Canada, China, and various countries in Europe and was released on British TV channels on 5th September 2022.

To date, Samantha has written 27 novels, 4 novellas, 3 collections, over 60 short stories, an audio drama, a *Doctor Who* spin-off, *White Witch of Devil's End* that went to DVD, as well as the screenplay for *The Stranger In Our Bed*.

The Stranger In Our Bed film was nominated and then won BEST THRILLER at the National Film Awards which was announced on 3rd July 2023.

A former high school English and Drama teacher, Samantha has a BA (Hons) in English and Writing for Performance, an MA in Creative Writing and a PGCE in

English.

An ardent supporter of charities, Samantha is Patron of advocacy charity POhWER and Survivor Ambassador for domestic abuse charity IDAS (Independent Domestic Abuse Services) which is based in Yorkshire.

Samantha lives in South Yorkshire with her husband, Historian, Writer and publisher, David J Howe and their cat Skye. She is the proud mother of a lovely daughter called Linzi.

For further information please visit:
www.samanthaleehowe.co.uk

Follow Samantha on social media:

https://www.facebook.com/samanthaleehowe/
Instagram: https://www.instagram.com/samanthaleehowe/
Threads: samanthaleehowe threads.com
Bluesky: @samanthaleehowe.bsky.social
TikTok: @samanthaleehowe
Mastodon: @samanthaleehowe@universeodon.com

ALSO BY THE AUTHOR

AS SAMANTHA LEE HOWE

The Stanger In Our Bed

HOUSE OF KILLERS TRILOGY
1: The House of Killers
2: Kill Or Die
3: Kill A Spy

COLLECTIONS
Crimes of Passion (13 Crime/Thriller Stories)

Criminal Pursuits: Crimes Through Time (Editor &
Contributor)

AS SAM STONE

THE VAMPIRE GENE SERIES
1: Killing Kiss
2: Futile Flame
3: Demon Dance
4: Hateful Heart
5: Silent Sand
6: Jaded Jewel
7: Midnight Masquerade (In 2024 TBC)

KAT LIGHTFOOT MYSTERIES
1: Zombies At Tiffany's
2: Kat On A Hot Tin Airship
3: What's Dead PussyKat
4: Kat of Green Tentacles
5: Kat and the Pendulum
6: Ten Little Demons
The Complete Lightfoot

(Hardback of the whole series with bonus chapbook)

THE JINX CHRONICLES
1: Jinx Town
2: Jinx Magic
3: Jinx Bound

STANDALONE NOVELS
POSING FOR PICASSO

COLLECTIONS
Zombies In New York & Other Bloody Jottings
Legends of Cthulhu
Cthulhu & Other Nightmares

CONTRIBUTOR

Terror Tales of The West Country (S. L Howe)
Terror Tales of the Seaside (Sam Stone)

Made in the USA
Middletown, DE
08 November 2023

42048416R00126